Autumn Tales

JOLYN & WILLIAM SHARP

Guideposts
New York, New York

Autumn Tales

ISBN-10: 0-8249-3180-7
ISBN-13: 978-0-8249-3180-3

Published by Guideposts
16 East 34th Street
New York, New York 10016
Guideposts.org

Copyright © 2012 by Guideposts. All rights reserved.

This book, or parts thereof, may not be reproduced, stored in a retrieval system, or transmitted in any form or by any means, electronic, mechanical, photocopying, recording or otherwise, without the written permission of the publisher.

Distributed by Ideals Publications, a Guideposts company
2630 Elm Hill Pike, Suite 100
Nashville, TN 37214

Guideposts, Ideals and *Tales from Grace Chapel Inn* are registered trademarks of Guideposts.

The characters and events in this book are fictional, and any resemblance to actual persons or events is coincidental.

All Scripture quotations are taken from *The Holy Bible, New International Version*. Copyright © 1973, 1978, 1984, 2011 by Biblica, Inc. Used by permission of Zondervan. All rights reserved worldwide. www.zondervan.com.

Library of Congress Cataloging-in-Publication Data

Sharp, Jolyn.
  Autumn tales / Jolyn & William Sharp.
    p. cm. — (Tales from Grace Chapel Inn)
  ISBN 978-0-8249-3180-3 (pbk.)
  1. Bed and breakfast accommodations—Fiction. 2. Autumn—Fiction. 3. Pennsylvania—Fiction. 4. Domestic fiction. I. Sharp, William. II. Title.
  PS3619.H35647A95 2012
  813'.6—dc23
                                    2012018418

Cover design by Müllerhaus
Cover illustration by Deborah Chabrian
Interior design by Marisa Jackson
Typeset by Aptara, Inc.

Printed and bound in the United States of America
10 9 8 7 6 5 4 3 2 1

Acknowledgments

The authors wish to thank Cynthia Manson, Regina Hersey, Beth Adams, Stephanie Samoy and David Morris, and especially Leo Grant, who had the vision.

—Jolyn & William Sharp

Grace Chapel Inn

A place where one can be
refreshed and encouraged,
a place of hope and healing,
a place where God is at home.

Chapter One

Saturday promised to be a fine day in Acorn Hill. There had been a hint of autumn chill first thing in the morning, but the sun grew strong in a clear, blue sky. All seemed right with the world as Alice Howard and her longtime friend Vera Humbert set out on a morning walk.

Whenever they could schedule it, the two women would walk together early in the day for exercise and companionship. At sixty-two, Alice, a nurse, knew the importance of staying physically active.

On today's jaunt they remarked on the likelihood that a beautiful afternoon awaited them, and they decided it would be good to plan something that would get them out into the countryside.

Fall was always a busy time at Grace Chapel Inn, the bed-and-breakfast owned by Alice and her two sisters, but when the weather was fair, their guests generally found lots to do on their own without relying upon the sisters to guide them toward entertainment. With that in mind, Alice thought that it would be easy to slip away for a few hours in the middle of the day. Her older sister would soon be making a trip to Maine. Alice assumed that she could depend on Louise for some extra help that day, because so much would fall on her own shoulders while her sister was away.

The upshot was that Alice and Vera decided to check out some yard sales. At this time of year, there were always many when the weather was decent. One just needed to drive around a bit and look for them. The women even convinced Vera's husband Fred to leave the hardware store in the care of his assistant and go with them.

They spent the entire afternoon driving from one sale to another and found some good items. Alice, dressed comfortably in jeans and a tan flannel shirt, loved to search for treasure and the opportunity to socialize. Eventually, however, they tired and decided that a yard sale north of town would be their last. That sale turned out to be the best one of the day. They did not encounter the usual cast-offs that one came to expect. Instead they found especially interesting and unusual items. Even though they were tired, they ended up spending quite a long time at the sale. There was just so much to see.

Vera found a large box of old tools, and she was feeling rather pleased with herself because she'd spotted it before Fred did. She thought she might be able to surprise him with it. Alice and Vera were sorting through this box, and just as Fred approached, Vera called out, "What in the world is this?" Immediately, several people crowded around to look at the strange object that she had found.

Vera held up a metal circle or band with a wooden handle perpendicular to the band.

It looks for all the world, Alice thought, *like one of those rings that you put into your frying pan to contain an egg in a circle when you cook it.* But it certainly wasn't one of those. It was too large and heavy, and the handle wasn't at the correct angle. Inadvertently, Alice disturbed her reddish-brown hair and scratched her head as she wondered about the strange object.

The woman running the yard sale said she had no idea what it was. She'd found it mixed in with the other tools, which had all belonged to her late father, and she had put it out to get rid of it.

As soon as Fred saw it, however, he got a funny look on his face, and he began acting nonchalant. "So, a mystery is it?" he said. "I always liked a good mystery. And I see you've got some other old tools here as well." In fact, he hardly glanced into the box.

Nevertheless, Fred began praising the box of tools. After a few minutes of that kind of talk, he made an offer on the whole box. By that point, it was obvious to Alice and Vera that Fred wanted the mystery object, whatever it was, but he was doing his best to conceal his interest. Despite his efforts, the woman running the sale seemed to have some suspicions, so she made an attempt to keep the price high.

Fred, however, called her bluff. He turned on his heel as if to walk away, and, as he expected, the woman got nervous about losing the sale. It was the end of the day, after all, so she gave in. Fred bought the box at a reduced price, tossed the strange object on top and sauntered off with the lot.

Back in the car, Fred began chuckling to himself in a self-satisfied way. "Can you believe no one knew what that is?" he asked.

Vera had been the object of some of Fred's jokes in the past. "Fred Humbert," she said, "you don't know what that tool is any more than I do. You didn't want it or the box. I know you: This is all just a trick to make us think you've made some great find. But I'm calling your bluff, just like you called that woman's."

At that, Fred grew quiet and adopted a detached air. Finally he said, "So, you don't know what that tool is?" And when Vera and Alice both said they didn't, he said, "And you think I don't know either?" He said it in such a calm way that Vera started to lose her patience.

"Well, if you know what it is, tell us," she said.

Fred gave an odd smile and replied, "I'm not sure I want to. My professional pride has been injured by your insinuation that I don't recognize the tool. I'm inclined to say you should just find out for yourself."

"Aha!" cried Vera. "I was right all along. You *don't* know what it is, or you'd say. You love to show off your knowledge about things like that."

Vera quickly realized that she had pushed Fred too far. His face clouded over, and he refused to say anything further about the tool for the rest of the ride home. After a period of uncomfortable silence, Alice led them into talking rather awkwardly about other subjects.

The next day, Vera told Alice that she felt guilty for upsetting her husband, but she couldn't figure out how to broach the subject because it seemed to have become such a sore point with him. Fred, however, raised the issue himself by announcing that he was going to hold a contest to see how many people in town knew what the tool was. "I think you'll find," he'd said to Vera, "that there are others in town who can also put this tool's right name to it. And then maybe the notion that *I* know what it is won't seem so . . . far-fetched to you."

Then he'd turned with an air of bruised dignity and, even though it was Sunday, went to the hardware store to prepare for his contest.

Vera, between stubbornness and guilt, couldn't bring herself just to come out and ask him what the doohickey—as she had started to call it—was, and Fred clearly wasn't going to volunteer the information, at least not until he'd had his contest. She suspected the point was to make her look silly. "He's probably hoping everyone else in town will know," she said, "just so he can tease me about it."

Alice shrugged. "Well, for whatever it's worth, you've got some company, because I still don't know what it is either. And remember, neither did the woman running the yard sale. So its identity can't be all that obvious."

Vera scowled, still frustrated. "I keep coming back to the idea that he doesn't know himself, and he just won't admit it. Maybe"—and she brightened with this new idea—"just maybe this whole contest is a ploy so that Fred can learn what the doohickey is himself."

Alice gave her friend a skeptical look. "Okay then, Vera, why don't you ask him sweetly if that's the case?"

Vera frowned, clearly not ready to confront her husband with this theory.

Alice sighed. "Personally, I'm getting antsy over this business. I think *I'm* going to ask Fred what the doohickey is."

Vera gave her a look in which hope struggled with dismay, but she said nothing.

Chapter Two

*L*ouise Smith stood in the inn's driveway Monday morning and watched the jitney bus back smoothly in an arc into the parking lot of Grace Chapel Inn. It was not a large lot—a tight space for even a small bus to turn in—yet the driver executed the maneuver with skill, swinging the bus around without hesitation, and he soon had the vehicle's nose pointing toward the exit, ready to pull out again.

Louise smiled. She appreciated people who were good at what they did.

The driver turned off the engine, and the lot was alive with birdsong. The air still held a bit of the crisp coolness of the autumn morning, but it was rapidly dissipating in the rays of the sun, and the bus seemed to sit and bask for a few moments in the warm light.

Then the driver's door popped open and a short, stout man sprang out. Clapping a cap onto his balding head, he bounced toward Louise with an energy that belied his stocky build. His eyes twinkled merrily.

"Tabard Tours," he announced. Both his hat and his jacket, not to mention the bus itself, also proclaimed the name. "Good morning. Got the right place, have I? Grace Chapel Inn? Will you be one of my passengers? I'm Harry Bailey, driver." He seized Louise's hand

and pumped it vigorously. "Is Mr. Gaunt around? He's the one who hired the bus."

"Louise Howard Smith," replied Louise, somewhat amused. "Yes, we're expecting you, Mr. Bailey, but I'm afraid the passengers are not all here yet, including Mr. Gaunt."

"Not a problem," said Harry, holding up both hands. "I'm early, I know I am. Just wanted to be safe. You folks take your time getting ready. I've got some paperwork I can do in the bus." He started to turn back to the vehicle.

"Oh, but won't you come inside to wait?" Louise said. "We can offer you some coffee."

As quickly as he had turned away, Bailey spun back with a smile. "Why, thank you, Mrs. Smith," he said, pausing to see if she would correct the "Mrs." When she did not, he continued, "I won't say no to that." He followed her happily into Grace Chapel Inn.

The inn was a massive, old Victorian structure. It had been the childhood home of the three Howard sisters, and when their father died, they decided to convert the building into a bed-and-breakfast in order to be able to retain it.

Louise led Harry to the inn's kitchen, where they found her youngest sister, Jane Howard, just completing her post-breakfast cleanup. The inn's current guests had all finished their breakfasts and gone out on day trips of their own. The dishwasher was gurgling, and Jane was wiping down the butcher-block counters.

Introducing the driver, Louise asked, "Do we have some coffee for Mr. Bailey? Or would you prefer a cup of tea?" she asked, turning toward him.

"Coffee would hit the spot, thank you," he said, looking around admiringly. "Do you ladies run this inn?"

Jane raised her forearm to brush a lock of dark hair back from her forehead and smiled warmly. "We do," she said cheerfully, gesturing him into a chair, "along with our sister Alice." She was already setting a mug, cream and sugar on the table, and she quickly had his coffee poured. "We have some apple-pecan muffins left over from breakfast," she added, whisking a plate of those onto the table as well. Harry smiled in delight.

"Jane, I'm going to leave Mr. Bailey here with you," said Louise, "while I go see what Alice is up to." Jane nodded, and Louise turned back to the bus driver. "I hope we'll be ready before too long, Mr. Bailey."

"Take your time," he replied, munching a bite of muffin and giving her a wink.

While Jane bustled around the kitchen, Harry picked up a brochure about the inn that was lying on the table. He read out loud: "Located in the picturesque town of Acorn Hill, Pennsylvania, Grace Chapel Inn enjoys a reputation as a haven for people looking to escape the stresses of modern life. It is a place where guests can find rejuvenation and renewal." He nodded in approval.

"This is quite an attractive logo and design," he said.

Jane looked over his shoulder and tucked a stray strand of hair behind her ear.

"Thank you," she said. "We're still tweaking the layout and text a little, though. I got the idea from a trade journal. We're not exactly hurting for guests, but I thought it would be good to start getting the word out farther afield."

Meanwhile, Louise had gone through the door into the main hall. As she entered, she spotted her sister Alice coming down the stairs from the second floor, lugging a large suitcase whose fabric sides showed a dark red-and-green floral pattern. Louise hurried past the inn's reception desk to meet her sister in front.

"Alice Howard, I can bring down my own suitcase," Louise remonstrated.

Alice ignored her sister's comment and said, "I heard the bus arrive." She gestured with her head in the direction of the inn's parking lot.

Louise grimaced at her sister's persistence, but because the suitcase was now downstairs, she decided not to pursue the issue. "Yes. I've just settled the driver in the kitchen with some coffee. Have you heard anything from John?"

Alice shook her head. "Not yet, but I'm sure he'll be right along." Alice gave Louise a searching look. "Do you feel ready for this?"

"I'm only going to Maine," Louise replied. "It's not an Arctic expedition." At sixty-five, Louise was the oldest of the three sisters, and in truth, it had been a while since she had done much traveling. Now she was about to go away for almost a week, traveling by bus. Her sister Alice had not been shy about suggesting that she might find the trip taxing. As a nurse, Alice had seen what became of people who pressed the limits of their abilities or endurance at the risk of their health, and she found it ironic that Louise was so often inclined to be critical of their younger sister's hectic lifestyle, though at fifty Jane was in fine shape and predisposed to be on the go.

"Aunt Ethel is going," Louise continued, "not to mention Florence. And Lloyd. Surely you don't think I'm more fragile than they?"

"Aunt Ethel knows her own limits," replied Alice serenely, "and as for the rest of them, well, that's their lookout. I'm asking about *you*."

Louise relented a little, knowing that Alice was motivated only by concern. "We'll be taking two days in easy stages, both up and back," she reminded Alice. "It will be fine."

Alice nodded thoughtfully and then smiled. "It's hard to believe this trip came together so quickly, isn't it?"

Only a few weeks before, in mid-September, the Howard sisters had first heard the news that would send Louise on the trip to Maine.

One of the innovations that Rev. Kenneth Thompson had introduced when he became the pastor of Grace Chapel was the "sharing of news and announcements" as a regular part of the service. Louise had mixed feelings about this practice.

She admitted that it frequently served a useful function, reminding people about church activities and obligations or sharing news of interest with the community. And yet Louise, whose father had been the pastor of Grace Chapel for so many years, felt that the practice somehow undermined the solemnity of the service. As people popped up in the pews to announce the weddings of nieces or someone's safe return from a trip abroad, Louise often found herself thinking that such information was better reserved for other times and places.

So it was always with a certain degree of chagrin that she heard news in which she was particularly interested. She recalled her friend John Gaunt rising in his pew and pausing before addressing the congregation. Any misgivings she harbored about the practice were overtaken by a keen curiosity in what the tall, dignified gentleman was going to say.

"Friends and neighbors," he began, "I am pleased and proud to announce that my nephew Jeremy, whom many of you have met, has completed his studies at the Maine Theological Seminary in Portland, Maine, and will be ordained as a minister next month, on October 11." John's face radiated love and pride as he made the announcement, and in response the congregation burst into spontaneous applause. Louise had always felt that applause belonged in the concert hall rather than the worship hall, and yet it seemed the most natural way to acknowledge their neighbor's news.

After the service, John was besieged by parishioners seeking further details. Everyone knew that Jeremy's parents—John's brother and sister-in-law—had died in a terrible car accident when Jeremy was a freshman in college. Ever since, John had looked out for his nephew and been a surrogate father to him, often bringing him to stay in Acorn Hill on school holidays. Those who had met Jeremy were thoroughly impressed with the young man.

"Yes, I'll be driving up," Louise heard him say as she approached. "I wouldn't miss this for the world."

"You'll have such a lovely trip too," exclaimed Florence Simpson. "Right around Columbus Day is just the time to be seeing the fall colors in New England."

John nodded happily, though his thoughts were clearly not only on the region's annual glory of colorful foliage. As he peered at his neighbors and understood the joy they felt in sharing this good news with him, he was moved to make an expansive gesture. "You know," he said, "if anyone else would like to attend the ordination, you'd be more than welcome to come along with me."

A calculating look appeared in Florence's eyes, but it was Lloyd Tynan, Acorn Hill's mayor, who spoke up. "You know," he said, adjusting his bright-blue bow tie, "we ought to think about sending a couple of representatives to this event, on behalf of both the town and Grace Chapel." He nodded as if agreeing with himself. "Yes, I think that would be a very nice idea."

Several other people spoke up in support of the notion, and Lloyd beamed, his green eyes sparkling with pleasure at having thought up such a popular plan. "Well, John," he said, "it looks like there may be more people than you can take in one car, but we'll get something worked out. Perhaps we can go up in a convoy. Will it be a problem to bring so many people to the ordination? We don't want to create any difficulties for Jeremy or his congregation."

John was deeply moved by this show of support and good will. "I don't know, Lloyd. I can't imagine it will be a problem, but I'll check with Jeremy just to be sure. In the meantime, let me say that I personally will arrange the transportation. I'll rent a bus, if necessary. It will be my ordination present to Jeremy. He'll be so touched that the people of Acorn Hill wish to come out and support him in this way."

Over the next few weeks, John Gaunt made all the arrangements. He'd determined the composition of the party that would be traveling, he had reserved a bus that would take them, and he had worked out a route that would follow both interstates for efficient travel and country roads for sightseeing. Through the excursion company he had also arranged for a hotel, where they could stop on their way up and back. The members of the party had drawn the line at allowing him to pay for the hotel; they all insisted that they would pay their own lodging.

Not only would Jeremy's congregation be delighted to welcome these guests from Pennsylvania, but the theological seminary from which he was graduating had two guesthouses on its grounds where they would be able to stay while they were in Maine.

And so the members of the party had agreed to meet at Grace Chapel Inn on Monday, October 9, to begin their journey to the hallowed home of Jeremy Gaunt and his fellow seminarians.

Louise wore a gray wool skirt and a blue sweater that matched the blue of her eyes and looked especially pretty with her short silver hair. She adjusted her wire-rimmed glasses before reaching down for her floral-patterned suitcase, but before she touched the handle, Alice snatched it up and began to head for the door, ignoring Louise's protests. Giving up, Louise returned to the kitchen, but she found that Harry Bailey wasn't there.

"Where's our driver?" she asked Jane.

Jane shrugged as she continued packing snacks into a cooler. "One minute he was enjoying his coffee and chatting away, asking all sorts of questions about the inn, and the next minute he jumped up and said he had to go see to his passengers." She smiled. "He's quite a character, isn't he? He's a retired teacher, so you should have an interesting trip with him as your guide."

Louise had the feeling that she was falling behind, so she turned to make her way back out to the parking lot.

She was surprised to find that all the members of the party had appeared as if by magic, and Harry was busily loading the suitcases into the back of the bus. In the parking lot, she found John Gaunt and his old friend Cyril Overstreet, a member of the church board; Florence Simpson; Lloyd Tynan; and her own aunt, Ethel Buckley. In addition, there was Alice, who had wrestled out Louise's suitcase, and Rev. Thompson, who had come to see the party off.

Ethel was gossiping with Florence, but to Louise, they hardly looked like they were both part of the same party. Ethel was dressed in comfortable cotton slacks and a cream-colored tunic that set off her red hair to great advantage. Florence was wearing a pink-and-black herringbone-patterned suit with a matching bag, and earrings more suited to a formal afternoon tea party than a day's ride in a bus. At least, Louise noticed, her shoes looked comfortable.

"Louise," called Ethel, "we've been waiting for you. Mr. Bailey has us almost ready to go." Louise counted to five to keep from retorting that none of them had been there just a few minutes before.

Jane, carting the large cooler in her arms, had followed Louise out to the parking lot. Looking over the group she exclaimed, "Well, and what a fine lot of pilgrims you are. I hope it's a good journey and a beautiful ceremony."

Harry quickly stepped up to relieve Jane of the cooler, and he smiled broadly when she explained that she had packed snack bags for the group, including one for the driver. She also pointed out that two coffee tins contained homemade cookies, and that she had remembered to pack water and juice, and an ample supply of paper napkins and towelettes.

Meanwhile, Rev. Thompson smiled as he shook hands with John Gaunt. "Congratulations again, John. You know how proud we all are of Jeremy." Looking over the group, he added, "I'm delighted that Acorn Hill and Grace Chapel can offer such a show of support for this happy occasion."

Alice and Jane crowded around Louise to wish her a good trip.

"It's a shame you won't have a chance to see Cynthia, since you'll be up that way," said Alice.

Though she would have welcomed a chance to see her daughter, Louise shook her head. "The hotel is in western Massachusetts," said Louise. "It would be too much of a drive out from Boston for her. And driving up to Maine would be even farther. I've paid all the bills that will come due while I'm away. I feel bad leaving when we're booked solid for the next two weeks, but at least you won't have to worry about trying to work in any new reservations. It just won't be possible."

Jane smiled and Alice said, "We'll be fine. Justine Gilmore is already coming in to help in the mornings, and as you know, the guests at this time of year tend to go out on their own. You should concentrate on having a good time. After all, you've been closer to Jeremy's uncle than either of us, and besides, you are expendable, while the inn and the hospital can't function without Jane and me." She laughed and gave her sister a reassuring squeeze on the forearm.

Louise's brow wrinkled at her sister's teasing, but before she could respond, Harry came bobbing in their direction. "About ready, Mrs. Smith?"

Louise introduced the driver to Alice and then joined the others as they began to board the bus.

Jane and Alice felt love and admiration—and a touch of sadness—as their tall, dignified sister turned to wave good-bye one last time.

The bus offered three rows of bench seating, each of which comfortably accommodated two people. John Gaunt and Cyril Overstreet had climbed gallantly to the most inaccessible seats in the rear, and Ethel and Lloyd, her "special friend," had claimed the middle row, leaving Louise to share the front bench with Florence Simpson. There were times when Florence could be a trial, but squaring her shoulders, Louise determined to make the best of the seating situation.

Harry had stored all the luggage in a cage at the rear, and he now bustled forward and into the driver's seat. "Okay, folks," he called out as he started the engine, "are we all aboard?" Not really expecting an answer, he was already moving the bus toward the street. "Let's wave to the good people who are seeing us off," he called as he pulled out of the parking lot, and he added a merry toot of the horn to the farewell.

As he deftly maneuvered the bus through town and toward the highway, he kept up a brief introductory patter. "I think I met everyone before we started, but in case you've forgotten already, my name's Harry Bailey and it's my privilege to welcome you to Tabard Tours.

"We're on our way to Maine, the Pine Tree State. We'll take two days going up and two days coming back, stopping over in Spruce Grove, Massachusetts, both ways. If you have any questions, if the bus is too hot or too cold, or if you need anything else, sing out! That's what I'm here for.

"Otherwise, sit back, relax, and enjoy the ride!"

Chapter Three

The first few miles of the trip passed in the blur of excitement that attends the start of any journey. John Gaunt reviewed all the arrangements for where they would stay and what their schedule would be. He also talked a bit about the course of study his nephew had pursued.

By the time they pulled onto the interstate, however, the departure excitement had subsided and the travelers were lapsing into a somewhat awkward silence. Lloyd and Louise kept up some desultory questions about Jeremy's studies and plans for the future, but even that faded out after a while. Soon, Louise began to fear that time might prove to pass very slowly on this trip.

After a particularly long silence, Harry spoke up. "Well, folks, we're on the highway now. But you know this trip is going to take a little time, and if you're all willing, I have a suggestion that will help make that time fly." He paused to see if this would draw any response.

Louise felt herself sinking into the lethargy of a long trip and couldn't seem to summon the energy to respond. A sudden dread that he would suggest singing songs clutched her heart. She shuddered at the prospect of endless rounds of "Row, Row, Row Your Boat." But John Gaunt spoke up with an eagerness that indicated he was concerned for the success of the trip that he'd planned so carefully. "What's that, Mr. Bailey?"

"As you might guess, I've been on lots of trips like this," Harry said, drawing out the suspense, "so I know what I'm talking about. And I've learned that oftentimes the old ways are the best ways. What's one of the tried-and-true methods that people have used to pass the time for hundreds of years?" He paused dramatically. "Telling stories."

Louise sensed a general skepticism among her companions, but Harry apparently had anticipated some resistance, because he continued without giving them a chance to object.

"Now, I know that many of you will say it's a lost art. You think that our grandparents, maybe, knew how to spin a yarn so as to while away a winter evening or keep the neighbors gathered on the front porch on a summer's night. You'll say those times are gone, that we don't tell ourselves stories any longer. We get our stories from books or the movies or '*teevee*.'" He stretched the last word with just the slightest tone of contempt.

"And I don't deny," he continued, "that we today may not have the skills that our grandparents did, but I tell you that I've been doing this awhile, and whenever I can get a group of travelers like yourselves to give storytelling a try, they always surprise themselves with what they can come up with." Louise saw Harry glance into his rearview mirror to observe what effect his words were having.

Louise gave a mental shrug. Why not? It might be interesting, and even if they tried it and it didn't work out, it would still serve to pass some time.

"Just consider the idea for a moment with an open mind," continued Harry, and Louise felt the prick of her conscience, because her own first response had been so dismissive. "Why, look at the stories we still tell every day, whether we're telling our spouses how our day went or trading gossip over the back fence." Louise thought of Florence Simpson beside her and of her aunt Ethel behind her. They were both inveterate gossips. Did that make them good storytellers?

"Think of it as a kind of game. As I say, any time I've tried this with an open-minded group such as yourselves, it has always worked. What do you say? Do you want to give it a try?"

There was an uncomfortable silence for a few moments, and then John spoke up with slightly forced enthusiasm. "Well, why not? What do you suggest, Mr. Bailey?"

Bailey's voice sounded genuinely happy. "Wonderful! You're gonna enjoy it, I just know. And all of you, please call me Harry. Now who's got one to start us off? Don't be shy now. Just a small one."

The embarrassed silence descended again. Finally, John Gaunt, showing himself to be a good sport, volunteered to be the first storyteller. "Well, since I'm responsible for having arranged this trip, I'll give it a try." Everyone else breathed a sigh of relief that someone else had agreed to go first.

"Like our friend Lloyd here, I take an interest in politics, and I like to read about systems of government from other parts of the world—how other people go about electing their leaders and whatnot. The story I'm going to tell you is something I came across in my reading.

"I don't know how many of you remember him, but when I was a boy, there was a fellow named William Stevenson, who was an explorer and anthropologist, a real larger-than-life character. His area of study was the Arctic, and he wrote a series of popular books. He had this phrase—'the abundant Arctic'—that he would use, trying to get people to understand that the Arctic was not some frozen wasteland, which was how most people thought of it.

"Stevenson would go on expeditions where he would live with groups of Eskimos—Inuit as they are properly called—for months at a time, studying their way of life. On one of these trips, he got to observe how a particular tribe went about choosing its leaders, and he later wrote about it in one of his books. When I read it, I found it just fascinating.

"Stevenson was making a return visit to a group of Inuit that he had studied and lived with previously. But when he arrived, he was greeted by bad news: The group's longtime leader had died. This fellow had always been friendly to Stevenson and encouraged his people to cooperate with the anthropologist. Stevenson was a little worried that, without the leader's support, he might not receive a warm welcome.

"The first thing he did was ask who the new leader was, so that he might speak to that person and try to win his support. But he was told that the new leader had not yet been chosen, and that the tribe was in the midst of preparations for the complex ceremony by which the new leader would be selected. Naturally, Stevenson asked if he could observe this process. After all, the previous leader had held power for years, and such an opportunity might not come again for a long time.

"After some hesitation, the tribe agreed, but they warned him that there would be some parts of the ceremony that would be off-limits. Naturally, Stevenson agreed to cooperate in that regard.

"When he asked about the ceremony, all he could get was that it somehow involved something called the Man of Ice, or the Iceman. Stevenson knew that this had been one of the ceremonial titles of the old leader. Before, it had never seemed especially important, but now this title seemed to have a significance for the people that he did not fully grasp. He decided to wait and see what happened.

"He saw that almost the entire village was involved in cooking up vast quantities of some special broth or potion. When he asked about this, he was told that it would be used in the ceremony. He got the impression that it was also some sort of medicine, but again, its exact role and purpose remained unclear.

"On the first day of the ceremony, almost the entire tribe got up early and went out onto the pack ice. There, all of the men, except for a few of the oldest and youngest, sat down on the ice, spreading out over about an acre. And then, they just stayed there. They didn't do anything. Naturally, this perplexed Stevenson. After all, there was supposed to be some sort of ceremony going on.

"As he watched, the women from the tribe made the rounds, giving each man a drink of the special potion that they'd prepared. Then the women stayed and watched the men for a while, and the men, as far as Stevenson could tell, just sat on the ice and stared off into space. Finally, everyone who wasn't sitting on the ice turned and went back to the village, leaving most of the men still sitting there.

"Stevenson was puzzled. Were the men meditating? Were they on some sort of spiritual quest? All the elaborate preparations suggested that the tribe expected the men to be out on the ice for a while. But so many of them? How was this going to help select a new leader?

"After extensive questioning, the best Stevenson could come up with was that the new leader would be selected through some sort of endurance test: Whoever lasted the longest out there would become the new Iceman. This seemed strange, but no matter how he phrased his questions, this was the answer the women gave him. Finally, they got sick of repeating it and walked away when he approached.

"The women, Stevenson reported, would send a small group out to visit the men several times a day. They would give the men more of the special potion and check on their overall condition. They never objected when Stevenson went along on these trips. The men would drink the potion when it was brought to them, but otherwise, they did not speak or move at all.

"This went on for days with no change. Every few hours, day and night, some of the women would go out and check on the men and then return. It was really quite a sight, he said, this expanse of ice with immobile figures spread out over it. Remember, this was most of the men who lived in the village.

"One day, just as the women were ready to return to the village, one of the men made a feeble gesture with his hand. Immediately, they bundled this fellow on a sled, dragged him back to the village, and took him into a special structure. Stevenson wasn't allowed to go in.

"They told him the man was being treated for what we would call frostbite and exposure. These people had lived in this environment for generations, so they knew how to treat these conditions effectively.

"Well, once one man came in, many more of them started to drop, and the women had to go out and check on them much more frequently. Each time, they brought back two or three more men, and they all had to be treated. But they also recovered quickly, so that the village soon started to fill up again.

"After another few days, just two men remained on the ice, and the difference between the two couldn't have been greater, Stevenson said. One, who Stevenson referred to as Good Choice, was a man who already enjoyed great influence and prestige in the tribe. He had been a valued advisor to the previous chief, and in the absence of formal leadership, he had helped organize this ritual in which he was now participating. Stevenson said that when he heard the old chief had died, he had at first assumed that this man would be the natural successor.

"But the other man, who Stevenson dubbed Bad Choice, was a notorious ne'er-do-well, a man who lived in large part at the tribe's sufferance. He never carried his weight in the hunting and fishing expeditions, despite the fact that he was large and strong. He never contributed anything of value to tribal discussions, and he mostly kept to himself.

"Stevenson went so far as to ask if Bad Choice would actually be installed as chief if he won the contest, and the villagers assured him he would be. More remarkably, said Stevenson, they didn't seem at all disturbed by that possibility, even though clearly they knew the temperaments and qualifications of the two men even better than he did.

"It got to the point where the entire village was making the trek out to check on the last two men, and one evening, they arrived to find Good Choice slumping forward where he sat. Good Choice made a feeble gesture with his hand, indicating he was ready to be taken back to the village. Bad Choice, meanwhile, took no notice, even when they tried to give him some more of the potion.

"*Well, that's it*, Stevenson thought to himself. He expected the tribe to take both men back and to begin some sort of celebration, because evidently the new leader had been chosen. But rather than show any signs of excitement, the villagers were even more somber and serious than before. They loaded Good Choice onto a sled, but they left Bad Choice alone and returned to the village without him. Clearly there was some further step or steps in the ceremony, but the villagers would only say that Bad Choice wasn't yet the Iceman.

"The next morning, the entire tribe went back out in a solemn procession. When they arrived at the spot where Bad Choice sat, they found his body frozen solid.

"By this time, Stevenson was very confused. Did this mean that Good Choice would be the new leader after all? Or would they have to start the whole ceremony over again?

"But the villagers were clearly in the midst of an important ritual, and he couldn't ask them. Instead, he watched as they chanted and carefully loaded Bad Choice's frozen body onto a sled. They brought it back to the village and took it to the healing shed. From that point on, nobody would answer any of Stevenson's questions. They acted as if he wasn't there.

"Stevenson began to suspect that Bad Choice's death had been an accident, that perhaps their ritual had somehow run off the rails and they didn't know what to do next. But surely, he told himself, this must have happened before. Such a difficult ritual in such an extreme climate must have resulted in the same tragedy on other occasions.

"After a few days, his friend Good Choice came to him one morning and declared that the new Iceman was with them. Stevenson's first impulse was to congratulate his friend, but Good Choice shook his head and led Stevenson back to the formerly off-limits healing shelter. There, to Stevenson's utter shock and amazement, they found Bad Choice sitting up in bed, with a long line of villagers queued up waiting their turn to speak with him.

"It turned out they were bringing every conflict and trouble that had arisen in the village since the death of the old leader for him to resolve. Bad Choice was indeed the new Iceman. And to Stevenson's amazement, he seemed to have been transformed. The Iceman listened carefully to all the cases that were brought before him, and he pronounced wise and fair judgments. He was no longer the selfish lout that Stevenson recalled.

"After a while, Good Choice explained the tribe's beliefs about the ritual. During the period of being frozen, he explained, the Iceman's soul wandered in the spirit world, where he was instructed in all the things he would need to know in order to be a good leader for the people. The Iceman almost always returned from this journey significantly changed from what he had been in his previous life. During the time his soul was in the spirit world, however, it was very important for the other Inuit not to talk about the Iceman or speak his name, lest his soul be called back prematurely, before he had learned the necessary lessons. That's why the villagers had ceased to speak with Stevenson over the past few days. They couldn't run the risk of breaking that taboo.

"Stevenson stayed on with the tribe for a few months, and he found that his initial impression had been correct. Whatever the truth of the Iceman's experience, he had become a good leader for his people. And he would continue to lead them until his own death, and then the Iceman ceremony would be performed once again.

"As was his custom, Stevenson held a press conference upon his return to New York in order to drum up publicity for his latest discoveries in the Arctic. Of course, he spoke about the Iceman ceremony, though the New York reporters were naturally skeptical. Finally, a reporter remarked that even if one accepted the idea that these Inuit knew much more about the effects of extreme cold on the body than we do, the whole process was a remarkably inefficient way to select a leader.

"After all, the reporter pointed out, it tied up everyone in the village for days, and every man in the village was exposed to dangerous conditions that might have lasting ill effects, all so that they could identify a single leader. It seemed to him that the process required too much in the way of time and resources.

"'Perhaps,' Stevenson responded, nodding his head thoughtfully. 'And yet you must agree that the process is ultimately founded upon a well-established principle.'

"'And how would you state that principle, professor?' asked the journalist.

"'Why,' said Stevenson, with a slight gleam in his eye, 'the principle that many are cold, but few are frozen.'"

The bus erupted in groans and jeers when John delivered the punch line to his tale. "It's a shaggy-dog story!" wailed Cyril Overstreet in mock distress.

John raised his eyebrows and spread his hands in a "what's all the fuss?" gesture, but his smile suggested that he was pleased with himself.

Louise shook her head but smiled as well.

Harry was laughing so hard he was bouncing up and down in his seat, though the bus never strayed off course, Louise was pleased to notice.

"Wonderful," said Harry, and then in his best Lawrence Welk impersonation added, "Wunnerful, wunnerful." Reverting to his own voice, he said, "That was an ice-breaker and no mistake. Thank you indeed, Mr. Gaunt."

"And a lesson to us all," he continued. "As Mr. Gaunt has so capably shown, one of our first goals in telling our stories should be to entertain our listeners. Although," and his voice dropped warningly, "we probably would agree that one shaggy-dog story per trip is sufficient."

The remarks that flew forward in response indicated that all were in agreement about Harry's concluding comment.

Chapter Four

As the bus continued north, Harry turned onto a secondary road that would enable the group to view an especially beautiful portion of their home state. They were grateful for the diversion and relaxed as they had a chance to enjoy the scenery. Alongside an orchard where trees bowed under the weight of ripe apples, a middle-aged couple applied a fresh coat of white paint to a farmstand, over which a sign let it be known that apples, cider and jellies could be purchased there. Farther on, several young men and women filled baskets with glowing apples and loaded them onto an aged flatbed truck.

Louise felt comforted by the scene and was moved to say a silent prayer: *Thank You, Lord, for such beauty and abundance. Truly, Your love for us is made manifest in Your creation.*

After a few moments, Cyril spoke up. "I'll tell you something that I'd like to hear," he said, "and that's the story behind this . . . doohickey, they call it, that Fred Humbert has on the counter down at his hardware store. Everyone at the General Store was talking about it when I picked up my morning paper. What is it, anyway? And what's this about some sort of contest? Is that gizmo the prize?"

"The contest is to identify the doohickey," Lloyd explained. "You write down your guess on a slip of paper and put it in that box he's set up. Fred says he's going to go through the answers on Friday, and from the correct ones, he's going to draw one winner who will get a gift certificate to the store. He says he'll have a little ceremony for the drawing on Friday afternoon."

"But why does he need a contest?" pursued Cyril. "Fred has all kinds of strange tools that nobody but he can identify."

"From what I heard," said Louise, smiling, "he may be trying to prove some point to Vera."

"Well, Fred sure seems to have stirred up some interest," remarked Cyril.

Lloyd nodded in agreement. "He's put a big sign up in the window: Enter the Doohickey Contest. I was by just after the store opened this morning, and he already had a lot of curious folks in. A gift certificate is a nice prize, but I think people are mostly just intrigued. Across the street in the Coffee Shop, I heard many a lively debate about the doohickey."

"But what *is* the doohickey?" Cyril asked again. There was no response.

"Alice was planning to ask Fred directly, out of Vera's hearing," Louise said. "She was going to confront him just after seeing us off. But now that he's made such a public fuss about it, I doubt that he'll tell her." She looked around at her companions. "Doesn't *anyone* here know?" They all shook their heads. "Then I guess we'll just have to wait until we return to Acorn Hill on

Friday. Perhaps we'll be back in time for Fred's drawing. After that, I imagine everyone will know."

"Or at least they'll know what Fred thinks it is," chuckled Lloyd.

∽

"He wouldn't tell me," Alice said. She watched the conflicting emotions on the face of her friend Vera. For one thing, Vera was dismayed that Alice had asked Fred directly what the doohickey was, because Vera felt it was somehow giving up a point in the contest of wills between her and her husband. Fred might even think that Vera had encouraged Alice to ask. But Alice also knew that her friend was frustrated that the attempt had been unsuccessful.

"*Hmmph!*" Vera finally fumed. "Well, that just goes to support my theory that he doesn't really know." She had added some sugar to her tea and was absentmindedly stirring it. The two were alone in the inn; Jane, as well as all the inn's guests, had gone out. Alice sat patiently while her friend scowled down into her mug.

Finally, Vera looked up again. "I tell you, Alice, this whole contest business is just a clever way for him to find out what the doohickey is without admitting his ignorance. Someone in town is bound to know."

"I'm not certain, Vera," said Alice. "As you say, it may be that someone in town will know what it is. But even if that's true, how will Fred know that they've given the right answer if he doesn't already know what it is? He's the judge of the contest, after all. He's the one who is going to say who gave the correct answer."

Alice gave a sidelong glance at her friend. Vera was taking this little misunderstanding rather too much to heart, Alice felt, and she didn't want to say anything that would upset Vera further.

Vera was momentarily stymied by this argument, but she quickly rallied. "Well," she said, "he's probably counting on the chance that the correct answer will be obvious once he sees it. Or maybe he'll take the one that seems most likely, then go to that person privately to see if they *really* know. Or if nobody seems to know, and the guesses all seem wild, then he can just pick whichever one he likes best and nobody will be the wiser."

Alice frowned at her friend. "Vera, you know how Fred feels about his tools. He loves precision, accuracy, and specificity in both tools and in talking about them. It wouldn't be in his nature to let everyone in town think that the doohickey is a—I don't know, a lathe or something—unless he knew that was true and accurate. He's not going to let people be misled or deceived about a tool, of all things." She set down her mug of tea with a definitive thump.

Vera pursed her lips unhappily but did not dispute Alice's assertion. Instead, after a moment, she said thoughtfully, "Maybe he's just buying himself time."

"Time?"

"Yes, of course," said Vera, warming to her new theory, "time to do his own research. He's probably looking it up on the Internet even as we speak. Or he's posting a digital photo of it to some tool discussion board, tapping their collective wisdom to tell him what it is."

Alice looked doubtfully at her friend. "Well, I suppose it's possible..."

Unheeding, Vera looked up with a gleam in her eyes. "What we need to do is find some way to monkey-wrench the doohickey contest."

"Monkey-wrench?"

"Sure, you know, throw a monkey wrench into the works. Mess with Fred's head a little bit." Her eyes narrowed as she schemed. "For instance, suppose we came up with our own answer to what the doohickey is. Something that's maybe slightly plausible, but unlikely. But then suppose the contest box was filled with guesses all saying that same thing. Even if Fred does find his answer on the Internet, that would throw him, wouldn't it? If he had a hundred guesses all saying that it's X when the Internet tells him it's Y, that would put him off balance, wouldn't it?"

"You want to stuff the contest box?" asked Alice dubiously.

"Well," replied Vera, draining her mug of tea, "it's one idea. There might be other ways to have some fun with this contest. I'll have to give it more thought."

"I don't know, Vera," said Alice, shaking her head. "It seems to me more likely that he's known what it is all along. In that case it doesn't matter how many false guesses you enter."

But Vera's face had assumed a satisfied look, and she rose from the table with only "We shall see." She looked at Alice appraisingly, and Alice could easily guess what her friend was thinking.

"Don't look at me, Vera Humbert. Whatever you come up with, I'm not going to help you do any monkey-wrenching."

Vera gave a shrug, smiled and turned away. As she took her mug to the sink, Jane walked into the kitchen carrying several bags of groceries.

"Alice, do you mind if we . . ." Jane caught sight of their guest. "Oh, hello, Vera. I didn't realize you were here. How goes the celebrated doohickey contest?"

"I've got some hopes," replied Vera happily and then laughed when Jane gave Alice a questioning look. "I must be off. Alice will tell you that I have a nefarious plan to implement." She made her farewells to the two sisters and bustled out of the kitchen.

Alice carried her own mug to the sink, and then began helping Jane put away the groceries.

"What was that all about?" asked Jane.

Alice shook her head. "I'm not quite sure. I think Vera's going off the deep end about this doohickey business. Both of them have really dug in their heels." She sighed.

Jane recognized the note of concern in her sister's voice. Casting about for a useful suggestion, she said, "Maybe Fred would tell you what it is."

But Alice shook her head. "I asked him." Bringing her attention back to the moment, she looked at her sister. "What were you saying when you came in?"

"Ah well," Jane faltered somewhat. "I wondered if you'd had a chance to figure out your work schedule."

Alice hesitated, looking thoughtfully at her sister. Finally she said, "Yes, I've talked with the duty nurse. I definitely can stick to the schedule we discussed." She sighed. "It's not that I object to minding the inn by myself occasionally, but I wish you'd tell me what this mysterious project is that's going to take you away afternoons."

Alice waited, but Jane did not respond. After a moment, she continued, "You implied that it's something that requires Louise's absence, which leads me to think that it's something to which she would object. And if it's something that Louise would object to, why should I feel otherwise?"

"Louise can be awfully set in her ways, Alice, you know that. She sometimes objects to something for the sole reason that it's not something she would choose to do herself. That doesn't mean it's not the right choice for someone else."

Alice knew well enough the justice of this observation; nevertheless, she shook her head. "I still wish you'd tell me what this mysterious *it* is."

Jane smiled. "Just think of it as a bit of personal growth or exploration. I don't even know if it's something that will work out. I may not . . . I may not be able to manage it. But if it does work out, I want it to be a surprise."

Alice sighed again and shook her head. "Well, you'll have the afternoons that you wanted free, so I hope your program of self-exploration proves fruitful."

Chapter Five

$\mathcal{I}$'m interested in what you said about the doohickey, Mrs. Smith," Harry was saying, "and the battle of wills it has sparked between husband and wife. The relationship between partners in a marriage has always been a great theme and subject for stories. I'm sure everything will turn out fine in their case, but the causes and complications of such marital misunderstandings make terrific fodder for tales, both comic and serious.

"I know that the rest of you have been diligently searching your brains for stories to tell." The driver's gaze swept over them in the rearview mirror. "If you're having trouble coming up with anything, you might try thinking along those lines. Sometimes it's easier to come up with a particular kind of story. Narrowing the range helps focus the thinking.

"Any marriage stories out there?"

Ethel cleared her throat uncertainly. "Well, I've been thinking about something that happened a long time ago. I don't know if it's what you'd call a marriage story. It's about a time when a wife almost got her husband into trouble, though quite by accident. But it's just something that happened. Not necessarily a story in any proper sense."

Louise, of course, had heard her aunt tell many stories about her life, and she immediately began racking her brains to guess what incident Ethel was referring to.

The driver was already encouraging Ethel. "Oh, pooh, Mrs. Buckley," said Harry, "I marked you as a natural storyteller the moment I met you. I'm sure you have a good one for us."

Ethel, who never objected to a bit of flattery, smiled demurely and said, "Well, all right then. As I say, this all happened a number of years ago. There was a farmer and his wife—we'll call them Dan and Evie—and they'd lived for years on their farm well out in the county. Their place stretched along the north side of a two-lane road. On the south side was another farm, owned by the Fullers, and they'd been there even longer than Dan and Evie.

"Both farms were pretty big, but it happened that the two farmhouses were quite close, almost across the road from one another.

"Bert Fuller was getting along in years and was reaching the point where he didn't really have the stamina for farming any longer. Both the Fullers' kids had moved to the city years before, because they had no interest in farming. Bert approached Dan and asked if he wanted to buy the Fuller farm, but Dan said no, he was content with his lot.

"So Bert pretty much retired from farming, and he divided some of his land for house lots, though he only sold off a few, and those were pretty remote.

"Finally, the day came when Bert and his wife decided it was time to retire to Florida, and they got ready to sell their own house and move away. They kept most of the remaining land, but they weren't about to keep the house. They didn't need it and they didn't want the hassle of renting it. But you can imagine Dan and Evie's surprise when Bert Fuller decided to sell that house to a hippie family named Tomasso.

"'They're young,' Bert said to Dan, 'they could use a little break starting out in life. They're—what do you call 'em?—Back-to-the-landers. Sure they've got some foolish notions about farming, but they're sincere. Give them a chance. You'll like them.' And so Angelo and Claire moved in across the street from Dan and Evie.

"Well, Evie just took against them right away. Most days, they wore normal work clothes around the farm, but whenever they went out, they wore these outlandish hippie clothes—what do you call them, tie-dyed? There was no issue about what they wore to church, though, because they didn't go to church. Even worse, they had two children, a little boy and a little girl, about three and four, and the parents didn't provide them with church-going either.

"And, land's sake, the way they lived! The Fullers, of course, had electricity and everything, but you wouldn't know it the way these hippies lived. They hardly ever turned on a light or used electricity for anything. Instead, they filled the house with kerosene lamps and used those for light. Evie said she couldn't see the reason of bothering with lugging the kerosene and trimming the wicks and cleaning the chimneys, not to mention the smell, for the puny light those lamps gave off, when they could have had nice bright light at the touch of a switch.

"They also installed wood stoves, both to heat and to cook with. Now a nice big iron cookstove can be very convenient, but it meant that Angelo had to spend all kinds of time cutting and chopping wood, in addition to his other farm chores and his regular job as a school librarian. Not that they were running the place as much of a farm. They had a couple of cows to milk, and a few sheep that they sheared, and some chickens and whatnot. But they didn't produce enough milk or wool or eggs to sell and support themselves. It was all for their own use. Well, that was fine. Evie could understand the convenience of having your own, though it involved an awful lot of time and effort that wasn't rewarded with some income from it as well.

"Evie even heard them once talking about an outhouse—as if the Fullers hadn't had indoor plumbing installed. They never built one, but still.

"Claire seemed to be some sort of writer, though just what she wrote, Evie was never sure. And they had the two children, as I said, and a couple of dogs. They sure kept busy, Evie had to give them that, but it grated on her that they would insist on doing things the old, difficult, time-consuming way when society had progressed to make many such chores easier and less labor intensive. It seemed downright stubborn to her, a willful rejection of progress. It seemed unnatural.

"The Tomassos were a great source of fascination to the folks in town. Evie had been accustomed to her friends dropping by in the afternoon on occasion to exchange gossip, but once the hippies moved in, her friends would visit even more frequently just for the chance to watch them from Evie's kitchen window. Evie used to joke to her husband that this increase in visits from her friends was the only good turn Angelo and Claire had done her.

"Dan, however, felt different. These young people really were very ignorant about even the basics of farming. Oh, they had read a lot of books and they even did a pretty good job of putting what they'd read into practice. But still there were lots of little things that just weren't included in their books or that weren't explained very well, and so they got in the habit of asking Dan about how to do things.

"This could have been annoying, of course, if they had come running to Dan every time they got themselves into a corner, but the youngsters really tried hard not to pester him too much. They'd try their best to figure things out for themselves before they asked his advice, even though they sometimes got themselves into trouble that way. They'd try to wait for a convenient time to approach him, and they were always very grateful for his help. And of course Dan's inclination was to help out his neighbors when he could, and since there was due consideration on both sides, and since the youngsters were always ready to help if Dan needed an extra pair of hands, all three got on pretty well.

"Dan even found he was taking a liking to these idealistic young people. More and more often, he'd wander across the road just to visit, though why he felt a need to be away from Evie, I'll never figure. If he got the sense that they were in over their heads on some project, he'd offer to help without waiting to be asked. He got in the habit of stopping across the road most days when he'd finished his own chores and chatting for a few minutes before going home to supper. He got to know more about the family and why they'd moved to the country. He heard about their unhappiness living in the city and why they didn't think it was a good place to raise their kids, and he decided that they'd been right to make the move, even if they didn't know much about country life. They were certainly eager to learn, he always said.

"Dan and Evie would often talk about the hippies, but the more Dan seemed to be sympathetic to their ideals and their goals, the more Evie spoke against them. She'd read about hippies in the newspaper and seen them on television. They often seemed disruptive, even anti-American. Dan took the position that he wouldn't make many of the choices that the youngsters did, but he could understand their reasoning, and it was certainly their right to make those choices.

"Evie continued to see their lifestyle as some sort of personal affront.

"But if Evie was frustrated by her husband's softhearted fondness for the hippies, she could take comfort in the fact that her cronies in gossip all agreed with her. It got to the point where the topic of conversation would rarely be anything other than the hippies. Whenever during these observation sessions they would see Dan heading across the street to chat with the youngsters, Evie would shake her head and bemoan the amount of her husband's time they were monopolizing. She would say, 'Most of these hippies have been spoiled since they were born, and now they think the world owes them everything.'

"Evie's friends clucked in sympathy. 'Why does he indulge them?' asked her friend Ruth.

"'He's just too softhearted,' said Evie. 'He feels kinda sorry for them. He says they're idealistic, and it's not their fault if they weren't taught the things they need to know in order to act on those ideals.'

"They sat silently for a moment. Ruth's cousin Tammy looked over at Evie. 'You ain't worried, are you, that those hippies might . . . you know.'

"Ruth, always direct, picked up the thread. 'You ain't worried about them being violent, are you? Planning riots right from across the road? I don't think Dan would stand for that.'

"'No, it's just the drain on his time and energy that I don't think is right. Like I say, they're just spoiled kids.' She got up to busy herself at the sink.

"'They told Dan that before they bought the Fuller place, they'd been thinking of joining a commune.' The women all considered this in shocked silence.

"'Why didn't they?' Ruth finally asked.

"Evie hesitated, wondering, *Did Dan say they had actually considered it? Or just that the subject had come up?* Finally, she replied, 'I'm not sure. I guess they couldn't find one they liked.' A new and terrible thought struck her. 'Oh my,' she said, 'what if they try to start one themselves? Right across the road here?' They contemplated this horrible possibility.

"Then Ruth said, 'They've been here almost a year now. If they were going to start a commune, they'd probably have done so by now. Besides,' she added uncertainly, 'I'm not sure the zoning would allow it.' They were all unclear about the details of zoning, a process that had only recently been adopted by their town.

"'They say hippies also take a lot of drugs,' said another friend. 'They all smoke pot.'

"Her friends looked expectantly at Evie, who seemed puzzled by the statement.

"'You know, Evie, marijuana. Ever see anything like that?' Tammy asked eagerly.

"'Well, no,' she admitted, 'and Dan wouldn't tolerate anything like that.'

"'Where would they get it anyway?' wondered Ruth. 'I'm sure you couldn't get pot around here.'

"'There are plenty of places up by the ridge where they could grow anything they wanted and nobody would be the wiser,' said Tammy.

"'Well, they did post all their land against hunters,' Evie said, 'and—'

"'Look, there they are!' exclaimed Ruth, pointing out the window.

"The women all fell silent while they watched the hippie family with deep suspicion. Unaware that they were under surveillance, Angelo, Claire and their two children left their yard and began walking down the road in the direction of a swimming hole about a half mile away.

"After her friends left, Evie continued to be concerned about this idea that the hippies might somehow be involved with drugs.

She brooded over it all the rest of the day, and finally, that evening she raised the question with Dan.

"For about five minutes, he laughed so hard that he couldn't even answer her. Finally he said, 'Evie, you've got the wrong idea about those people. They are much more the my-body-is-a-temple type. If a doctor prescribes them medicine, they'll *probably* take it, though only with reluctance and probably for only about half as long as instructed. But they won't take aspirin or any other pill you can buy over the counter, they don't drink alcohol, they have no use for tobacco. Drugs would run counter to everything they believe.'

"Evie felt relieved. Though she didn't really like the hippies, and though she had been quick to run with the idea that they might be doing something illegal, she hated to think that anyone she knew, any neighbor of hers, would actually be involved with marijuana or the like."

"I've met some people like that," Florence said under her breath. "They *are* strange." From the look on her face, Florence seemed to sympathize with Evie's distrust of the hippies.

"The next day, Evie was in her kitchen working on an apple pie when she heard the wail of a siren. This was an unusual sound out on her road, so she registered it immediately and wondered what the problem might be. Her first thought was that there must be a fire someplace, so she looked out the windows of the kitchen but couldn't see any sign of smoke in the sky. As she moved through the house to look out other windows, the sound of the siren got louder. In fact, she now thought she could hear two sirens.

"*It must be something bad,* she thought to herself. *I wonder what it is.*

"She was about to call for her husband but then realized that she'd seen Dan heading across the street to the hippies' house about a quarter of an hour before.

"The sirens were now very loud, and as she returned to the kitchen, she was astonished to see two police cars coming down the road, their lights flashing. She soon saw that the lead car was from the county sheriff's office.

"It moved by her house and came to a stop, facing the Tomassos' house. The other cruiser, following, also turned toward their house as it slid to a stop.

"The cars' sirens stopped, though their lights continued to flash. Then the driver-side doors of both cars opened, and two officers exited cautiously.

"One officer remained by his car, while the other scuttled in a crouch around to the trunk of his car. He opened it, reached in and pulled out a bullhorn, and then returned to his post behind his open car door. Evie saw him raise the bullhorn to his mouth, and as he did, she recognized that he was Charlie Pearson, county sheriff in those days.

"'This is the police,' the bullhorn boomed. Privately, Evie thought that the moment for that announcement had passed, but the officer continued, 'Come out with your hands up.' For a while nothing happened.

"Then the door to the hippies' farmhouse banged open and her husband Dan came striding out, yelling, 'What on earth is going on here?'

"His appearance produced an instant reaction in the sheriff. He threw his bullhorn into his car, pushed his glasses farther up on his nose and waved his gun in the air. Evie didn't know much about guns, but pointed toward her husband, it looked large and black and very deadly. Now, without benefit of the bullhorn, the officer was yelling, 'Stay where you are, stay where you are,' at the top of his lungs.

"Dan stopped with a shocked look on his face, and then slowly raised his hands in the air. 'Charlie,' he said to the sheriff, 'what on earth is going on?'

"'I think you'd better just stand still for a minute, Dan.' But now the sheriff had another matter to contend with.

"Once she had gathered her wits, Evie had come storming out the kitchen door, and she now marched up to ol' Pearson. The deputy kept his eyes on Dan.

"'Charlie,' scolded Evie, 'what's going on here? Why are you two pointing guns at my husband?' And turning to the other officer, she shouted, 'Put that gun down! That's my husband.'

"Sheriff Pearson turned to her with an exasperated but determined look on his face. 'Get back, Evie,' he warned, 'this is official police business. Dan will be fine. We don't want him, we want the Tomassos.' Turning away, he called, 'Where are they, Dan?'

But Evie quickly demanded, 'What do you want them for?'

"Exasperated, Pearson hissed, 'Drug raid,' over his shoulder, 'as if you didn't know. You're the one who said they were running folks off their place so they wouldn't discover they were growing pot. We're here on the strength of your . . . observations.' But a look of dawning unease was in his eye.

"Evie's heart sank into her stomach. 'My what?' she cried. 'I don't know about any observations.' She was aware of Charlie's reputation for honesty and hard work, but she also recognized that he was getting old for his job.

"With a visible effort, Sheriff Pearson reined in his emotions. 'Evie,' he said as calmly as he could, 'didn't you tell Tammy that the Tomassos are growing pot in a field somewhere up by the ridge? Because that's what she told me. And when I happened to mention it to Stu here,' he nodded in the other officer's direction, 'well, he was eager to check things out as soon as possible.'

"But Evie was shaking her head long before he had finished. 'I never told anyone that, Charlie. I was just, just speculating with a group of gossiping women. When I mentioned it to Dan, he said there was no way in the world it could be true.'

"The sheriff stood for a moment looking back and forth between Evie and Dan, and then heaved a long, deep sigh. 'Better stand down, Stu,' he called over to the other officer. 'It looks like there's been a misunderstanding.'"

"Well, I'd say so," said Cyril, with a little guffaw.

"I guess those boys were a might quick on the draw," Lloyd added.

"You can't be too careful," Florence retorted with a small sniff.

"The Tomassos had been in the house all along, it turned out. Their children were frightened by the arrival of the police, and when Angelo had wanted to go outside, Dan had insisted that he go instead and see what was going on. The whole family had been rather shaken by the sight of the police cars screeching to a halt in front of their home and armed police officers pointing their guns toward the house.

"The sheriff explained as soothingly as he could that they had received faulty information, and he acknowledged that they had been overzealous in acting on it without first checking it out thoroughly. His apology was clearly sincere, and the Tomassos, once they had recovered from their original shock, accepted it graciously. Sheriff Pearson had left Evie's role in the business unmentioned, but she knew that, if she was going to continue to be their neighbor, she had to confess what she'd done.

"So Evie's apple pie didn't stay at home that night. Instead, she took it across the street in order to give herself a pretext for visiting before she confessed her secret.

"They took the news surprisingly well. Indeed, they seemed to regard the whole thing as a bit of a lark, as no harm had been done.

"'We're under no illusions about what people in town think of us,' said Angelo. 'Or some people, not everyone.' He looked at Dan, who had come across the street with Evie. Angelo gave a small shrug. 'We're . . . not what those around here are used to. And the unfamiliar can make people nervous.'

"Evie wanted to ask why they couldn't reassure their neighbors a little bit by acting more normal, but she reminded herself that she was there to apologize rather than chastise. Biting her tongue, she looked around the dining room, which had been so familiar to her when the Fullers had lived there.

"The Tomassos insisted that Dan and Evie stay and share some of the pie, and Claire brewed coffee to go with it. The children were very excited at the prospect of the unexpected treat, and they sat quietly at the table with shining eyes.

"As Claire handed around mugs, Dan said, 'So you drink coffee? I thought it might be one of the things you didn't touch.'

"Claire smiled. 'Even we have our limits. I don't know how we'd function without it.'

"'Your children are very well behaved,' ventured Evie, still looking at their expectant faces.

"Claire smiled more broadly, and Angelo rubbed his son's head. 'One of the advantages of living the way we do,' he said, 'is that we get to spend more time with them. Not just time: We're able to do more as a family.' He gazed at his children with evident pride. 'I think that sort of focused and . . . mindful attention is good for kids. It lets them know in the deepest possible way that they're loved.'

"And then, to Evie's astonishment, Angelo looked at them with an apologetic expression and said, 'I realize it's not a complete meal, but would you object to our saying grace? Thankfulness is one of the things that we try to teach the children.'

"And they all bowed their heads.

"The next week, the Tomassos reciprocated with a pie of their own, and soon the traffic back and forth across the road was pretty steady, not just for Dan but for Evie too. She found herself sharing her knowledge and experience with them the way Dan did. She loved talking about canning and preserving or homemade recipes for household cleaners. She still maintained that she'd never want to go back to those old-fashioned ways herself, but recalling them reminded her of her childhood, and she found that she enjoyed teaching the Tomassos the things she remembered. It was satisfying.

"Evie's friends found her more subdued after that when it came to the sharing of gossip, but most remarkable, thereafter she would never allow a word to be spoken against her neighbors across the road."

Chapter Six

When she finished her story, Ethel sat back with a satisfied expression. Louise was rather astonished. She was sure that the incident described had never really happened; her aunt's hint that it was a true story had just been a bit of craftiness on her part. Nevertheless, the story demonstrated a greater degree of self-awareness than Louise usually gave her aunt credit for.

On many occasions Ethel's own gossiping had led to uncomfortable or embarrassing moments for herself and her sisters—though none, thank goodness, that had brought the police with lights flashing and sirens wailing. The Howard sisters would remonstrate with their aunt when these incidents occurred, and Ethel was always sincere in her apologies and dismay. But try as she might, she could not keep the impulse to meddle curbed for long.

Louise admired her aunt for telling a story that underscored one of her own weaknesses. The other passengers, who were all aware of Ethel's penchant for gossip, seemed unsure how to respond.

Louise heard Lloyd clear his throat. "Well, Ethel," he said gently, "that was certainly an instructive story. Naturally I can only agree that gossip can sometimes result in unforeseen complications. But I have to say that I think you're being a little unfair.

"Gossip, after all, is a form of communication, and often a very helpful one, I would argue. It promotes bonds between people, it disseminates information that the community may need to know, it helps define the standards of what is and is not acceptable within the community.

"As a matter of fact," he continued, "I've got a story that might be thought of as the flip side of the one that you just told, and if nobody objects, I'm going to go ahead and tell it."

There were a number of encouraging comments, and so Lloyd settled back to begin.

"My story is also about a husband and wife, and this wife also loves to gossip. In fact, if anything she's an even bigger gossip than Evie. We'll call this couple . . . George and Maxine, and Maxine, I'll have you know, is at the center of pretty much every gossip network that exists in their town.

"Maxine is one of those high-energy people, always on the go, always talking, and especially always talking about the other folks in town. To a large extent it's just a natural outgrowth of her exuberance, her joy in being alive. Gossiping makes her feel connected to people, part of the fabric of the community. She's not malicious about it—though she's happy enough to spread the bad along with the good, don't get me wrong. She has a whole round of people whom she checks in with every day, whether in person or on the phone. And if anyone in town needs information about something, Maxine is generally the first person they go to.

"Maxine has the perfect job for her personality: She works as a clerk at the post office. This means that she sees most everyone in town at some time or another, and many people stop by on a daily basis to pick up their mail. So she's always in the center of the information network.

"It also means that she was one of the first people in town to meet Douglas. He was just moving to town and he came in to open a post office box. Naturally, Maxine took a neighborly interest in his story—where he moved from, and so forth—but she found that he's not very communicative, and she likes to think she's not the type to pry. And I'd just like to point out that enjoying gossip is not the same thing as being nosy, even though people often equate the two. I find that many gossips are content to take the stories that come along without going out of their way to poke into their neighbors' affairs.

"Anyway, George and Maxine live in a nice little house in town with their son Adam. There's a house on the corner of their block that's owned by a fella who's moved to Florida, and he has arranged with a local Realtor to find renters for the place, but these, of course, tend to come and go. It takes Maxine almost a week to realize that the new tenant who has rented the house is this Douglas who came into the post office, and that her son's new friend in the neighborhood is Douglas's son Brian.

"Once she realizes who he is, Maxine also notices that this new neighbor keeps to himself. He doesn't seem to go out to a regular job, and nobody knows what he does for a living. He comes into the post office every day to pick up his mail, but he never seems to receive anything except the usual bills. Any time someone in town tries to strike up a conversation with him, that person doesn't get very far. He avoids any direct questions about himself or his past, and soon people get the idea that such inquiries are not welcome.

"On the other hand, Maxine often finds Brian at her kitchen table when she gets home from work, studying with Adam. But Brian is a painfully shy child, and whenever she tries to talk to him and draw him out, he turns beet red and starts stuttering. She can't see putting the poor kid through that.

"The youngster is a good kid, but his father quickly develops a reputation in town as a mysterious misanthrope. Only Maxine, who sees him regularly in the post office, and who knows his son, at least a bit, doesn't think he's quite as odd as people make him out to be. He's certainly not friendly, he's private, even, but she doesn't get the sense that he hates all humankind, as some in town would have it. She doesn't hesitate to say so when the subject comes up.

"One day Maxine comes home to find Adam at the kitchen table studying alone. 'Where's Brian?' she asks. 'Did you two have a fight?'

"'No,' says Adam, shrugging.

"But Maxine can tell that there's something going on. 'What then?' she persists.

"With an exaggerated sigh and rolling of the eyes, Adam says, 'He stayed after school for a Latin Club meeting.' He stops, but Maxine waits patiently for the other shoe to drop. 'There's a girl he likes.'

"*Ah,* she thinks, *my son's feeling abandoned by his friend, who has betrayed him with this interest in the opposite sex.* She smiles. 'Well, you know,

Adam, as you and Brian and your other friends get older, you'll all probably want to be spending more time with girls.'

"Adam gives a noncommittal shrug. 'Maybe,' he admits.

"Thinking her son could use some company, Maxine pours two glasses of milk and pulls out some Oreo cookies she'd hidden in the back of the cupboard. Mother and son talk their way through some cookies, and then Adam begins to tell her a bit about his friend Brian.

"Before moving here, he says, Brian had lived all his life with his parents in a small town out West. Brian's mother fell ill the year before, and his father took family leave to care for her. But she died suddenly, and father and son found themselves somewhat at loose ends.

"'Then out of the blue, Brian's dad comes home one day and says he's rented a house here and they up and moved.' Adam shakes his head, apparently sharing in the bewilderment his friend had felt when he confided this.

"'But why here?' Maxine asks.

"'Brian says his dad grew up around here. But they've been looking for his relatives ever since they came back, and they can't find them.'

"'Can't find them?' repeats Maxine, but she is even more surprised by the idea that Douglas has some connection to the area. She's never heard anyone say anything to suggest that. 'That does seem strange. But do you think Brian is unhappy here? I don't know what his life is like, but at least he's made a good friend in you. Even if he did stay after school for Latin Club,' she added.

"Adam flashes her an appreciative grin for the sympathy but then speaks seriously again. 'I think he misses his old school sometimes, and his mom, but I think overall he's pretty happy here. He says at least the teachers aren't always giving him the "poor thing" look, 'cause of his mom, you know.'

"Maxine nods and makes a mental note not to give him that look either.

"Not too long after that, George is coming home from work one day, and he sees Douglas trying to carry a chest of drawers into his house all by himself. Naturally, George goes over to help him, and between them they soon get it inside. George isn't as withdrawn as Douglas, but he is a pretty quiet guy himself, and he and Douglas have the friendship of their sons in common, so they actually hit it off pretty well. From that day forward, they become friends too.

"After some time, Douglas starts to open up to George a little bit about his past. He confirms what Brian told Adam. Douglas grew up in a town not too far away. He ran away from home when he was fifteen, it turns out, and he's had no contact with his family since. Now that he's a widower and a father, he regrets this, and he's moved back to the area to try to find out what became of his parents and his brother and sister.

"But his tendency to be aloof has been hampering his efforts, he admits. Rather than move to his actual hometown, for instance, he's moved to this one instead, two towns away. He's tried looking up his family in the phone book, but there's no listing. He's driven past his old house several times, but he doesn't recognize the people who live there.

"George suggests talking to people in his old neighborhood or at the town hall, but Douglas won't—or can't—make those sorts of approaches. His shyness, coupled with his embarrassment over the fact that he ran away from home, prevents him. He's happy to pursue any leads that involve no more than looking up information, but the thought of just walking up to strangers and asking questions paralyzes him.

"George shakes his head as he tells Maxine all this. If Douglas really wants to find his family, George feels he should be willing to put himself out there more. But Douglas is adamant that he won't do this. He doesn't want to call attention to himself. 'And,' says George warningly to Maxine, 'if that's the case, I think we need to respect his privacy.'

"Maxine purses her lips but nods in agreement.

"A few days later, however, George and Maxine are amazed when Douglas comes to call. He has big news: His sister has contacted him. She now lives in the next county. She's his only surviving relative, it turns out, but she had heard that her brother was back and was looking to contact the family.

"Well, Maxine had inadvertently activated the gossip network back when Adam first told her the story. She hadn't even really intended to, but she was so surprised by the idea that Douglas had local connections that she started asking everyone she knew if they could place him. Naturally, the rest of the story came out as she was making her inquiries.

"She did not, in fact, speak directly to anyone who remembered Douglas or his family, but nevertheless, the story started to get around. Finally, it reached one woman who did remember the family, and who knew the sister, her married name, and how to contact her.

"The result of all this was a happy reunion for Douglas, a host of new relationships for Brian and the beginning of a happy new life for them both.

"So you see," concluded Lloyd, "sometimes a little gossip is a good thing. Not everyone can be counted on to speak up for himself, and sometimes it's necessary for others to do the talking for him."

Ethel beamed and patted his knee. She knew that he had told this story as an implied defense against anyone who might criticize her own habit of gossiping. He could be such a dear.

Florence, however, who was every bit as much a gossip as Ethel, leaned over to Louise and said in a stage whisper, "I still think it's a terrible habit."

Louise searched Florence's face for even a trace of irony, but she found none.

Chapter Seven

*J*ane found herself driving uncharacteristically slowly as she followed the country roads some miles outside of town. Though it was a beautiful day for a trip through the Pennsylvania countryside, she was distracted and unable to enjoy the pleasures of the drive. Her nervousness over her upcoming appointment was causing her to reduce the pressure on the gas pedal.

She had told Alice that this was a project of "personal growth," which she supposed it was, though the closer she got to her destination, the more it felt like foolish fantasy—a potentially dangerous, foolish fantasy.

She found the road she wanted and turned left onto it. Open fields stretched along both sides. On the left, the land was somewhat rugged, but on the right, the terrain was unnaturally flat. A long ribbon of pavement ran down this field, parallel to the road, and on the far side of the pavement, propeller airplanes were lined up in a neat row. They squatted in the sun like odd, brightly colored insects.

Several low buildings clustered about a quarter of a mile away at the end of the airstrip, and when Jane arrived at them, she entered a small parking lot. After she turned the engine off, she sat quietly for a few moments, breathing deeply. She said a quick prayer for the strength to see her decision through, then stepped out of the car and closed the door with a decisive thunk.

The gray, nondescript building toward which she walked could easily have seemed ominous, but someone had gone to the trouble of planting flowers by the door. Incongruously, lacy café curtains hung in the windows. And a sign on the door, handmade but colorful, announced, Skydiving Class Today. Welcome, Students!

Jane felt oddly reassured. She squared her shoulders and approached the door.

Inside, seven or eight people milled about. The coffee urn on a far counter looked decrepit, but the coffee aroma was alluring. As Jane stood looking about for a moment, trying to get oriented, a young woman with a clipboard approached her. She had an open face and a friendly smile, and she moved with athletic grace.

"Hi," she said, "are you here for the skydiving?" She gestured with the clipboard to indicate that students had been required to sign in for the class.

"Yes, I'm Jane Howard." She said it with a rising inflection at the end, as if asking a question.

The woman glanced down at her clipboard and made a small notation. "Yes, got it." She looked up and smiled again. "Welcome, Jane. I'm Miranda Maples. I'm going to need you"—she was fiddling with a stack of papers—"to sign one of these release-and-waiver-of-liability forms, please." As she turned toward Jane, she added with a wink, "After all, we are going to be jumping out of airplanes."

Jane guessed that other students had reacted to the release form just as she did: It wasn't exactly unexpected, and it was certainly understandable, but it somehow made her intentions more immediate and dramatic. Jane gave what she hoped was a brave smile—though she suspected her face telegraphed absolute terror—and accepted the paper.

She cast her eye over it while barely registering its contents. But Miranda waited patiently, and Jane fought the urge to sign without looking, just to get it over with. Finally, she wrote her name on the line at the bottom and handed it back with a weak smile.

"Thanks," Miranda said brightly. "If you like handouts, there are informational packets over there, or if you prefer, you can go straight for the coffee. We'll start with an orientation in just a few minutes." Jane noticed a handful of folding chairs set up in the back of the room.

Normally, she was an outgoing person, but having to sign the release form left Jane feeling a little subdued, so she picked up one of the packets and began flipping through it, as much to avoid her fellow students as anything else. When she moved to one of the folding chairs, she inadvertently set off a general movement in the same direction, and in a few minutes they were all sitting and waiting quietly.

Jane looked about at the other students. The first thing that struck her was that there were more women than she expected. Somehow, she'd assumed that skydiving would appeal to more men overall than women, this despite the fact that she herself had always wanted to try it. In addition, many of the students were older than she had expected.

Miranda stepped in front of the group and smiled reassuringly. "Welcome again, everyone, and congratulations on taking the first step to an experience you will never forget.

"Almost everyone who comes here says that skydiving is something they dreamed about for years before they ever worked up the nerve to try it. So if that sounds like you, you should feel proud that you've taken a step to realize your dream.

"Almost everyone who comes here *also* says, right about now, that they're feeling a bit apprehensive." This drew some nervous chuckles from the crowd. "That's fine. It's perfectly normal to feel that way, but I'm going to be sharing some information with you that I think will allay your nervousness.

"Now, as I think you all know, we can take up a limited number of people on any given trip. Some larger facilities bring people in, go through all the training, and go right up that same day. We don't work that way. We like to ease people into the experience a bit more slowly. We've asked you all to attend the two orientation-and-training sessions, this one and the one on Wednesday. Then we'll schedule you individually for your actual jump according to the day that is best for you.

"The first thing to address is the kind of jump you'll be doing. Many of you have probably seen or heard about tandem jumping. That's where you jump strapped to an instructor in a special tandem harness. Those are popular because there's very little for the student to do. The instructor does all the work, and the student is basically a passenger. As a result, very little training is required, and you can get to the jump itself very quickly.

"We don't do tandem jumps at this facility. As I say, you're basically a passenger in that kind of procedure. We think that you, the paying client, should have the chance to do a bit more. That's not to disparage tandem jumping or those who enjoy it. If that's the experience you are looking for, go for it. It's just not what we offer.

"You may also have heard about static-line jumping, or instructor-assisted deployment. These aren't quite the same thing, but they both are based on the chute opening automatically, activated either by a line or by the instructor as the student exits the aircraft. We don't do these either.

"The jumps we do are solo free-fall jumps. That doesn't mean, however, that we toss you out of the plane on your own." This provoked further nervous laughter. "No, you will be jumping with two instructors, myself and my coinstructor Dale, and we will be holding onto your harness as we go out." She held her clenched hands out before her, miming the tight hold she would have on the student's harness. "We will free-fall like that until it is time to deploy your chute.

"Once your chute opens, we will let go, and you will fly your chute down to the ground on your own. We'll be talking to you over a radio the whole time, to help you steer your parachute down to the drop zone. And, of course, we'll have Raffi, our trusty cameraman, on hand to film your jump, so that you'll have a memento of the experience.

"I've got a video to start us off," she continued as she rolled out a tall cart with a monitor perched on it. "Don't worry," she said, before turning it on, "there will be plenty of time for all your questions."

Chapter Eight

The travelers had arrived at New York State's Tappan Zee Bridge over the Hudson River. The bus rolled along the seemingly endless causeway, and conversation died out as the passengers admired the mighty river and its picturesque shoreline.

Harry shook his head. "This bridge is so impressive. It's hard to believe that it's essentially obsolete."

"What do you mean, Harry?" John asked.

"They built this bridge to carry a hundred thousand cars a day at peak capacity, but traffic's now well in excess of that, if you can believe it. Look at it now. It's certainly not yet rush hour, but the traffic is still steady. They're going to have to do something about it—replace it or build a tunnel or something."

"I hope they keep a bridge here," said Cyril. "I love the view from the middle of the river."

"Now then," said Harry, as they approached the eastern side of the bridge, "speaking of stories. You know, of course, that one of this country's earliest great storytellers was Washington Irving."

"Rip van Winkle," Florence said promptly.

"And the headless horseman," added Cyril.

"Exactly," nodded Harry, "Ichabod Crane and *The Legend of Sleepy Hollow*. Well, as a matter of fact, Sleepy Hollow, New York, is just to the north of the bridge there, off to your left. We are passing through a very storied part of the country here."

Everyone gazed downriver as the bus completed its crossing of the bridge. "All this country must have looked very different in Irving's time," said John wistfully. "Wilder. Fiercer."

"That's true enough," said Harry, "though don't forget that many of Irving's stories looked back to yet an earlier time. Even in his day, people were worried about the spread of civilization. Be that as it may," he continued with an air of getting down to business, "who's hungry? We should eat before we get on the parkway."

It was, in fact, well past lunchtime, but this was a compromise they had made in planning the trip. Rather than start at what some might regard as an unreasonably early hour, they agreed instead to eat a late lunch.

"Well, there's an area coming up in a few miles that has a pretty good selection of restaurants," Harry said. "Seems to me it's time to stop and stretch and refresh ourselves. How does that sound?"

It sounded appealing. It was quite evident that everybody was hungry.

"In that case," continued the driver, "what are you in the mood for? There's the usual run of fast-food places, and there are regular sit-down restaurants. There's Italian or Chinese. What's your pleasure?"

"We'll be spending a fair amount of time on this bus," said John. "No offense, Harry," he continued in a jocular tone, "but it seems to me we could have a little break and go to one of the sit-down places."

"We can sit down in a fast-food place too," Florence said, thereby continuing a pattern that had characterized much of the planning of the trip. Most of those who had agreed to go were content to leave the planning largely to John. And John had been scrupulous about checking with his fellow travelers before committing to the route, timetable and places to stop.

Florence, however, balked at just about every proposal that John made, usually complaining about either the expense or inconvenience involved. Each time Florence complained, John tried to accommodate her, which meant he then had to go back to the other travelers and clear the new plan with them as well.

John was unfailingly polite, even cheerful, throughout the process, but the others could see that he had to spend twice as much time and energy planning this trip as should have been necessary.

Louise sighed. *And here we go again,* she thought.

"Well, you know, Florence," said Ethel, "I think I'd prefer something other than fast food myself." Louise smiled, ducking her head so that Florence wouldn't see her merriment. At times her aunt could really come through in a pinch. As Florence's friend, Ethel could most easily get away with openly disagreeing with her, and indeed, Florence now pursed her lips but said nothing more.

"It's settled then," said Harry after a moment. "I know just the place."

Unfortunately, their expert guide failed them in this case: The restaurant he had in mind was closed. In fact, it gave every appearance of having gone out of business.

Harry pulled the bus into the empty parking lot, climbed out of the driver's seat and stood with his hands on his hips, studying the restaurant as if he could tell why it had closed just by looking at it. After a few moments he climbed aboard, shaking his head. "It was a good place, very nice people," he muttered as if to himself. "I can't imagine what happened to it." He looked up at his passengers with a troubled expression. "Well, folks, I'm not quite sure what to suggest next."

"We passed several places right back there," Florence said. They had all been cheap fast-food places.

Everyone was silent for a moment, and then John said, "Well, we don't want to waste half the day looking for a restaurant. We probably should go with the bird in the hand."

The other passengers, with no great enthusiasm, agreed. Florence sat back in her seat with the glow of a minor triumph on her face.

Louise ate without enjoying her meal. She picked at her french fries, then put them aside in favor of a plastic container of salad.

"Oh, cheer up," said Ethel, sitting across from her. "You've eaten fast food before. It isn't going to kill you." Ethel herself had clearly decided to make the best of it, biting into her burger with vigor.

Louise shifted uncomfortably in the hard, plastic chair. She smiled weakly at her aunt, trying to emulate Ethel in her positive thinking. Of course she'd eaten a great deal of fast food in her life. Who hadn't? The convenience had much to recommend it, even if the greasiness and the bright fluorescence of the restaurant did not. She merely replied, "It's not like our Jane's cooking."

"Of course it's not, dear," said her aunt brightly, "but then, little is." Ethel smiled at her niece.

The party had settled into a long bank of two-person tables along one wall of the restaurant. At the far end, Harry was engaged in lively conversation with John. Harry was, Louise reflected, one of those people who would be completely at home in almost any situation. Well, she supposed, in his job he must inevitably eat a lot of fast food himself, though she had the definite impression that it wasn't his first choice for a meal either.

Lloyd sat next to Ethel, and Cyril was across the small table from him. But Lloyd had scooted closer to Ethel while Cyril was somewhat turned in his chair and engaged in the conversation between John and Harry. Florence sat closest to Louise and her aunt, looking smug.

"I'm with Louise," said Lloyd, who had heard her comment about the food. "This can't hold a candle to Jane's cooking."

"You're turning out to be quite a storyteller, Lloyd," said Louise. "You're a man of hidden talents." Lloyd beamed, but even as she said it, Louise reflected that her comment about hidden talents wasn't really true. Lloyd had always been a talker, a bit of a raconteur. Louise had just never thought of this behavior in terms of *storytelling*.

"I think this Harry Bailey is wonderful," said Ethel, lowering her voice. "He knows how to make the time fly on a trip like this."

Lloyd nodded. "He's quite a character," he said. "We're lucky to have him."

Louise glanced down the row in Harry's direction, and just as she did, he looked up and caught her eye. Even as he kept up his conversation, he gave her a wink as if he knew what they were saying about him at their end of the tables.

Harry brought the bus as close as he could to the door of the restaurant. He'd already brought the heat up, and Louise actually felt quite snug as she settled into her seat. The food may not have been great, but it was better to have a full stomach than an empty one. The other passengers were quiet, and she sensed that, as she was, they were feeling content.

Louise watched the landscape as they made their way back to the highway. It was both unknown to her and completely familiar, because it contained exactly the sort of development that one finds off highway exits everywhere. Undoubtedly it was on the outskirts of whatever town they were near, but it had its own concentration of restaurants and service stations for the benefit of those, like herself and her companions, who had pulled off the road for a quick break.

A whisper from Florence broke into her observations. She leaned close to Louise and asked, "Dear, do you think that any of the others resented stopping at the fast-food place?"

"What on earth would make you think that, Florence?"

"Well, a couple of the men didn't finish all of their food. And for that matter, I noticed that you didn't eat all of your french fries."

"Why, Florence, did it ever occur to you that I wanted to leave room so that I could have croutons with my salad?"

"My goodness, I suppose I just imagined that people were upset with me."

"Florence, you are truly remarkable."

"Thank you."

Chapter Nine

Once Harry had brought the bus to the steady hum of highway speed again, he began commenting on Lloyd's story as if he'd just finished telling it.

"I was glad you brought some children in, Mr. Tynan," he said. "I mentioned the relations between husbands and wives as a popular subject for stories, but, of course, the relations of parents and children are often part and parcel of that. And besides, I have a particular fondness for stories about kids myself. Does anyone else have a good story that involves children?"

"As a matter of fact"—Cyril cleared his throat—"I have a story that I was thinking about over lunch, and it does indeed involve kids. I don't know if you'd call it a story about family, per se, though it does feature two families who were very close. And—I don't know—I thought you all might get a kick out of it."

"By all means, Mr. Overstreet," Harry responded. "Let's hear it."

"This is a story from a time when I was a teenager and you good people were just babies. It's about two families who were neighbors and good friends. Each family had several children, and the whole gang of them grew up together and were very close. There were seven kids in all, but there was only a little more than four years between the oldest and the youngest, so they all made good companions. The ringleader was the oldest of the group, a girl named Morgan.

"Since the families were so close, the kids came and went between the two homes with equal familiarity, and any or all of them might as likely be found in one house as the other. And though each child had a room to himself in his own family's house, every child had some bed that could be used in both houses, so there was always a certain improvisational element about who might be sleeping where or who might show up for meals on a given day.

"As they got older, these kids would often play up and down the neighborhood as a group or go to the park together. And while each had friends of his own in school, they all remained loyal to one another even as teenagers. As they aged, they also grew fond of pulling off jokes and pranks as a group. Their peers in school referred to them playfully as Morgan's Gang, but it became a name that they themselves embraced.

"Of course, they weren't a real gang, in the bad sense. They were essentially good kids, though as I say, with a fondness for pranks. They played some pretty good ones over the years, and the best ones were always those thought up by Morgan. Their first victims were their own parents, as you might guess. One time, for instance, when both sets of parents were away for a day, they swapped the entire contents of the living rooms of the two houses, re-creating each room in the other house as closely as they could. The parents laughed as hard as anyone, though, of course, they made the kids put everything back.

"They would often swap places themselves as well, so that an inattentive parent who thought he was talking to one child would suddenly find himself addressing a different child, not necessarily his own. Another time, they piled the entire contents of both families' garages into one, leaving the other completely empty. The family with the newly clean garage was thrilled, but the thrill didn't last.

"One time, a brush salesman called at one of the houses when all the kids were home with one of the fathers, who had carelessly drifted off in his easy chair. They invited the salesman in and made him show off all of his wares, spending an hour explaining everything, but then they declined to buy anything. They recommended, however, that he try the neighbor's house, since those people often bought from salesmen. Then one of the older kids kept the salesman distracted for an extra few moments, while the rest managed to race next door. The salesman, when he arrived, found himself facing the same group of children, all swearing earnestly that no, they hadn't just been at the house next door, they didn't know those people. The poor fellow didn't fall for their act a second time, but he didn't make a sale either, and I suppose that's as close to mean as the group's pranks ever got.

"Now, every autumn"—Cyril gestured to the autumnal weather outside the bus—"football was a big thing in this town. The high school team, the Cyclones, was consistently good, and it had a few state championships to its credit over the years. The Morgan's Gang kids were not particularly interested in football themselves, but they would often attend games with their friends, and they shared the local pride in the success of their team.

"One year, football fever was very high indeed. The team had been strong the previous season, most of its best players had returned, and it was undefeated after its first few games. People in town started talking about another state championship for the Cyclones. The biggest obstacle was going to be the team's hated rival, the Stevenson High Knights, which was also starting the season strong. And the Stevenson game was fast approaching.

"So in the spirit of pitching in, the Morgan's Gang kids decided to see what they could do to help.

"On the day of the Stevenson game, spirits were high. This was a critical game for both teams: Barring a tie, only one would emerge with an undefeated record, and a loss could stall the momentum that each team was building toward the championship. Boosters of both teams were pulling out all the stops. The Cyclones had an advantage because the game was to be played on their home field.

"As the visiting Stevenson fans arrived, however, they found that someone had gone to a lot of trouble to provide some school spirit even to this away game. As they took their seats in the visitors' sections, young people were handing out large colored sheets of cardboard. These were to produce one of those mosaic effects you often used to see at games: Each piece of cardboard was a single color, but when the entire visitors' section held them up at once, the Knights' fans were informed, the total display of cards would spell 'Go Knights.' It was sure to antagonize the Cyclone fans on the other side of the stadium.

"This was the first time in years that either school had tried this procedure at a football game, but this was such an important game that the Stevenson supporters were feeling very smug that their side had thought of this morale-boosting tactic. The young volunteers—there seemed to be half a dozen or so—made their way through the crowd, making sure that everyone had the correct color cardboard and understood when to hold it up.

"When the Knights got possession of the ball, the fans were told at the end of each play that they should hold up their signs to send the 'Go Knights' message.

"As it happened, the Cyclones got the first possession, and they marched down the field for a score. Emotions were already running high on both sides, and the Knights fans were eager to see the score evened up. The Cyclones kicked to the Knights' receiver, who made a decent return before being brought down.

"Excited, the Stevenson fans yelled and shouted and, as they'd been directed, held up their placards. Immediately, a roar went up from the home-field seats, though some Knights fans did notice that, rather than a roar of defiance or dismay at the 'Go Knights' message, it sounded more like laughter. And then a very strange thing happened. The Cyclone fans apparently had signs of their own, because they now held up their own placards, which produced the message 'We know.'

"Many of the Knights fans took little notice of this, but a few began to wonder. The action resumed and all eyes turned back to the field. The Knights tried a running play and gained a few yards before their halfback was tackled. Dutifully, the Knights fans all held up their placards again, and again, the message flashed from the Cyclone side, 'We know.'

"Now one of the Knights cheerleaders had been frowning at the displays in the opposing stands, and the next time her team's fans flashed their placards, she watched their display, and an expression of outrage crossed her face. She immediately began shouting into the ears of the other cheerleaders, and then, amazingly, they all began climbing into the stands. The young volunteers, the ones who had been helping to direct the flashing of the placards, took note of this, and decided it was time to make their way toward the exits.

"The cheerleaders initially had a hard time getting their message to the folks in the stands, so that at the end of the next play, more than half of the visitors once again dutifully held up their placards. It was still possible for the home-field fans to make out one last time the barely legible message, 'We're losers,' that the visiting fans had unknowingly been flashing.

"The Cyclone fans responded with a final 'We know' and a chorus of jeers before putting away their placards for good.

"Were the Knights demoralized by the trick that had been played on them? Certainly the visiting fans were noticeably more subdued for the rest of the game, and the Cyclones went on to a decisive victory.

"But after the win, the Morgan's Gang kids, who had dreamed up and implemented the prank, were almost as widely celebrated by the Cyclone fans as the players themselves. In fact, many folks who attended the game can't remember the score but still remember in detail the great flash-card caper."

Chapter Ten

Everyone on the bus had a good chuckle over the story of the Morgan's Gang and their prank—everyone except Florence, who merely gave a small sniff and expressed the opinion that the gang's prank was in poor taste.

"Oh, lighten up, Florence!" a muffled male voice said behind her.

She turned about to spot the culprit, but all three men had ducked down in their seats. Ethel laughed and pointed toward Lloyd, but remarkably, Florence also laughed in spite of herself and announced, "Somebody better behave himself."

Louise let out a slow breath, an indication of her relief.

"Entertainment is all well and good," Florence said, "but the best stories should also teach a lesson. They should show us something of what's necessary to do in life, even if those lessons are not cheerful or happy.

"For instance, I've always hated those stories about true love at first being thwarted and then somehow triumphing. The fact is that young people often want to marry someone who is completely unsuitable, and when that happens it is the responsibility of their parents to set them straight, to help them avoid making a major mistake."

"Well personally, I like a story about kids just being kids," John replied, perhaps feeling defensive on behalf of his friend Cyril. "So much of what you hear today is about children who grow up too fast or in terrible circumstances or who make bad choices that they come to regret. You wonder sometimes if kids have any chance just to have fun any longer, or if they've all been brainwashed into thinking that shoot-'em-up video games are the height of human pleasure." He shook his head.

"It's a different world from when we were young, John," said Cyril. "You've got to expect some changes."

John grimaced. "I realize that. But still, there's a degree to which kids will be kids in any age. Your story shows that."

Cyril nodded thoughtfully. "I guess you're right. Our attitudes depend on whether we want to emphasize the similarities or the differences in the experience of childhood from one generation to the next. You're arguing that as a society we put too much emphasis on what's different, and you think we're not sufficiently aware of the things that are the same."

"Exactly," said John, nodding vigorously.

"I think the only difference is in the parents," Florence persisted. "They've gotten much too permissive. If you hear more than you used to about children who get into trouble, it's because they haven't been raised with a firm enough hand to begin with. It's the parents who have changed," she said with conviction. "They've gotten lax."

Spoken like someone who's never had children, Louise thought to herself. She would never give voice to such a thought, but as a mother, it did seem to her that a gap often existed between those who had actually been parents and those who had not. Even as she thought that, counter examples on both sides of her imagined divide came to mind. *If you don't like it when Florence makes sweeping generalizations,* she upbraided herself, *then you shouldn't make them yourself.* She felt guilty, too, because she knew that their own failure to have any children had been a source of great distress to Florence and her husband.

"Well, I don't know, Florence," Cyril was saying. "I think part of it is just a greater degree of openness. Even when we were young, kids got into trouble. It just wasn't talked about. And kids who got into serious trouble were sent away. But that doesn't mean it didn't happen."

"Of course there have always been bad parents," retorted Florence. "But the fact that there's now more 'openness,' as you call, it is just a symptom of what I'm talking about. Back in our day, people didn't talk about a child who had gone astray because they were ashamed—as they should have been. Nowadays, poor parenting has become so common that there's no longer any stigma attached.

"You mark my words," she continued, "if parents would just take their responsibilities more seriously, kids today would be a lot better off. Sometimes—usually, even—parents see more clearly than their children what needs to be done, what the correct course of action is. And when that's the case, it's the parents' responsibility to show the children the correct path."

"Mrs. Simpson," called Harry, "it sounds to me like you might have a story for us along those lines."

Florence seemed taken aback for a moment. "No, I don't have a story on the subject. I was just trying to make a point."

Ethel spoke up from the middle seat. "Well, you've made me think of one, Florence," she said. "Perhaps you'll like it."

Louise watched a look of curiosity cross Florence's face as Ethel began another story.

"Florence has put me in mind of a story about a mother whose daughter wanted to marry an unsuitable man. Theirs was a nice family, well off. Their name was ... Beck. The father was an executive at a major corporation and the mother was a member of the most prominent social organizations—indeed, she was president of her town's garden club. They had a lovely house in the suburbs, with the most gorgeous flowers you ever did see, and their daughter Iris had been raised with all the advantages.

"So what did Iris do? She decided she wanted to declare her independence by marrying a ne'er-do-well musician. This young man was a wily fellow with no means of his own and no roots. He spent weeks on the road with his band, and was employed part-time—if at all—between gigs, usually as a busboy. Everyone called him Mikey, as if he were twelve years old.

"It was clear to Iris' parents that Mikey was only interested in her for her money. And really, if Iris had been honest with herself about her own motivations, she would have realized that she was more interested in upsetting her parents than in marrying this young man.

"But her vision was clouded, and Iris was all set to make a terrible mistake, until her mother Emma found a way to intervene.

"When Iris had first started dating this young man, her parents both objected. But the contrariness of youth is such that their objections only made her more determined. Well, Iris' parents had run up against that kind of behavior from her before, and so they soon pulled back and ceased to warn her about Mikey.

"Unfortunately, that strategy didn't work either, because it just left her all the more open to his lies and flattery. And so before her parents knew what was happening, Iris started talking about marrying Mikey.

"Her parents, shocked, had hoped that the infatuation would blow over once they ceased to speak against it, but now they were in trouble. They still had the same problem: If they openly opposed young Mikey, they would only make their daughter more determined to stay with him. But marriage to this layabout was a mistake that they couldn't allow.

"'Hold your friends close and your enemies closer,' Iris' mother declared, and so she began inviting Mikey to the house more regularly in order to study him and plan her strategy. 'If you're this serious about him, dear, we must get to know him better,' Emma told her daughter. She began inviting him not only to parties but also to family meals and excursions. And she watched him like a hawk.

"Mikey didn't have much on the ball to begin with—a good nose for an opportunity maybe, but if he truly had gifts he wouldn't be living the kind of hand-to-mouth existence that he was. In fact, the family's increased interest raised his daily standard of living considerably, and he undoubtedly thought that he was already beginning to reap the rewards of his scheming for innocent Iris.

"Then he began to get careless. Like many other coarse young men, Mikey had a wandering eye. So Emma arranged opportunities for young Mikey to spend time in the presence of attractive young women—at parties or playing tennis or what have you. She suspected that he would be unable to resist the temptation to let his attention stray. And stray it did.

"Just as she expected, Mikey was a cheat and a flirt. Emma was careful never to show that she had noticed his flaws, and he did manage to keep his behavior hidden from Iris, so Mikey came to believe that he was being sufficiently crafty. Emma, however, kept every wink and flirtation filed away mentally for future use.

"Soon Emma began to think that she could see her way clear to opening her daughter's eyes about Mikey. And yet, she wondered if this would be enough. Even if Iris could be induced to throw the scoundrel over, there might soon be another Mikey, and another and another. The poor woman began to see that she not only needed to nip this marriage in the bud, but she also needed to arrange a more permanent solution to the situation.

"Well, Emma thought, if Iris had decided she was ready for marriage, then marriage is what she would get.

"The truth is, Emma had had her eye on a suitable candidate for some time. Winthrop 'Win' Sanderson was the son of Emma's good friend Emily. When their children were younger, Emma had often dreamed that Iris and Win would someday marry, but when Win left for Harvard, her fickle daughter mostly forgot him. After his graduation, however, he returned. He now was working very successfully in the city, and he was unmarried. Emma decided that this represented a special opportunity.

"Mikey's presence on the scene provided an excuse for Emma to arrange more than the usual number of social activities for Iris under the cover of introducing Mikey to their friends and family. But Emma realized that she could also use these occasions to bring Win back into the picture as well, and she was quick to do so. Emma daydreamed that a simple side-by-side comparison of the two men would be enough to make Iris see the error of her ways.

"It did seem a mismatch when the two young men first met at a lawn party on a mild summer evening. It was the first of two parties that weekend to celebrate the birthday of Iris' father, and numerous family friends and neighbors had been invited. Win was casually dressed in a button-down shirt, chinos and loafers. Mikey was a few notches below casual in his T-shirt, shorts and flip-flops. Emma, in a pale-green sundress, circulated with lemonade and fancy cookies. She managed to get most of the other guests involved in a game of croquet, after which she settled down to chat with Win, Mikey and Iris.

"Win, of course, had the easy manners and pleasant nature of those sure of their place in the world. Mikey was vastly overmatched: He was crude and uncultured and even lacking the wit to recognize his better. Win treated Mikey with the consideration required by good manners, but Mikey was too oblivious of their respective social positions to even understand this. With some surprise, Emma realized that Mikey truly did consider himself to be on the same level as Win.

"Win, of course, was too well bred ever to behave in a manner that would suggest his superiority.

"Win's good manners often led him to inquire about another person's interests, and Emma listened as Win drew Mikey into a conversation about music. They managed some common ground on the subject of the music popular with young people, though as Win sought to expand the conversation to other types of music, it quickly became obvious that for all his alleged professional interest in the subject, Mikey was narrow in both his tastes and knowledge.

"Iris dutifully praised Mikey's own band, but even she found herself quickly moving beyond her boyfriend's limited range of musical experience.

"Emma hadn't thought that Mikey's musical tastes would be anything like her own, but she had at least wanted to give him credit for a broader knowledge of what was, after all, supposed to be his chosen field. Finding that his knowledge barely exceeded the average fan's, she was appalled by his claims to be a professional.

"Win next tried Mikey on films, but though he had seen most of the current special-effects blockbusters, he seemed to have little to say about them beyond the opinion that they were 'cool.' Oddly, they *all* seemed to be cool, and Emma wondered if Mikey saw anything at all to distinguish one from another. As it happened, Emma had seen one of these films herself, and so she offered the opinion that this film seemed to have some obvious plot problems, despite its exciting pace and special effects.

"Win added some of his own observations to support this point, and even Iris made a joke at the film's expense, but when Emma pressed Mikey to comment, the idea that its plot had been weak seemed to come as a revelation to him. 'I hadn't thought of that,' he observed. The others had already guessed as much.

"Fortunately, Win was ready to pick up the ball again, to point out that not every blockbuster was poorly written. He cited one or two other examples—movies, again, which Mikey claimed to have seen, though apparently without coming to any conclusions about their being good or bad.

"Worse, to Emma's way of thinking, he seemed uninterested in the question. It seemed that if Mikey liked a movie, it was judged to be cool, and any additional reflection about its merits or shortcomings he regarded as a waste of time. Asked by Emma to name a film that *wasn't* cool, Mikey happened to mention one of Iris' favorites. Iris said nothing, but Emma watched the line of her mouth narrow.

"Emma, Win and Iris moved on to books, but it was clear that Mikey had no contribution to make on this subject whatsoever. Asked if he had read this or that best seller, Mikey always said no, and it was only with difficulty that Emma refrained from asking him to name something he *had* read. She wondered if he would have been able to come up with a title.

"The conversation continued in this manner for some time.

"By the end, Emma's hopes were high. She didn't see how Iris could fail to notice the huge gap between Win and Mikey. Emma was aware that she was open to being thought of as a snob—I'm sure she probably was—though she preferred to think in terms of 'having standards.' But her standards were not the issue here. The question was about Win's behavior, and Win, she felt, had been perfectly polite and civil to Mikey, never talking down to him. Win, at least, was not open to a charge of being stuck up.

"The fact was, Emma told herself, that while snobbery might generally be considered a bad thing, people had to make judgments about other people all the time. On those occasions when little depended on the outcome of those judgments, then one could afford to overlook whatever failings had been revealed.

"But on occasion a great deal depended on the judgments one made about others. There was no room for being careless in picking a spouse: One looked for the perfect candidate. *Of course* one needed to make judgments. One couldn't function in the world without making judgments about other people, for better or worse.

"The next morning, sad to say, Emma almost lost her advantage: She made the mistake of trying to lead Iris into making a negative remark about her precious Mikey. It was too soon. Iris bristled and even flew into a rage in Mikey's defense, though Emma consoled herself with the thought that her daughter protested too much. Emma quickly backed down. Her blockbuster was planned for that afternoon, and she knew she should wait for the right moment.

"The previous evening's lawn party was going to be followed by a Sunday afternoon pool party, though only a select few from the previous evening's guests had been invited. The only new face was a stunningly attractive young woman whom Emma introduced as Arabelle and casually described as 'the daughter of a friend of a friend.'

"Mikey, Emma noted with satisfaction, perked up considerably when Arabelle came on scene.

"The charming Arabelle took quite an interest in young Mikey, and as the young people all lazed by the swimming pool in the heat of the afternoon, she flirted outrageously with him. Cad that he was, Mikey responded in kind, despite the presence of his fiancée. After first ignoring it, Iris several times tried to drop a hint about his behavior. Mikey shrugged off Iris' attempts, and the lovely Arabelle proved unwilling to back off.

"By the middle of the afternoon, Iris was jumping up every five minutes to stomp back and forth between the pool and the house, seeking some outlet for her anger without making a scene. The bottles in the refrigerator rattled loudly when, on one of her trips inside, Iris yanked the door open as angry as she ever had been: When she'd left, Mikey and the luscious Arabelle had been splashing in the pool together.

"'My goodness!' exclaimed her mother. 'Whatever is the matter?'

"Iris seemed on the point of saying something but then merely replied, 'Nothing,' as she poured herself a glass of juice.

"Emma let that slide and said, 'Iris, could you be a dear and help me with these sandwiches? I wanted to offer them to your friends outside.'

"'My friends?' snapped Iris.

"Her mother shrugged. 'Well, the other young people. Could you give me a hand with them?'

"Iris heaved a sigh and moved to the counter where her mother was working. She tried to focus on the sandwich ingredients, and her mother knew better than to interrupt her thoughts. They worked side by side for a few minutes, and finally Emma said, 'There, that should do it. Would you take them out and offer them around, my dear? You're such a gracious hostess.'

"In fact, there was little grace in the way that Iris yanked the plate of sandwiches off the counter and marched outside.

"Emma never inquired into the details of what happened. All she knew was that, in the end, Iris failed in her desire to avoid a scene. Within a week, the wedding had been called off. Within two months, Emma had the satisfaction of announcing her daughter's engagement to Win Sanderson.

"And, land's sake, a month after that, she had the pleasure of attending—alone—a little piece of experimental theater produced by and starring an aspiring actress named Arabelle."

Chapter Eleven

"Wonderful!" crowed Florence. "Thank you, Ethel. That's exactly the sort of thing I meant. Now there's a dutiful mother. She's looking out for the best interests of her child and doing whatever is necessary to protect those interests." She lifted her chin with a satisfied expression.

Ethel said nothing, and Louise twisted in her seat to look at her aunt. Ethel wore the bland smile and middle-distance gaze of someone who is choosing to be quiet rather than disagreeable. Louise was quite sure that Ethel had intended the story as an extreme example that would highlight the limitations of Florence's ideas about child rearing.

Instead, Florence had embraced the story wholeheartedly. *At least she's consistent,* thought Louise.

For herself, Louise was inclined to be mildly upset at first by the bad light cast on a "fellow musician," but later more so because of the lesson presented by the story. Well no, she was forced to admit to herself, the truth was that she felt she *ought* to be put off by the story, but while she didn't agree with the lesson Florence drew from it, she understood too well the temptation to step in with determination to prevent a child from making a bad decision.

Louise was a mother herself. What parent would not understand the desire to save a child from making a terrible mistake? When her daughter was little, Louise reflected, that's exactly what she had spent much of her time doing—setting rules and limits designed to keep Cynthia safe. One of the hardest parts of parenting for Louise had been to gradually let go of that protective impulse as Cynthia grew older.

Louise firmly believed in the necessity of allowing children the chance to make their own decisions as they matured and, yes, their own mistakes. But believing in that principle did not make it easy to put into practice. The only difference between herself and Florence, Louise concluded, was that Florence continued to endorse a parent's natural protectiveness even when the child became an adult.

From the silence in the bus, Louise suspected that the others had the same mixed feelings as she did about Florence's enthusiasm for the story.

Cyril cleared his throat. "I don't know, Florence," he said tentatively. "Don't you find the mother's attitude in that story a bit . . . cynical?"

"Absolutely not," she replied. "She was acting in the best interests of her daughter. How could that be cynical? If anything, I would call it noble."

Ethel still maintained her quiet reserve.

"I guess it depends on how you define 'best interests,'" said Cyril.

Florence snorted. "Spoken like a man. Look, I understand that a bad marriage like the one Iris almost made can be hard on both of the people involved, but I still say that it tends to be harder on the woman than the man." Louise was reminded again that Florence's own marriage had been through a rough patch. "Even in this day and age," Florence continued, "men have much more freedom to get out of the house and seek their happiness elsewhere when the marriage is unhappy.

"If the marriage goes sour, it's the wife who ends up locked in a bad situation. Of course a mother like Emma is going to want to protect her daughter from that."

Louise sighed. It was one of the great conundrums of parenthood, she felt. She still believed deeply that parents must allow their adult children to make mistakes, even terrible ones. It was better for the child in the long run, she felt.

John cleared his throat. "I think what bothers me," he said, "is the kind of family dynamics that are implied by the behavior of the characters in that story."

Florence stiffened slightly. "What do you mean by that?"

"Well," said John, "the way that the mother acts unilaterally, manipulating rather than talking with her daughter."

"Talking," sneered Florence. "That's the thing about kids these days: They're so spoiled that they cannot recognize when something is opposed to their best interests, even when you point it out to them. They are so accustomed to getting their own way that even trying to talk them out of something just makes them all the more determined to do it. Just like in that story."

"Perhaps," said John, "it depends on how you go about the talking." Florence drew a breath to retort, but John continued.

"You know, I think I have a little story to share, one that touches on just this issue."

"Please go ahead, John," said Ethel, "I'd like to hear another point of view." She turned and smiled at her wise and dignified companion.

"Thank you," replied John. "In some ways, Florence, I agree with you, at least about the potential for sadness. Is there any greater sorrow for a parent than to see a child making a mistake that could affect the rest of his or her life?

"It's all too common, of course. Parents, in their desire to protect their children, often seek to stifle rather than direct the natural energy and curiosity of youth. In the attempt to shield a child from the dangers of the world, they try to control that child, too often producing a dangerous counter-reaction as the child grows older and naturally seeks to take greater control of his own destiny.

"Yes, children need limits and boundaries to test themselves against, but those limits and boundaries need to change over time as the child becomes more capable. Some parents, dismayed to see their children grow up so quickly, and eager to protect them as long as possible, fail to move those limits progressively outward, as we shall see.

"The Clarks had but one son, Malcolm, whom they doted on. When he was small, they were diligent to build a world around him in which he could move about safely, learning and growing while unaware of the cocoon of his sheltered environment. His parents were not overprotective necessarily, but they saw to it that nothing truly threatening ever entered little Malcolm's world.

"As he grew older, however, he began to strain more insistently at the constraints that made such protection possible. And his parents, rather than accommodating themselves to changing conditions, sought ever more eagerly to preserve the rigid structure.

"They worried desperately that any harm might come to him, yet eventually harm and unhappiness are the lot of everyone in life, and in their desperation to protect their beloved son, they failed to expose him to that important life lesson.

"Malcolm was aware on some level that his parents were just trying to protect him, but as he got older, he chafed more and more against strict parental controls. As before, the reaction produced by this chafing was a reflexive tightening of those controls, especially on the part of his father, so that after a while every interaction between them became a struggle for control.

"Sometimes when you walk a dog, you have to keep him on a short leash, but sometimes the best way to maintain control is to give a little slack. Malcolm's father could not bring himself to do the latter. It's not that he didn't understand the value of this strategy, but in truth, it simply scared him. What if something dire happened to his son as a result of his being too permissive?

"And so father and son found themselves locked in a negative situation, and as I say, their every interaction become a struggle. The son felt compelled to deny his father's authority when he could, and his father's unvarying response was to tighten the screws.

"This unhealthy dynamic began to affect every aspect of the boy's life. His grades in school slipped. He began hanging out with unsuitable friends. He was in minor but regular trouble with his teachers and school administrators. It only provoked his father to try to assert ever more control over his son.

"One evening, Malcolm was out at the mall with some friends, and they decided to go on a little shoplifting spree. It began because Malcolm wanted a new CD but didn't have the money for it. His friend David, in that half-joking, half-challenging manner of kids trying to get up the nerve for something, suggested the 'five-finger discount.'

"Slightly horrified, but also slightly thrilled at this prospect of rebellion, Malcolm reminded his friends that stores have security systems to protect against theft, especially those, like CD stores, where theft is easy and common.

"But David said he knew a way around this. The CD store, he knew, had an unwatched, unguarded back door that led out into a deserted hallway in the mall. It could only be opened from the inside, but when the store was staffed with the minimum number of employees, as it would be on a Tuesday night, there simply weren't enough people to keep track of that back door and the storage area that led to it.

"The youngsters spent another twenty minutes talking themselves into it.

"The entire group went into the store and spent time browsing and discussing the various options. Then several of the boys distracted the employees, who were kids not much older than themselves, while David, Malcolm and another boy, loaded down with disks, slipped into the storage area to make for the unguarded door.

"It was their bad luck that another young man was also indulging his rebellious urges. An employee of the store, he had snuck into the storeroom to have a cigarette. One might think that a spirit of solidarity with other boundary-pushers might lead this teenage smoker to allow the shoplifters to pass with a wink and a nod. But no, everyone has the line he will not cross, and for our smoker, it was stealing.

"The CD thieves had almost made it to the rear door when Captain Nicotine spotted them and sent up a shout. Naturally, they panicked and went barging through the door as fast as they could. But the smoking sentinel followed, and they all went pounding down a corridor to the main part of the mall, where they promptly ran into a pair of strolling security guards. All three would-be thieves were taken into custody.

"Now it was not the policy of mall management to call the police for every youthful transgression. The three friends were marched to the mall security office, where the head of security determined that they were not habitual offenders. Rather than bring in official backup, he settled on a policy of first-offense leniency.

"The boys called their parents, who were instructed to come down and meet with the security chief before escorting their would-be delinquents home."

"Why wouldn't they call the police right away?" demanded Florence.

"Don't want to be too quick to ruffle parental feathers," said Cyril with a shrug. "Might drive away customers."

"When the Clarks arrived, they found Malcolm sitting in a dirty orange molded-plastic chair under the bright fluorescent lights. He was pale and he slumped in his seat, his fingers pressed to the bridge of his nose. His companions had been picked up by their parents hours before, but the Clarks had been delayed, and Malcolm sat long enough to be thoroughly miserable.

"His parents pulled open the glass door and walked into the security office. They moved to their son and stood looking down at him for a moment, but he couldn't meet their eyes. Quietly, Malcolm's father asked him if he was all right, and Malcolm nodded. They turned away from him then and stepped up to the chest-high counter that ran the length of the room. They identified themselves and were led through a door at the far end of the room.

"After about twenty minutes, they emerged, escorted by the security chief, who murmured some parting words in a confidential fashion and then shook their hands. They approached their son once again. He had not moved in the interim.

"Clearing his throat, Mr. Clark said quietly, 'Mr. Brownlee says the CDs were all returned? There's no restitution required?' Malcolm nodded. 'Okay, then. Let's go home.'

"In the car, Malcolm slumped in the backseat, closing his eyes and saying nothing. He had the air of someone awaiting an inevitable storm, trying to will it away but knowing that was hopeless.

"When they got home, Malcolm thought about trying to escape upstairs to his room, but his parents directed him into the living room, where they all sat down. Though Malcolm had elected to remain silent, his parents' use of the same tactic was beginning to wear on him. They sat and looked at him patiently.

"Finally he said, 'It took you long enough to come get me.' Even as he said it, he realized that an accusatory tone on his part was not a good strategy. Nor, he had to admit, did he have any real justification for feeling put out. In part, he just wanted to trigger the inevitable outburst from his parents and get it over with. The waiting was killing him.

"But the Clarks merely looked mildly at each other. 'Did the other parents come more quickly then?' asked his mother.

"Suspicious of where this might be heading, Malcolm gave a cautious nod.

"'And how did they seem when they collected their children?' asked his father.

"Surprised at the direction the conversation was taking, Malcolm nevertheless thought about the question. 'Well, they were mad, I guess, for the most part.' He shrugged.

"'Did they yell at their sons? Right there in the mall?'

"'No, it was mostly silent-treatment mad, the just-wait-until-we-get-home sort of mad.' Malcolm shrugged again. 'David's father seemed more annoyed than anything else, like he just didn't want to have to deal with it.' Malcolm was still waiting for his own tongue-lashing to begin.

"'As a matter of fact,' his father said, 'we deliberately waited before going to get you.'

"Immediately, a sense of grievance welled up in Malcolm. They had let him just sit there all that time, his own parents. 'Why'd you do that?' he complained.

"His parents glanced at each other again, and then his mother said, 'It was Rev. Gladwell's suggestion.'

"Malcolm's head snapped up. They had talked to the minister? Why? Malcolm had the odd sensation that he'd been told on, ratted out. Were they trying to embarrass him by telling everyone about the incident? No charges had been filed, after all.

"But his father was already continuing his explanation. 'He thought it would be better for everyone. Better for us, to give us a chance to cool down before we saw you. Better for you, to give you a chance to think about what happened while the experience was still fresh. He sat here and prayed with us.'

"'He came over to the house?' asked Malcolm, shocked. All this seemed worse than going to jail. His parents weren't that religious. Did they really feel so desperate they had to call in a minister? The degree to which this seemed uncharacteristic of his parents threw him.

"'He was very helpful, very supportive,' said Malcolm's mother. 'He offered to go down to the mall with us, but we decided against it.'

"'Now,' said his father, 'why don't you tell us in your own words what happened.'

"Malcolm thought about what to say. In some ways, he would have preferred the tongue-lashing. 'I wanted the new Persimmon CD,' he finally admitted.

"With interest, Malcolm watched his father start to respond and then check himself. He began to appreciate the effort this was costing his parents.

"Finally, his father said, 'And you didn't have the money?'

"Malcolm shook his head.

"'But you know that we would give you money if you need it, don't you?'

"'But you don't!' Malcolm fired back. He'd been ready for that one. 'I asked you for some money last week and you just asked me what happened to my allowance.'

"His father's eyes flashed. Malcolm watched him go through the start and stop routine again. His mother reached out and almost put a restraining hand on her husband's arm but didn't.

"His father pursed his lips. 'All right,' he said at last, 'fair enough. We don't always give you money every time you ask for it. But we do give you an allowance, and one of the things that we're trying to teach you is how to manage the resources that you have. So sometimes when you ask for extra money, it seems important for you to learn that money isn't always there just for the asking.

"'And yes,' he admitted, 'we make judgments. Or at least I do. When it seems to me that you want extra money for something frivolous, I'm less likely to give it to you. But in fairness, I think you have to acknowledge that there are many times when you've asked for extra money and made a good case for it, and I've agreed.'

"Malcolm slowly nodded.

"'But that's not the main issue,' his father continued. 'Malcolm, do you think'—he looked his son in the eye—'that just because you want something and don't have the money for it, it's okay to steal it?'

"Well, of course he didn't think that, but even to say so was to have to admit what he'd done. They already knew what had happened. Why couldn't they leave it at that? But his parents waited patiently, and finally he shook his head.

"His father released a long-held breath. 'No, I didn't think you did. So how did it happen?'

"Tears were beginning to roll down Malcolm's cheeks. How *had* it happened? 'I dunno,' he started, but the effort to speak made it even harder to control the tears. 'We just . . . we just thought we could get away with it.'

"His father rubbed his face with his hands for a moment. Finally, he said, 'Malcolm, I don't believe that you think the ability to get away with something wrong justifies doing it. Do you?' Malcolm shook his head. 'I think that you were a group of kids with time on your hands and an itch for some kind of excitement, and you managed to talk one another into doing something you shouldn't. You're hardly the first.'

"Crying more freely now, Malcolm nodded.

"'Okay then,' said his father, standing up, 'we're going to trust you that this won't happen again.' He paused a moment and added, 'We love you, son. Get on up to bed.'

"Malcolm rose and left the room, but outside the door, he stopped and looked back. He was surprised to see his father slump back into his chair, as if exhausted. His mother laid a comforting hand on her husband's forehead, and Malcolm was even more surprised to see his father reach up and wipe away a tear.

"More than the hours in the security center, more than the lecture, more even than the forgiveness, it was the memory of his father's tear that came to his mind any time that Malcolm felt tempted to try something stupid once again."

Chapter Twelve

There were murmurs of approval when John finished his story, but a shake of her head from Florence.

"Well, it would certainly be nice if people in real life were as polite and reasonable as that," she said, "but in my experience, they're not."

"Perhaps not," said John softly.

The bus began to slow down, and they could hear the tick of the directional signal as Harry prepared to exit the highway.

"Welcome to Massachusetts, folks," he called. "Well, actually, we passed the state line a ways back, but I didn't want to interrupt. In any event, we are almost done with our first day of travel." As he spoke, he navigated the bus through smaller, local streets. Louise realized that dusk was upon them.

"As you know, we have reservations at the Purple Fox," continued Harry. "It's not fancy, but it's clean and convenient, right in the heart of downtown Spruce Grove."

Louise had tried to help John locate a nice bed-and-breakfast for them, but this was foliage season in New England, and especially with a party their size, they had to sacrifice charm for convenience and availability. The excursion company recommended this place and helped secure the reservations.

Soon, Harry was guiding the bus under the small portico of the Purple Fox Hotel. Louise heard Florence mutter, "Not exactly the Ritz," under her breath.

Harry helped them unload their bags while John went in to confirm their reservations. The lobby of the hotel was clean enough but small and sterile; the lights were too bright and glared off the tan floor tiles. A single plastic plant, some sort of palm tree, offered the only, rather incongruous, visual relief.

Louise and Ethel had decided to double up for the sake of economy, and John and Cyril had done the same. Lloyd and Florence were each taking their own rooms. Harry's room was factored into the cost of the bus rental, but Tabard Tours had an arrangement with the hotel chain so that he stayed at a reduced rate.

Because they were paying their own way, they each had to register separately. As they stood in line, Harry said, "Well, we've all had a long day together. We could arrange to go out for dinner as a group if you like, but my experience of these sorts of trips suggests that we might all be better off making separate plans. That way, those who want to turn in early can do so.

"The hotel here has a small restaurant." He gestured in the direction of its door. "Or there are several other places within a block or two. See me if you'd like a recommendation." Slowly, everyone registered and headed up to the rooms.

Louise sat on one of the twin beds, surprised at how tired she was. She briefly considered skipping dinner, but she could imagine the disapproval in Alice's voice if she knew about such a plan. She sat looking blankly about the room and waiting to ask what her aunt wanted to do. Just as Ethel returned to the room with extra towels, however, the phone rang. Louise picked it up. It was Lloyd asking for Ethel.

Ethel listened for a few moments, and then said, "No, that's fine, Lloyd. No, I'm much too tired. You go ahead. We'll be fine. Have a good time. Good night." To Louise's questioning look, she said, "The men are going out to some lodge restaurant nearby. Harry is leading them, but Lloyd didn't want to abandon us. He's very thoughtful." She looked shrewdly at her niece. "Is that okay? You look almost as tired as I feel. I thought perhaps we could have a little something at the restaurant downstairs. You don't mind missing the night life?"

Louise smiled. "No, Aunt Ethel." Determined to be polite, she steeled herself to ask, "What about Florence? Shall we call her room and see if she wants to join us?"

"If we see her downstairs, we'll invite her, naturally," said Ethel, "but if I know Florence, she'll be ordering room service."

Somewhat ashamed of herself for feeling relieved, but feeling relieved nonetheless, Louise said, "Shall we call Alice and Jane before we go down or wait until after dinner?"

Ethel frowned. "Oh, don't these hotels charge an arm and a leg for long-distance calls?"

But Louise was already rummaging in her purse. "Not to worry. Jane got us a prepaid calling card. We only need to call a toll-free number, and the charge for the call is deducted from the card."

"How marvelous. In that case, let's check on those sisters of yours." She sat down on the other bed to wait while Louise placed the call.

Jane and Alice were eating dinner in silence in the kitchen of Grace Chapel Inn. Earlier, Jane had spent an hour reading through the instructions and safety materials from her skydiving class, and she was beginning to have doubts about her ability to go through with her plan. She had hurriedly stuffed the materials into a drawer when Alice returned to the inn and then felt guilty about not having dinner ready.

For her part, Alice was brooding over the tension between Vera and Fred Humbert regarding the doohickey business. She was frustrated by her inability to resolve their problem. Of course, once Fred ran his contest, they would undoubtedly put it all behind them, but in her own way, Alice was as stubborn as the two Humberts: She wanted the tension resolved *now*.

And both sisters were missing Louise, who never would have allowed them to remain in such self-indulgent funks. "How do you think Louise is getting along?" Jane finally mustered the energy to ask.

Alice shrugged. Her concerns about Louise's absence rushed in on her again, displacing her worries about the Humberts.

"I'm sure Aunt Ethel will look out for her," Jane said reassuringly. They lapsed into silence once again.

The phone rang. Alice jumped and Jane nearly dropped her spoon. "Grace Chapel Inn," said Alice. "Oh, Louise, we were just wondering how you were making out. You've arrived in Massachusetts then? How's the hotel?" Alice's voice was animated, and she and Jane smiled at one another, their blue mood broken.

Jane watched Alice talk with Louise, trying to deduce what Louise was telling her. It sounded like lunch had been less than satisfactory. Something about telling stories? Jane couldn't quite make out what that was about.

But she was glad that Louise had called. She knew that Alice was worried about Louise's making this trip. For her own part, Jane thought it would be good for Louise to get out and see some new sights, but Alice had been fretting that Louise would try to push herself too hard. Jane didn't quite see why she might think this, but she realized that worries about loved ones are often not necessarily rooted in rationality.

She could tell from the conversation that their aunt Ethel had come on the line. She shook her head, smiling, when Alice gestured to learn if Jane wanted to take the phone. She would get all the news after Alice hung up.

Finally, Alice said, "Okay, Aunt Ethel. Sleep well." When she hung up the phone, she said to Jane, "They both send their love. Aunt Ethel is very impressed with the phone card you provided."

Jane laughed. "How's the trip?"

"Louise seems to be holding up well," Alice said with satisfaction. "Apparently that driver, Harry Bailey, is quite a character. He's got them all telling stories to pass the time. It sounds like he's turned it into something of a game."

"And Louise is enjoying this?" asked Jane with some skepticism. She tended to view her oldest sister as quite a reserved woman.

"What, you don't think Louise knows how to have fun?" chided Alice. "She sounds like she's really enjoying it."

"Okay, okay." Jane held up her hands in a gesture of surrender. After a moment, she said, "Speaking of games, how is Fred's contest going?"

Alice shrugged. "It's all I hear people talking about. I guess we'll have to wait and see."

In Spruce Grove, Louise and Ethel returned to their room after a quiet dinner in the hotel's restaurant. As they prepared to make an early night of it, the phone rang. Ethel answered.

"Oh, hello, dear," she said. "Yes, fine, thank you. And how are you? Wonderful! Yes, she's right here, I'll put her on." With a smile, she handed the phone to a puzzled Louise.

"Cynthia!" exclaimed Louise as soon as she heard her daughter's voice. "What a lovely surprise. How did you know where we were?" Glancing up at Ethel, she provided the answer. "Jane told her."

As Louise continued talking with Cynthia, Ethel turned away with a satisfied nod and a smile. For Louise, it was the best possible end to the day.

Chapter Thirteen

The next morning, the group gathered in the hotel's restaurant for breakfast. Though the hotel was nothing fancy, neither was it as unappealing as Florence had feared. The rooms had proven to be clean and comfortable, and everyone felt refreshed after a good night's sleep. They enjoyed a wholesome breakfast from the restaurant's buffet.

"Why do all hotels seem to serve breakfast buffet style now?" wondered Cyril.

John shrugged. "It must save them money. The offerings are more limited compared to the variety you'd find on a menu, and they probably don't need anywhere near the same number of waiters and waitresses this way."

"But I think there's also a psychological appeal for the customer," said Lloyd. "I look at this spread and I feel like it's quite a bounty, even if a menu actually offers me a wider range of choices."

"As long as there's coffee," said Harry, winking as he passed them, "I'm happy."

Soon they were back on the road, feeling contented from their rest and their breakfast and looking forward to reaching their destination by the end of the day.

Louise watched the landscape with great interest. Today was a bit cooler, but the sun shone brightly and foliage blazed in red, orange and yellow. They were now sufficiently far north that the change in the foliage was significant. To Louise, it didn't look like the colors had quite reached their peak, but what she observed was beautiful and inspiring. Harry reported that Portland, Maine, would be at peak beauty when they arrived.

For a while, the travelers were content to watch the passing colors, set off by picturesque New England villages with white colonial churches and quaint houses dating back to Revolutionary times.

"I must congratulate you all," said Harry after some time had passed. "You all told some interesting and thought-provoking stories yesterday. I appreciate the way you all took to my proposal with enthusiasm. Did you enjoy it enough to tell some more today?" There was a chorus of assents. "Wonderful! I can't wait to hear what's in store for us today.

"Before we start off, I thought I would throw out this idea for you to ponder. Your stories yesterday were all very realistic. By that I mean they involved people and places that any of us might expect to encounter in our daily lives, and they involved familiar dynamics like our relationships with family and neighbors. And, of course, these are all very important matters.

"But another pleasure in listening to and reading and telling stories is the opportunity to experience, by way of the imagination, places or times or events that we can't possibly know any other way. I'm sure you've seen movies set in distant galaxies or read books set in some early historical era or heard ghost stories around a campfire at night. They all deal with things outside our daily experience, and on that basis, these kinds of stories can provide a distinct pleasure.

"I'd encourage any of you who feel so motivated to try your hand at that kind of story today."

Louise was feeling a little self-conscious about the fact that she had not yet contributed a tale, so she was quick to say, "Well, as a matter of fact, I'd been thinking about a story that would transport us back to classical times."

"Excellent," cried Harry. "By all means, let's hear it."

Louise took a few moments to gather her thoughts.

"In ancient Rome, there was a slave called Servillius. He was a Greek who had originally been bought by the Martinius family to be a tutor to their son Marcus. As Romans went, the Martinii were neither particularly harsh nor particularly lenient with their slaves. In the case of Servillius, the family had agreed to free him when Marcus came of age, which was not an unusual practice.

"Marcus' father, however, died when the boy was just twenty, old enough legally to be the head of the family, but young enough to still be very reliant on the advice and guidance of his tutor. Even though Marcus continued to promise Servillius his freedom, he kept putting off the day, unwilling to face such a drastic change in the life he knew. Servillius bided his time, but he began to chafe at the delay, and though he was fond of Marcus, having virtually raised him, he began to grow resentful as well.

"One day Marcus surprised his tutor by announcing that he had made up his mind to get married.

"'Indeed? Congratulations, Master. Who is the fortunate girl?' asked the tutor, who had mastered the art of disguising his skepticism.

"'Pulchritudia Poltinius,' Marcus announced with a suitable air of solemnity.

"Servillius paused and then said, 'I wasn't aware that the master knew the young lady. Or indeed, any of the Poltinii.'

"Marcus waved his hand dismissively. 'That's not a problem. We know many families in common who will be able to introduce us.'

"'I see,' replied Servillius slowly. 'And how did you come to decide on Pulchritudia Poltinius, may I ask?'

"'I saw her today. She was at the temple with her family. They were making a sacrifice in honor of someone's birthday, I think. The whole clan was there, and as soon as I saw her, I knew she would be the wife for me.'

"'I see. Have you opened negotiations with the family?'

"'Not yet, but I don't think it will be a problem.' Marcus had sufficient modesty to refrain from elaborating, but his father had left him well-off, and though perhaps he was immature, he was sober in his habits. He was considered a good catch by most of the families in Rome with unmarried daughters.

"'And what about winning over the young lady?'

"This brought Marcus up short. 'What do you mean?'

"'Well, her parents are said to dote on her and to indulge her. I don't suggest that they would consent to just any love match, but neither would they be willing to commit her to a marriage that she did not herself desire. I believe you'll need to win her approval in addition to her family's.'

"'Well, that's fine,' said Marcus, recovering. 'It's not that unusual, after all. I'm sure I can convince her of my suitability as a husband.' He paused, then exclaimed, 'Poetry!'

"Servillius raised his eyebrows.

"'That's how all the young men are conducting their wooing these days,' continued Marcus. 'It's quite the fashion. Women wish to be won over with poetry.'

"Servillius squinted at him. 'Fads,' he said. 'And isn't that mostly young men seeking young lovers? Are you sure you want to seek your intended wife in the same manner?'

"Marcus laughed. 'No, no, Servillius. You must keep up with the times. Poetry's not used exclusively for flirting. This season it is quite the thing to use poetry in marriage negotiations as well.'

"'I assume you're not thinking of writing this poetry yourself, are you?'

"'Of course not. That's not how it's done. Professional poets supply all the young men. Servillius, I want you to do a little research. Find out who the best of these love poets is and what his prices are. Meanwhile, I shall arrange an introduction to the family.'"

"The way to a woman's heart is through her . . . ear?" asked Lloyd teasingly.

"Those were simpler times," remarked John.

Louise ignored them both.

"Now Servillius, as I mentioned, was getting impatient for his freedom. If Marcus would not grant it, his only recourse was to attempt to buy it. But that required money, and Servillius had few opportunities on a day-to-day basis to acquire any. This new task he'd just been given, however, seemed to open up fresh possibilities.

"And so, Servillius sought out Rufus Quintillius. Rufus was actually a distant cousin of Marcus, but from a branch of the family that had fallen on hard times. For a time, when Rufus was young, Marcus' father had taken the boy into his own household, as a gesture of kindness, and Servillius had acted as tutor to both boys.

"After a few years, Rufus' father had reclaimed him, but Rufus continued to live a much more precarious existence than his wealthy cousin. Nevertheless, because he had been under Servillius' care during a formative period in his life, the two had remained close. So Servillius went to him and told him of Marcus' marriage plans.

"'I'm sure it will be a good match,' said Rufus. 'Have you succeeded in locating a suitable poet?'

"'Here's my thought,' said Servillius, lowering his voice. 'What a surprise to find that one of Rome's most sought-after love poets is Marcus' own cousin, Rufus Quintillius, who is so successful,' he continued, dropping his voice even further, 'that he is able to charge very high fees for his work.'

"Rufus gave him a sad smile. 'It's an interesting idea, but I can't write poetry. Just ask my last tutor. He'd be able to tell you.'

"'Ah, but I'm thinking it's your old tutor who'll be doing the writing. I'll pass the poems along to you, you'll deliver them to Marcus and collect the fee, and you and I will divide that fee. Where's the harm? He's going to have to pay for his poems anyway.'

"'Why not just sell them to him yourself? You'd keep all the money that way.'

"'Rufus. This is Marcus we're talking about. He'd never be willing to pay me for something. His attitude would be that I'm his property and that any poems I wrote would be his property as well. He'd give me some small reward, certainly, but not money.'

"Rufus smiled and nodded. 'Yes, and the reward might be an extra serving of fish for the next month. You're right.' He hesitated. 'But still, do you think we should? I mean, are you any better at poetry than I am?'

"'As it happens, I'm a decent enough poet, and I have the models of my illustrious countrymen to draw upon. But more to the point, fads and fashions are fine, but ultimately, if the lady is interested, or is not, it won't be because of the poetry.'"

"I'm with him," Cyril said. "Poetry is all well and good, but it's not going to win over his intended."

"Hush!" scolded Ethel. "Every woman likes a bit of poetry. It's romantic."

"'Rufus?' cried Marcus. 'Is he really that skilled? Well, good for him.' He paused and added, 'Do you think he'd give us some sort of family discount?'

"Servillius blanched but managed to say, 'I'm not sure it would be appropriate to ask, Master. It is his livelihood, after all.'

"'Quite right, quite right. Well done, Servillius. Thank you. We shall certainly be engaging cousin Rufus.'

"'Have you been in contact with the Poltinius family then?'

"'I have, and I must say her father seemed quite receptive. I've been invited to dinner as a means of getting to know the family and the young lady better. In fact, I shall take Rufus as my guest. Surely it will sharpen his poetic insight to have some firsthand experience of the lady, don't you think?'

"'I expect so, Master.'

"That first dinner did not go well, however. As Servillius later heard it described, first by Marcus and then by Rufus, the young lady seemed dismayed to find herself being ogled by strangers—as she was heard to mutter to her cousin—and remained sullen for much of the evening. Even worse, she was apparently under some confusion as to which of their guests was Marcus and which was Rufus.

"Also present were the girl's parents, her brother Dominus—'a spoiled brat,' said Marcus, to Servillius' amusement—and her cousin Julia, apparently an orphan now officially under the care of Pulchritudia's parents. They were comfortable but by no means wealthy, and the father, at least, seemed eager to encourage the match. Despite the evening's halting conversation, Marcus appeared to be optimistic.

"'On the positive side,' said Rufus after making his report, 'I may be able to get us more work in a similar vein.'

"Servillius looked up sharply. 'What do you mean?'

"'I was telling some of my friends that Marcus will be paying me to write his poems, and it seems there are others in the market for such works as well.' Noticing the slave's scowl, he added, 'Everyone knows these poems are written by hired hands. It's no secret.'

"'No, but *my* involvement must stay secret,' said Servillius, 'or it will get back to Marcus.'

"'Please have more faith in me. I kept that part quiet. I just thought, if this works for Marcus, maybe we could branch out.'

"Servillius sighed. 'Let's focus on the immediate commission first.'

"Since Marcus wanted poems that were personalized for Pulchritudia, Servillius charged Rufus to be especially observant of the young lady's habits and qualities. After a full debriefing, Servillius got to work. His first efforts were duly passed on to Rufus, who sold them to Marcus, who had them delivered to Pulchritudia, who apparently received them with favor, for both Marcus and Rufus were invited once again for dinner.

"This pattern of events was repeated over a number of weeks.

"The day came, however, when Rufus made a surprising announcement to Servillius, who was making his usual secret visit in advance of his master's in order to deliver the poems.

"'I'm not going to go on doing this,' Rufus announced.

"Servillius checked his impulse to protest and looked carefully at Rufus. Finally, he said, 'Why, what's the matter?'

"Rufus gathered himself and said solemnly, 'I'm in love with Pulchritudia myself.'

"Servillius closed his eyes and sighed. Of all possible complications, emotional ones were the worst. They could lead young men into doing all kinds of foolish things. He pursed his lips and thought a moment. 'So are you going to set yourself up as Marcus' rival? That seems indefensible. One, he's your kinsman. Two, you've only been invited to the house as his guest. Three, how's it going to look to your beloved when she learns that you've been actively supporting his courtship?'

"Rufus' face showed disappointment, as if his worst fears were confirmed. 'I've thought of all that,' he said. 'I agree that I have no standing to woo her myself and would have little chance anyway, since Marcus is so much wealthier than I am. But at the same time, I just can't keep helping him when I feel that I should be doing the courting.

"'You should hear how she goes on about the poems he sends her. "The poet who wrote this must be a man of great honor and maturity. The poet who wrote this other must be a man of refinement. Certainly a man who could express himself thus is a man any woman would honor as a husband." He's wooing her under false pretenses with my poems.'

"'*Your* poems?'

"'Well, not his poems, anyway. Poems I helped supply. Poems that he thinks are my poems, but which he's happy to use anyway. It's such a deception.'

"'So you're thinking of backing out? Telling Marcus you'll no longer supply any poetry?' Servillius was already racking his brains for another suitable front to sell Marcus the poems, but he didn't know any other candidates.

"'That's right,' said Rufus. 'As a man of honor, I can no longer participate in this deception. And, Servillius . . .'

"'Yes?'

"'You must give me your word to say nothing of this. I know I have no chance with Pulchritudia, but I would not have my unhappiness in love bandied about as forum gossip.'

"Servillius sighed. 'Yes, yes, you have my word. But what about these?' He brandished a sheaf of new poems. 'It's unfair to me to spring this sudden change. I think that, as a man of honor, you have a responsibility to carry out this one last transaction before you drop out.' In truth, Servillius was just trying to buy time to think of a new plan. Fortunately for him, Rufus agreed with his argument."

"There you go!" called out Harry. "Love, not as the grand culmination but rather as the unwanted complication. A classic twist."

"I suspect there's another twist coming," predicted John.

"'The problem, Servillius,' said Marcus out of the blue when they met later that day, 'is that I am a man of honor.'

"*Uh-oh,* thought Servillius, *that's the second time today I've heard that. That can't be good.* However, he merely raised his eyebrows and said, 'Master?'

"'If I were not a man of honor,' Marcus continued reflectively, 'I would withdraw my suit for the hand of Pulchritudia.'

"'Excuse me?'

"'But at this point, I've gone too far. I cannot withdraw from the commitments I have made.'

"'And why would you want to?'

"'Because after all these evenings spent in their presence, I realize that it is not Pulchritudia that I love, but rather her cousin, Julia.'

"'Great Jupiter!' exclaimed Servillius.

"'Yes, having led the poor girl on like this, I certainly cannot abandon my suit now. Duty trumps desire, as it must for any Roman. And Servillius,' he added in a grave tone, 'I command you to say nothing of this to anyone. I won't have the girl hearing rumors that my suit was anything less than sincere.'

"*Blast them both and their promises of silence,* thought Servillius. *There's got to be a way around this.*

"On his next visit to Rufus, without betraying his master's confidence, Servillius suggested as delicately as he could that it might be a good idea for Rufus to press his own suit with Pulchritudia after all.

"Rufus had the air of a man clutching a lifeline. 'Do you think I could? Do you think there's some way to get her to notice me rather than Marcus? I have little means, but I would reward you well, Servillius.' Servillius knew more than Rufus realized about the state of his purse, but he let that slide.

"'What we need,' said Servillius, 'is a fortune-teller.'

"'What on earth for?' asked Rufus.

"'To tell the young lady that she shouldn't be paying attention to Marcus' suit, but that she should be looking to you instead.'

"'What makes you think she'll believe a fortune-teller?'

"'Most Roman women believe in fortune-tellers. We've just got to find the one whom she consults and persuade her to deliver the message that we want. And we've got to find her quickly, because you and Marcus are invited to dinner again the day after tomorrow.'"

"Believing in fortune-tellers! Why that's nonsense," said Florence.

But Louise was unrepentant. "Just because a character in a story believes something doesn't make it true. Besides, listen to what happens next.

"'She doesn't believe in fortune-tellers?' exclaimed Servillius with dismay. 'What kind of woman doesn't consult a fortune-teller?'

"The man across the table shrugged.

"Servillius sat in the slave quarters of the household of the Poltinii. He'd decided that since his master was courting the young woman of the house, that gave him sufficient standing to strike up an acquaintance with some of the household slaves. The slaves had proved receptive enough, especially when he produced a skin of his master's wine, but the information he was hearing was not to his liking.

"'Well,' said Servillius after a pause, 'who does she listen to then?'

"'Her cousin Julia.'

"'And who does Julia listen to?'

"'Her cousin Pulchritudia.'

"Servillius heaved a deep sigh. He felt he was running out of options. Accordingly, when he got home, he asked Marcus if he could be taken along on the trip to Pulchritudia's house for dinner.

"'Take you along?' said Marcus. 'Whatever for?'

"'To provide . . . music,' said Servillius, a note of desperation in his voice.

"'The Poltinii have musicians,' said Marcus. 'Better ones than you, I might add.'

"'That's not the point,' said Servillius. 'It's the gesture. You're enjoying their hospitality, so you show your gratitude by providing some fresh entertainment.' Marcus required some persuading, but in the end, Servillius was carting his lyre as he trudged along behind his master on the way to the house of the Poltinii.

"When the meal was done, Marcus, Rufus, Pulchritudia and Julia gathered in the inner courtyard to hear Servillius perform. Servillius felt that he had outdone himself in preparing for the occasion. Working all night, he had composed a song whose lyrics were designed to push Pulchritudia into the arms of Rufus and to propel Julia into the arms of Marcus. Given how successful his poetry had been, despite his own initial cynicism, Servillius felt that his song could not fail.

"He gave his all to the performance. He was not able to deliver his message plainly, of course, but he thought that the carefully hidden hints and suggestions would speak clearly to the young hearts of his audience. He sang as he never had before, and he found himself transported into the lofty realms where true love always finds a way.

"He finished the song and realized he'd been singing with his eyes closed. He opened them to find all four of the young people scowling at each other.

"For long moments, nobody moved.

"Finally, Servillius took a deep breath and began his song again. Perhaps they needed another exposure to its coded message.

"'Silence, slave!' snapped Pulchritudia. 'You just sang that song.' Servillius stopped, and Pulchritudia glanced at her cousin as if seeking encouragement. Finally, she said, 'Marcus, I understand that you are not the true author of the poems that you've been sending me.'

"Marcus was flabbergasted.

"Before he could respond, Julia added, 'Come, come. It's all over the forum.'

"'Well, that's true,' said Marcus, bewildered. 'But did you really think I was? I mean, that's just not how it's done. Surely you're not surprised?'

"'Well, no,' Pulchritudia had to admit. 'But even so . . .' She faltered, looked to her cousin for support and then rallied. 'But even so, the knowledge has caused us to question your sincerity.'

"Marcus, who, after all, was no longer sincere, had no answer to that. But Rufus could stand the tension no longer. 'Well, do not question *my* sincerity,' he cried, falling to his knees, 'for *I* love you.'

"'You do?' called out Marcus in surprise.

"'You do?' said Julia, smiling.

"'You do,' sighed Pulchritudia, as if a dream had been realized. Then she snapped back to business. 'You foolish fellow,' she said. 'I knew all along that you were writing the poems. Why didn't you declare yourself? I gave you enough opportunities.'

"'Well, I—I . . . ,' stammered Rufus. 'How could I . . . ?'

"Pulchritudia turned to Julia, who said, 'You see? I told you he was in a difficult spot.' Turning to Marcus, Julia continued, 'Oh, Marcus. You can see how it is, can't you? I'm sure it's very painful for you, but still, you wouldn't stand in the way of two people in love, would you? Especially when one of them is your cousin?'

"'Well,' said Marcus, speaking slowly for effect, 'as you can imagine, it is quite a blow to me. Of course, I don't wish to stand in the way of their happiness. Still'—he looked up slyly—'it would ease my pain, Julia, if I could come and talk with *you* from time to time.'

"Julia smiled. 'I think that could be arranged . . . from time to time.'

"Two months later, as a double-wedding present, Servillius received his freedom."

Chapter Fourteen

"I love a happy ending," Ethel said when Louise finished. She reached forward and proudly patted her niece on the shoulder. Ethel was a great reader of romance novels, so Louise's love story had particularly appealed to her.

"Just so, Mrs. Buckley," said Harry. "There's nothing like a good all's-well-that-ends-well story, whether it's set in contemporary America or ancient Rome. Even if the trappings are a little different, we can all relate to the outcome."

"Love conquers all," Lloyd said, "including our own clumsy efforts to bring it about."

Louise was pleased. She had especially wanted her aunt to enjoy the story.

"Ancient Rome is certainly a locale that we can now visit only in our imaginations," observed Harry. "How about some others? Does anyone else have a tale set in an exotic time or place?"

"What about you, Harry?" John asked. "You haven't told a story yet, but I bet you know quite a few. If you're taking requests, I like stories that have a bit of adventure to them."

"Well, now," said Harry. "As a matter of fact, our trip through New England does put me in mind of a story. And I think I can satisfy your desire for adventure, Mr. Gaunt, because this is a pirate story.

"You probably all remember pirate tales from your childhoods. And the fact is, piracy was a big problem on the Atlantic, especially in the seventeenth and eighteenth centuries. The British were the lords of the seas, and there was a great deal of traffic back and forth between England and her colonies in North America.

"Almost every American port was besieged by pirates, and it got to the point where trying to sail into or out of any of those ports involved making a run through the pirate lines. The sea is pretty big, of course, and most ships did manage to slip through, but there was constant danger, and obviously, the pirates caught enough ships to make their efforts worthwhile.

"One of the busiest ports in colonial New England was Portsmouth, New Hampshire. Many of New Hampshire's famous birch trees were shipped through Portsmouth on their way to England, where they were prized for making wonderful masts for British ships.

"A few miles off the coast of Portsmouth, there's a group of islands called the Isles of Shoals. There was a small fishing community on the islands in those days, but otherwise they were mostly barren and deserted, and therefore a favorite stopping place for pirates. It's said that the pirate Edward Teach, better known as Blackbeard, buried some treasure on one of these islands, but it has never been found.

"Be that as it may, there was at least one occasion when the Isles of Shoals failed to provide a refuge for pirates.

"One year a merchant captain named George Fairweather was bringing a cargo of finished goods from England into Portsmouth, and he was attacked by pirates on his approach.

"Captain Fairweather was a tall, lean man, more given to contemplation than conviviality, but he nevertheless commanded the unwavering respect and loyalty of his crew. His near-constant companion was a blue and green parrot named Hera, and she also was a great favorite of the men.

"Fairweather of course had anticipated the possibility of a pirate attack, and his ship, the *Halcyon*, was provided with defenses, and his men were trained to fight as well as to sail. But what Fairweather didn't know was that the New England coast at that time was bedeviled by a particularly wild and cruel pirate named Rennis.

"Fairweather had found that a demonstration of his willingness to fight was often enough to drive off pirates. Pirates, he had found, were generally a pretty cowardly lot, and they saw no reason to challenge a ship that was prepared to defend itself, because there were so many others around that would not. Pirates most often left Fairweather alone in favor of easier pickings.

"But Rennis was different. Today we would probably call him a sociopath. He was short and solidly built, with wild black curls and soulless black eyes. He was reckless in battle, exuding a ferocity that alone could chill the blood of his enemies.

"His crew feared and hated him. He would attack any ship, no matter how well defended it was, and he would fight for the sake of mayhem and destruction, long beyond the point needed to relieve a vessel of its riches. Rennis was so fierce that even other pirates were wary of him, and at this time, he could command any portion of the American coast that pleased him, while other pirates would seek their booty elsewhere.

"This is the pirate that Captain Fairweather encountered on his way into Portsmouth.

"Fairweather had not yet heard of Rennis, but he saw immediately that this pirate intended to engage the *Halcyon* despite her defenses, and he gave his orders accordingly.

"It was a terrible battle. In the end, Rennis carried the day because of his savagery and his recklessness. Fairweather made the mistake of expecting an attack based on logic and strategy, but Rennis was simply wild, willing to throw his ship, his crew, and himself into harm's way; and it was this unexpected ferocity that overcame the plans of Captain Fairweather.

"Soon, Fairweather and his crew were tied up on their own deck, watching the pirates unload their valuable cargo for transfer to the pirate ship. As Rennis swaggered about on deck, Fairweather began to get a sense of the true brutality of the man. As they waited for the theft of the cargo to be completed, Rennis would occasionally confront one of Fairweather's captured crewmen, accusing him of cowardice and ridiculing him for his helpless condition.

"He did this because he could see the effect it had on Captain Fairweather. The first time it happened, Fairweather struggled to his feet with a loud cry of protest, only to be struck down to the deck once again. But he could see in Rennis' eyes the pleasure that his anguished objection had inspired, so thereafter he remained silent in an effort to offer no further provocation. Nevertheless, Fairweather was unable to keep the anger from his face each time Rennis mistreated one of his men.

"When the pirates finished, Rennis waved his sword threateningly near Fairweather's neck, but he knew he did Fairweather more damage by letting him live with the memories he'd supplied. He ordered his men to lay waste to the *Halcyon*—not to the point of sinking her, but leaving her to flounder, sorely wounded. The pirates, laughing and jeering, left Fairweather and his crew still bound, with several sailors in need of medical attention.

"Once the pirates were gone, Fairweather and his surviving crew managed to free themselves, and Fairweather set about directing repairs with urgency and an inspired, improvisational use of the materials at hand.

"During the fiercest fighting, Fairweather had lost Hera, who flew away in alarm. Now he dispatched a crewman to try to find the bird. After some time, the man returned bearing a sodden and battered mass of blue and green feathers. 'She was tangled in the ratlines, sir,' he said. 'She's hurt bad.' Since the ship's surgeon was busy with the wounded from the battle, Fairweather himself bundled up the bird and tended to it even as he oversaw the hasty repairs.

"Fairweather and his carpenter were both knowledgeable about ship construction, and they were able to make sufficient repairs to the *Halcyon* so that they could sail her into Portsmouth. She limped into harbor as probably the least seaworthy craft ever to float up the Piscataqua River.

"As he watched his wounded and bedraggled men taken off the ship, Fairweather, still holding a carefully wrapped Hera in his arms, burned with a fury that would not abate. The dangers of piracy he knew and could accept: To sail through their regions of activity was a calculated gamble, and sometimes a merchant lost. But the flagrant aggression and cruelty of Rennis were beyond the pale as far as Fairweather was concerned.

"Fairweather represented important merchants in Portsmouth, and he came from an influential family. It was an easy matter for him to gain an audience with the royal governor of New Hampshire in order to air his grievances.

"None of them came as any surprise to the governor, of course. Rennis' depredations had been a cause for concern for some time. In fact, when Fairweather entered the governor's office, he met an admiral of the British Royal Navy who had been specifically charged with the capture or destruction of the notorious pirate."

Harry paused, and in the solemn silence that engulfed the bus, Lloyd asked in a quiet voice, "Was the bird okay?"

Harry gave them a reassuring smile in the rearview mirror. "Hera survived," he advised them, "though not unscathed. Her wings were badly damaged, and though Fairweather was able to nurse her back to health, she was never able to fly again."

John said, "I don't think this Fairweather was a man you'd want to provoke with something nasty like that."

"Very true, Mr. Gaunt," said Harry, nodding. "But that's only one side of the story.

"Before his encounter with Fairweather, the pirate was accustomed to letting his reputation do his work for him. Most ships, realizing that it was the ferocious Rennis who approached, would simply bow to the inevitable and surrender. The fact that Fairweather had fought, and fought well and hard, stuck in the pirate's craw. Indeed, the captain had come closer to winning that fight than even he had realized. He had succeeded in inflicting more damage on Rennis' ship and crew than was immediately apparent.

"As a consequence, Rennis nursed a grudge against Fairweather. His own crew was aware of how close a call the battle had been, and he felt that his iron control over them had slipped somewhat as a result. He brooded over this. He wished now that he had completely destroyed the *Halcyon* . . . and dealt more severely with all on board.

"And so he stayed in the vicinity of the Portsmouth shipping lanes, brooding and hoping for another chance at Fairweather. He knew that the *Halcyon* had made it to Portsmouth, but her condition made it unlikely that she would sail again any time soon—if ever. And yet something made Rennis persist.

"One day, he was amazed to see the *Halcyon* sailing out of the mouth of the Piscataqua. She was still battered, but somehow Fairweather had managed to make the craft seaworthy. In addition, he had rechristened her the *Phoenix*, but a new name was not enough to prevent Rennis from recognizing her. Fairweather, it would seem, was going to attempt his return voyage to England while the weather held.

"Rennis was overjoyed. He determined to destroy Fairweather and his ship once and for all, and thereby reestablish his position with his own crew. At once he set his course to overtake the *Phoenix*.

"Much to his gratification, the *Phoenix* began to tack as soon as its crew spotted his *Running Dog*. It seemed obvious that Fairweather had no appetite for a second engagement. Instead he maneuvered in an apparent effort to flee. But Rennis had no intention of letting this ship get away. He would chase it across the Atlantic if he had to.

"The *Phoenix* put on all sail and was making decent headway. Given the ship's damaged condition, Rennis judged that she was probably now making her best speed. But the *Running Dog* was faster, and inexorably she closed the gap. When it was clear that Fairweather could not outrun Rennis, the *Phoenix* began to tack in a wide arc. Fairweather was going to try to slip past him, Rennis reckoned, and make a run back to Portsmouth.

"Rennis recognized the desperation in such a move. Since the *Running Dog* was coming up from behind, the *Phoenix* would have a difficult time getting past her to begin with. And even if she did, the distance between the two ships would be considerably reduced, so that the *Dog* was almost certain to catch her quarry before she made it back to safe waters.

"Coolly, Rennis ordered a course correction to intercept the *Phoenix*, but as it happened, Rennis had not been directly behind his adversary. Actually, he had been coming up on it from an angle. Since the ship had tacked away from the *Dog*, she had just enough room to slip past the pirate ship in her attempt to return to Portsmouth.

"This quickly became clear to Rennis, who silently admired the skill with which the reverse course had been effected, but he was still confident of overtaking the *Phoenix* before she reached safety.

"And indeed, the *Running Dog* was now almost upon the *Phoenix*, which changed objectives and desperately tacked again, now making for the nearby Isles of Shoals. Rennis laughed: Fairweather would find little shelter there. The Isles of Shoals were a familiar stopping point for all pirates, and the small community of fisherfolk who lived there were sufficiently cowed that they would offer no help to Fairweather against Rennis.

"The *Running Dog* was closing in on the *Phoenix*. At the last moment, the *Phoenix* heeled about and prepared to fight. At close range, Rennis laughed to see the battered condition of the opposing ship. She wasn't going to be up for much of a fight, he figured. Captain Fairweather should have yielded immediately, Rennis thought—though that would not have stopped the pirate from executing his destructive plans.

"Rennis approached and raked the *Phoenix* with a broadside from his cannons, and he was satisfied to see that Fairweather could only muster a small and poorly timed return. Half the cannon ports on the *Phoenix* were still closed, and the state of the ship's defenses seemed every bit as poor as the rest of her. Rennis decided to move alongside and ordered grappling hooks thrown out.

"As the pirates used the grapples to pull the two ships together, Rennis noticed that the decks of the *Phoenix* had cleared almost completely and that a fire was burning high up in her rigging. The crew was undoubtedly cowering below. He felt hot satisfaction course through him as he led the first boarding party across.

"Fairweather stood before him on the deck. A weak but defiant Hera perched on his shoulder, but the captain, it seemed, had otherwise been deserted by his entire crew. He held a sword in his hand, but it was at his side, and Rennis thought he recognized the signs of imminent surrender.

"'Captain Fairweather,' said Rennis, 'how good to see you again, and so soon too. But I seem to recall that the last time we met, you were surrounded by more of your men.'

"Fairweather said nothing.

"'Of course, I can understand how their previous defeat might make them timid on this occasion.'

"'Your barbarity certainly had an effect on them,' Fairweather said.

"Rennis chuckled. 'And well it should. Too bad it didn't have as strong an effect on you, Captain Fairweather. Your men do right to hide, not that it will save them. I do not intend to show the misguided mercy that I did last time. This time, you and your men will be put ashore on these hellish islands, and your ship will be burned when we're done.'

"He paused and then lifted the corners of his mouth in an evil smile. 'Your parrot I may keep for myself,' he said softly. 'Every pirate needs a parrot, and you and your men will be an example to others.'

"'Are you quite sure that you will not be the example? Of what happens to pirates?' Fairweather slowly raised his sword. 'What if I were to succeed in taking you prisoner? Do you think your men would be so distressed at your capture as to exact vengeance? Or would they thank me for removing you from their midst?'

"'My men?' He shrugged. 'My men signed on for plunder, and plunder is what I make sure they get.'

"'Well, I see that your men are sufficiently eager for that plunder. They all seem to have come over to my ship and left yours untended.'

"Rennis laughed. 'And what of it? Do you really think that any of your crew could make it across to the *Running Dog*? Turn the tables somehow? Do you think . . .'

"But the reference to the pirate ship had caused some of its crew to turn around and look in her direction, only to be shocked by the sight of a naval warship bearing down on the *Running Dog*. The ship had been waiting on the far side of the island, which provided just enough cover that the pirates had not noticed its masts amid a cluster of fishing vessels.

"No sooner had the warning cry gone up among the pirates than Fairweather raised his sword into the air with a yell, and Hera gave a great squawk. At the captain's signal, a mass of British marines in their distinctive red coats came boiling out of every hatch that gave access to the deck. For a moment, the pirates thought of resisting, but better judgment led them to surrender.

"Soon, all were disarmed. Rennis himself sat on the deck with a wounded arm. With a yell, he had charged Fairweather directly and was relieved of his sword for his trouble. Fairweather now stood over him, his sword pressed against Rennis's neck. Hera's cold eye gazed with unblinking avian intensity at the defeated pirate.

"Fairweather put just an ounce of additional pressure behind the sword, enough to start the thinnest trickle of blood from a small cut, but then held his hand. 'That's where the rope will go,' he said, 'when they hang you for piracy.'

"He turned away from Rennis, but Hera swiveled her head for a last, contemptuous look at the pirate, who sagged where he sat, defeated and without hope."

Chapter Fifteen

"Good for Hera!" Lloyd called out. "And that was a fine story, Harry."

John and Cyril nodded.

"And good riddance to that awful pirate," said Florence.

"Are there really any Isles of Shoals?" asked Ethel.

"Oh yes," said Harry. "I read about them when I was researching this trip. It's a small group of islands off the New Hampshire coast. Nobody lives there permanently these days, but there was a fishing village there once upon a time, and pirates did indeed use it as well. In the nineteenth century, there were some hotels built on the islands, and the area became famous as something of a resort.

"A woman named Celia Thaxter grew up out there. It was her family that built the hotels, but she was famous in her own right as a poet. She cultivated a garden in that difficult terrain, and apparently there are fans who maintain the garden to this day."

"Isn't that wonderful," said Lloyd. "Even with adventure stories, you still learn something."

"Yes, indeed, Mr. Tynan," agreed Harry.

"Pirate stories are a popular genre," said Cyril, "but I can think of another type of story that perhaps has even more resonance in the American imagination."

"Oh, I believe I can guess where Mr. Overstreet is headed," Harry said. "Is it time to go west, young man?"

"Just what I was thinking," said Cyril. "Is there any better example of an adventure story than a western? And yet you may find this one a bit different from some that you've read or seen. For one thing, our hero is a minister.

"It was a hot, dry day in the western town of Cinder Creek, and inside the hotel's modest eatery, the sheriff stood talking with Brady Wall, the hotel manager, while a handful of patrons enjoyed the establishment's hospitality. As the two men stood passing the time of day, a rangy man dressed in black stepped through the doors and stopped to survey them.

"'Well, I'll be a—' began Brady, before catching himself. Then, grinning and nodding, he said, 'Afternoon, Reverend. Been a while.'

"The sheriff also had broken out in a broad grin. 'Tom,' he said, holding out his hand, 'it's good to see you. How've you been?'

"Rev. Tom Pilliston smiled in his turn, approached the bar and shook their hands. 'Brady. Sam. Good to see you both. You look like you're doing well.'

"A light was dawning in the sheriff's eyes. 'Did they send you out here to replace Horace, the silver-tongued wonder?'

"The preacher laughed and said, 'Horace has been called to higher things back East. You should be careful what you say about him, Sam. He is considered to have a bright future before him.'

"'No one is more convinced of that than Horace himself,' said the sheriff. 'He made it quite clear that his posting to our little town would be a very brief step in his ascent. But I'm surprised they had the sense to send you to us.'

"'The synod thought that my familiarity with the area might be a help, though it's not yet clear that I'll be the permanent replacement.'

"'I see,' said the sheriff, 'still on the bad side of the powers that be?' Pilliston smiled noncommittally and shrugged.

"'Can I get you some sarsaparilla?' asked Brady, holding up a tall glass.

"'I'd like that, thank you, Brady. But just a small one.'

"'Same as always,' said Brady, pouring. 'Moderation in all things, eh, Tom?'

"'It's a philosophy that has served me well,' said the preacher. 'Gentlemen, your good health.'

"The three stood talking, the sheriff and the manager catching up the preacher on the news of the town.

"'Do you like the idea of serving in town, Tom?' asked the sheriff after a while. 'It must be awfully different from the missionary work that brought you our way before. We'd hardly see you for weeks on end while you were out with the Indians, and then you'd come back to town, resupply, and head out again. Now you'll be staying right in town, preaching to the local flock. I always thought you enjoyed being out with the Indians, so I'm a little surprised that you've turned to town life.'

"'My superiors decided I enjoyed it *too* much, being out with the Indians. My happiness and, yes, my admiration for them, was interfering with my ability to minister to them. Or so it was thought.' He shrugged. 'I miss it, certainly. And since they removed me from missionary work, they've been sending me around from parish to parish whenever someone is needed, so I haven't really been able to enjoy the benefits of settled life, either. But I must say, having spent so much time with them, I'm looking forward to renewing my acquaintance with Chief Red Sky's tribe.' He paused and asked, 'Is Red Sky still chief?'

"'Oh, sure,' said the sheriff. 'He's still going strong. I get some news of what's going on out there, though nothing like when you were here. That was useful, that connection you made between the town and the tribe.'

"'You ought to meet this Hammond fella that came to town recently,' Brady said as he stacked some dishes. 'He's real interested in Injuns. Trades with 'em. Travels all over. Interestin' fella, though kinda cocky. He was gonna go out and talk with Red Sky and his tribe, and I guess he did. Came riding back in at dawn this morning, and he looked all worn out. Took a room and said he was going up to have a sleep. He'll be down sooner or later, and if anyone'll have news about Red Sky, he will.'

"The preacher frowned slightly. 'What kind of trade is he doing with the Indians?'

"Brady shrugged. 'Wants their baskets and pottery and jewelry mostly. The thing is, he says that back East and in Europe, stuff made by Injuns is in high demand. He says it's in vogue. Anyway, he represents dealers that sell it to rich folks for lots of money, and he gets a nice cut of it.' He shrugged again. 'Looks like he's pretty prosperous, I'll say that.'

"Pilliston looked at him steadily. 'Brady, do you think he's out there selling them liquor? Alcohol is the bane of Indians, and some unscrupulous people are making a great deal of money supplying it to them.'

"'I see what you're getting at. But no, I don't think that's what's going on. Mind you, I think he'd swap liquor for the baskets and pottery and such as quick as anything else, but liquor's not his game. I think he finds it easier to pay cash money or to trade in metalwork. But, no, I think he was telling the truth about the baskets and such. When he came to town, the first thing he did was put a big load of that stuff on a stagecoach heading east. He said he was shipping it to a consolidator who would package it up with the stuff sent by others like him, and it would all go to the coast on the train. No, I think he's doin' what he says he's doin'.'

"Pilliston nodded, relieved."

"I hope this story isn't going to have any clichés about 'savage' Indians," said John.

Cyril smiled enigmatically but went on without answering.

"An hour or so later, Pilliston got to meet this Mr. Hammond himself when the young man came down from his room apparently feeling much refreshed. The preacher found Hammond to be much as Brady had described him—cocky, arrogant even, but apparently engaged in exactly the business he described.

"'You wouldn't believe it,' he told the minister, 'the prices these Indian goods command in New York and London. They're crazy for this stuff.' He had indeed been out to visit Chief Red

Sky's tribe, but though he had successfully traded with them, he didn't seem to have actually learned much about them. Pilliston was disappointed in his hope for news of the tribe.

"As the sheriff and the preacher talked with Hammond, it became apparent that self-congratulation was very much a part of his personality. He became more and more loquacious as he spoke of his accomplishments, and soon he was bragging about his successful trading experience to the point that Pilliston began to worry the young man had cheated the Indians in some way. Knowing the canny chief as he did, this was hard to imagine, but Hammond clearly felt that he had secured the best end of the deal.

"Leaning close to Pilliston and speaking in a confidential whisper, Hammond said, 'Hold on. I'll show you. This stuff will fetch a fortune. In fact, I'm going to take it back personally in order to obtain the best terms possible.'

"Rising from his chair, Hammond made his way to the stairs at the rear. Pilliston watched him with an uneasy look on his face.

"'Don't worry,' said the sheriff. 'Probably Red Sky has pawned off some piece of junk on him and convinced him it's a valuable Indian artifact.'

"'I'm not sure I find that thought any more comforting than the possibility that Hammond has cheated the Indians,' replied the preacher.

"The sheriff shrugged. 'Even if Red Sky did pull a fast one, that doesn't exactly make it cheating. Chances are, young Hammond can take it back to New York, tell the same story, and get all the money he's dreaming of for it.'

"'So it's okay as long the pain gets passed along to a rich person?' The minister frowned.

"'What I mean is, the value of something is what people are willing to pay for it. If Hammond can find a buyer offering the price he wants, then there is no cheat.'

"The preacher looked at the sheriff with a slight smile. 'Well, I don't deny that that's the common understanding. Yet I can't help but think that my Bible—a nice one—cost me fifty cents, and I don't think that defines the value of it any more than a high price defines what a trinket is worth.'

"The sheriff grimaced as Hammond came back with a small sack. He set it on a table and began removing carefully wrapped bundles. He opened one to reveal an exquisitely beaded pouch, inside of which were a number of herbs and various odd bits difficult to identify.

"When he saw them, the preacher leaned back with a small gasp. 'You traded for these?' he asked, a note of incredulity in his voice.

"A look of dismay flashed over Hammond's face. 'Well, well sure. Of course I did. How else would I have gotten them?'

"'What's up, Tom?' demanded the sheriff. 'What are they?'

"Pilliston shook his head. 'They're trouble.'

"As if on cue, there was a tremendous commotion outside: men shouting, horses galloping, women screaming. The sheriff and the preacher jumped up and headed for the door.

"Riding down the center of the street were more than a dozen Indians decked out in war regalia, shouting and looking mighty fierce. People scattered before them in terror.

"'Sam,' said the preacher quietly. 'I trust you're noticing that they aren't doing any real harm.'

"'I'm noticing,' the sheriff replied grimly. 'But I'm also noticing that they *are* in a position to do a lot of it if they choose to.' He stepped to the top of the stairs that led down to street level, and he stood with his arms folded across his chest. With a great noise, the Indians came down the street and stopped in front of him.

"Soon most of the Indians had drawn up in front of the saloon, with Red Sky leading, mounted on his fine horse. He held up his hand, and his braves fell silent.

"After a moment, the sheriff spoke, making his voice as calm as possible under the circumstances. 'Hello, Chief. What seems to be the problem?'

"'We want the stranger, Sheriff,' said Red Sky. 'He has stolen from us.'

"Before the sheriff could reply, Red Sky waved his gun menacingly over his head, but the lawman had already leaped down the steps and into the street.

"If he thought the sheriff was charging him, Red Sky showed no sign of losing his composure.

"The sheriff stood alongside Red Sky. 'Now then. What is this about? Who stole from you?'

"Pilliston had been standing by the doors to the hotel, but he now stepped forward into the light. He addressed Red Sky in the chief's own language: 'It's been a long time, my friend.'

"The chief raised his hand in greeting. Pilliston, who knew him well, was oddly gratified to see the faintest hint of a pleased smile on the chief's mouth as he recognized the preacher.

"But this wasn't the moment for reunions. Before the chief could respond, the preacher said in the same language, 'This is about the bundles, isn't it?'

"'You know about this?' the chief asked.

"The preacher was already shaking his head. 'I've just now learned of it. If I'd known earlier, I would have acted earlier. But let me see what I can do now.' He stepped closer, and he and the chief conversed further. Finally the chief nodded.

"Pilliston walked over to the sheriff, who still stood in the middle of the street between the Indians and the hotel. 'Tom?' asked the sheriff under his breath.

"'Trust me,' replied the preacher in the same low tones. Then, in a louder voice that would carry to the spectators, he said, 'Sheriff, would you be so good as to bring Mr. Hammond out here? I'll stand here in your place.'

"Puzzled, the sheriff entered the hotel and soon came out dragging Hammond by his shirt collar. He walked the man into the street, and Pilliston stood directly in front of him.

"'Mr. Hammond,' said the preacher. 'You must return the medicine bundles that you stole from these Indians.'

"Belligerent, Hammond squawked, 'I didn't steal anything. Those are mine.'

"'Mr. Hammond, those medicine bundles are sacred possessions of the tribe. I know for a fact that they never would have willingly parted with them. Therefore, you must have stolen them, and they must be returned. Furthermore, you must make restitution to the tribe for the desecration of their sacred objects.' As Pilliston spoke, Red Sky shifted in his saddle and cocked his head to one side.

"'Never,' said Hammond, though the cockiness had gone out of his voice considerably.

"'Mr. Hammond, you can return the bundles and make restitution, or you can face the Indians, who want to exact their own punishment for desecration. Take my word for it: You want to take the first option.'

"Hammond twisted his neck from right to left, seeming to count all the Indians who'd converged on the town and who were now pressing forward to get a better look at the agitated trader. Hammond tried to show bravado and raised his fists, but as the reality of the situation sank in, he lowered his hands and sank back against the sheriff for protection.

"In the end, Hammond returned the medicine bundles and turned over the cash he had in his possession. Before he left, Red Sky told the preacher that he hoped he would visit soon. Then the Indians rode off in peace and with dignity.

"That night, the preacher and the sheriff sat talking in the sheriff's office. Turning to the day's events, the sheriff said, 'You know, Tom, that business about turning young Hammond over to Red Sky was dicey. He may well have deserved it, but turning someone over to the Indians for punishment, well, I wouldn't really have been able to do it.'

"'I know that,' nodded the preacher, 'and Red Sky knew it too. He never even asked for that. But it was just the final shove needed to tip Hammond over into cooperation.'

"'I see,' said the sheriff. 'And you, as a man of the cloth, had no compunctions about twisting the truth like that.' But his tone was teasing, for he agreed with his friend's handling of the situation.

"But the preacher shrugged. 'It wasn't the only lie I told.' And when the sheriff raised his eyebrows, he added, 'Red Sky never asked for restitution, either. He just asked for the medicine bundles back. But I thought he deserved restitution nonetheless.'

"'For heathen religious objects?'

"'For Red Sky's people, those bundles are very powerful, very holy, not to mention old and irreplaceable. As you were saying earlier today, it's a question of knowing the value of things.'"

Chapter Sixteen

"That's terrible!" exclaimed Florence. "A minister lying like that—that's a dreadful message for a story to send."

Cyril, however, smiled. "I wondered how people would respond to that."

John seemed taken aback by the vehemence of Florence's reaction. "I don't think you're supposed to see them as *lies*, so much," he said.

"That's what the minister himself called them," Louise pointed out.

"Well, yes, but I mean they weren't self-serving. They were more in the nature of a bluff. He was trying to resolve a dangerous situation, and that was an expedient way to do so."

"But the Indians didn't even ask for restitution," Florence said. "That was all his own idea."

"But they deserved it," John insisted. "As a minister he probably knew how he would feel if his church's sacred objects were stolen. How would you feel if someone stole things out of Grace Chapel? He was trying to right a wrong."

Louise frowned, uncertain regarding the argument: She was generally unimpressed with the argument that the ends justify the means.

"He was faced with a dangerous confrontation between a lot of upset people, most of whom had guns," John continued. "He had to resolve it as quickly and as peacefully as he could. You could almost argue that he had an obligation to bend the truth, because by doing so, he defused the standoff."

"Ministers shouldn't lie," said Florence emphatically. "They are men of God."

"Nobody should lie," Lloyd said, "but do you really think that ministers never do? They're only human."

"If that was typical of his behavior," said Louise, "perhaps that's why he was in trouble with his superiors."

"I still say he achieved a good resolution to the crisis," said John.

"That's the thing about stories," said Harry. "The characters don't always behave as we think they ought to, because people in real life don't always behave as we think they ought to. But as readers of, or listeners to, stories, we have the opportunity to decide what we will take from them. We can take the grain and leave the chaff, as it were. As for Rev. Pilliston, well, he'll have to answer for his lies to a higher power someday."

Florence nodded in satisfaction at that.

The exciting stories and the discussions they had inspired helped the morning pass quickly, but as lunchtime approached, Louise began to wonder if they would have a repeat of the slight unpleasantness of the previous day. However, before such a discussion could begin, Harry announced, "I hope you good folks don't mind, but I've got a lunch spot picked out. It's a nice little place just north of Portsmouth, New Hampshire, and since we've already heard about that town in our stories today, it seems especially appropriate. This is a place that I visit any time I'm up this way, and if you all have no objections, I'd like to suggest that we go there."

There was a general chorus of agreement. Louise sneaked a glance at Florence, but her expression was serene.

So Bailey got them off the highway and took them to a charming seafood restaurant where wide, tall windows overlooked a small rocky harbor only large enough for a few small fishing boats. Lobster traps were stacked along the wooden piers, and on the far rocks, cormorants perched with their wings spread to dry in the sun.

The friends feasted on lobster and scallops, coleslaw, maple-flavored baked beans, and delicious herb-cheese muffins that Louise thought would make a wonderful addition to the inn's menus. She wondered if Jane might be able to recreate the muffins from her description alone, but she put those thoughts on hold when the server arrived with steaming dishes of dessert: Indian pudding with homemade vanilla ice cream melting on top. All agreed that Harry's recommendation had been outstanding.

Back on the road, Florence scoffed good-naturedly at the adventure stories told that morning. "Boys' adventure tales," she teased. "Where's the romance? Where's the beauty?"

"What would you prefer, Florence?" asked John. "A fairy tale about a princess?"

"Why, yes, since you mention it. A story about a princess would be very nice."

"Be careful what you wish for," said John, laughing. "The thing that always strikes me about fairy-tale princesses is how passive and helpless they are. Always waiting for some knight to come and save them. Not exactly paragons of self-determination, are they?"

"I don't know, John," said Florence thoughtfully. "I'm not sure it has to be that way. Indeed, I believe I know a rather different kind of princess tale. Just give me a moment." She closed her eyes briefly, then opened them and raised a hand to indicate that she was ready.

"Once upon a time—I've always wanted to say that—there was a beautiful princess. She lived in England, and handsome knights were always vying for her hand, especially since she was the king's only daughter and destined to be queen. And yet, though they certainly were handsome, not to mention charming, the knights who courted her always lacked a degree of imagination and creative spark that she wanted in a husband.

"Nevertheless, as she grew older, her father the king grew more and more concerned to see her safely married, the better to provide any necessary heirs that the kingdom might need. And so the day came when he announced a great tournament for the hand of his daughter. Knights from all over the kingdom and beyond would compete to win the fair Princess Faith.

"'Father,' stormed an exasperated Faith. 'How could you do this to me? I'm being shunted off as some sort of prize, and you didn't even consult me.'

"'Well, dear, something had to be done. You've had many suitors in the more usual manner, but you refuse to accept them. This seemed to me a way to bring a happy resolution.'

"'None of them is right for me. What's the rush, anyway? I'm not under a deadline to get married.'

"'In a sense you are. Leaving the royal line uncertain in any manner is asking for disaster. There's always some other king who will think it his responsibility to come on in and straighten things out by putting his own offspring on the throne. No, it is not in the interests of our nation to leave you unmarried any longer.'

"Princess Faith thought that over for a moment and then tried a new tack. 'But this tournament is open to anyone. One of the knights that I've already rejected could win.'

"'I suppose, yes.'

"'And what kind of a marriage is that going to be? Some knight bitter over the first rejection now will have his opportunity to take revenge.'

"'I'm sure they won't behave that way, dear. One will still be prince consort after all. He will have a certain standard to maintain.'

"Well, Princess Faith was far from satisfied, but the king had already made his royal proclamation, and once it was publicly announced, there was no going back on it. Even she could see that rescinding a royal proclamation would only breed uncertainty and confusion among the populace.

"And so Princess Faith went off to brood.

"Her father thought it quite likely that his daughter would come around in the end. After all, she was a wonderfully intelligent princess, highly knowledgeable regarding all of the skills that distinguished knights. In the past, she had taken a lively interest in jousts and tournaments, commenting on technique and cheering on the best competitors.

"Besides, her dad had a plan. There was a young knight, Sir David, whom he had already picked out as excellent son-in-law material, and it was his intention that Sir David should win his daughter. Sir David was cultured and intelligent, and he was not one of the previously rejected suitors that the princess was concerned about.

"Sir David was an extremely skilled knight in his own right and would no doubt win most of his matches on his own. But just in case, any knight who might pose a challenge was to be warned in advance, just as a precautionary measure, that the king would be displeased by any upset and that he had set aside generous portions of land in the northern and western parts of his kingdom with which to reward compliant knights.

"The king's hopes for his daughter's acquiescence were dashed, however. She refused to attend the games any more than she absolutely had to. She agreed to put in appearances at the very start of competitions, but then she slipped off, presumably to pout. The absence of their prize only seemed to push the knights to greater efforts. To a man, they performed exceptionally well in their contests, and none better than Sir David. Only once or twice were the royal advisers required to remind a knight who had been persuaded not to give his best effort of his commitment.

"As the competition continued and the ranks thinned, however, one other knight seemed to be emerging as a possible competitor for David. A certain Sir Fidelus, about whom very little was known, had come out of nowhere—some guessed France—to dominate every match in which he appeared. With rapid dispatch, Sir Fidelus overcame one opponent after another, and soon only Sir David stood between him and the king's daughter, a fact that caused the princess to complain passionately about the prospect of being 'won' by an unknown competitor who might be ugly, foolish or vicious, as far as the king knew.

"To make matters worse, the royal advisers had been unable to pin down this Fidelus and talk him into an arrangement regarding his bout with Sir David. Sir Fidelus seemed to appear out of nowhere at the start of every match he was slated for, and to disappear as mysteriously when it was over. The king pressed his advisers to find out all they could about this Fidelus as quickly as possible, but they came up empty-handed.

"Soon, the day of the final match arrived, and as expected, the contest came down to Sir David and Sir Fidelus. The king wasn't too worried: As much as he liked young David, if Fidelus bested him fair and square, the king would have a prize son-in-law. Young David would be disappointed, of course, but that's a risk of marriage plans based upon a series of skirmishes.

"Mostly the king favored David because he thought that this young man would be one to meet his daughter's high standards.

He'd not said anything like that to her, of course. That would just have set her against the young man all the more firmly. The king had merely contented himself with remarking over dinner how well the handsome young knight had performed that day.

"And now there was a chance David would lose to the mysterious stranger. The king was prepared to make the best of whatever resulted. If this Fidelus really was French, he thought, perhaps there would be a diplomatic upside to the competition.

"The king sat impatiently through the entertainment provided before the title match, but at last, Sir David and Sir Fidelus were led into the lists. The king leaned forward in his seat. He glanced about him: He had thought that his daughter might show up for this event if no other, but no, she was not to be seen.

"And then the knights were off. Both drove their horses at top speed down the lists, their lances fixed and their shields gripped tightly. With a clang that could be heard for a quarter mile, lances and shields made contact and both knights rocked back in their saddles. But both stayed seated and cantered on to the ends of the lists to turn around and try again.

"The second encounter was, if anything, even fiercer than the first. Two blows were resoundingly delivered and, amazingly, solidly absorbed. Both knights were still mounted and they prepared for a third run.

"This was fiercest of all, and though skillfully executed on both sides, to the amazement of the crowd, Sir David found himself knocked out of his saddle by his opponent's lance. He crashed to the ground behind his horse.

"Sir Fidelus immediately wheeled his horse and rode to the fallen knight. He jumped from his saddle—not an easy thing to do in armor—reached down and helped Sir David to stand. Clearly shaken, Sir David was nevertheless unhurt, except perhaps for his pride. With dignity he accepted the helping hand of his victor.

"Sir Fidelus turned to the king in the stands, swept the helmet from his head, and declared in a loud voice: 'The prize for this tournament was to be the Princess Faith. I hereby claim my prize. I claim myself.'

"All in attendance were in shock. It was indeed Princess Faith who, bright, skilled and determined, had prevailed."

"Ha!" exclaimed John Gaunt. "Talk about taking control of your own destiny."

"But it doesn't solve the succession problem," Lloyd pointed out. "I don't think we've reached the end of the story yet."

Florence maintained an unsmiling silence for a moment before she continued.

"'It simply won't do,' exclaimed the king that evening as he paced in agitation. 'The point was to get you a husband. The point was to produce an heir. The point was to ensure the stability of our house and our kingdom. All that money and planning for nothing,' he roared.

"'It was a lovely festival,' said his daughter mildly. 'Everyone had a good time. Bread and circuses, remember, Father?' When he did not respond, she turned to Sir David, who had been asked to attend the king. 'Didn't you have a good time?'

"Sir David winced. 'Up until the end, My Lady.'

"'See?'

"The king turned angrily on his daughter. 'Give me one good reason why I shouldn't just declare Sir David here the winner,' he demanded.

"But it was Sir David who spoke up, saying, 'Because I didn't win, Sire.' Princess Faith looked at him in surprise.

"'I wasn't talking to you,' the king responded, but the knight's answer, so baldly put, had taken the wind from his sails. 'Look, my daughter,' he said finally, 'don't you see it's not good for the kingdom to leave your future in this state of uncertainty? Something must be done.'

"'I quite agree,' said his daughter.

"'I mean, it's not just the internal stability, there's also the question of foreign . . . what did you say?'

"'I said I quite agree. Indeed, my objections were to the procedure you chose for deciding the issue, and, more importantly, to the fact that I was never consulted in the process. After all, it is my marriage that we're talking about.'

"The king drew a deep breath. 'All right then. What do you suggest?'

"In two weeks, his daughter had an answer to that question.

"'Tests?' The king screwed up his face.

"'Both written and practical.'

"'Tests for what?'

"'Intelligence. Creative thinking. Ability to make decisions under pressure. Diplomacy. You know, the sort of skills one might need to help run a kingdom.' Princess Faith was getting tired of explaining it.

"'All these?' Her father flipped to the third page of the plan she had prepared. 'Who's going to prepare and administer all this? Who's going to be the judge?'

"'You and I will judge,' she said, 'along with an expert or two in each relevant area. As for the administration, Sir David has been a tremendous help already and has promised to continue to be so.'

"'He's not a sore loser. I'll say that for him,' muttered the king as he continued to flip through the plan. 'But, my dear, are you being realistic? What sort of paragon could win a contest in all these different areas?'

"'None, of course, but that's the point. It's not a simple-minded win-or-lose distinction. I'm not a carnival prize. It's a matter of ranking relative abilities across a broad range of criteria. It's all about identifying a blending of capabilities that will offer the promise of a positive outcome.'

"'Positive for whom, I wonder,' the king muttered, but not so his daughter could hear."

"In terms of finding a husband," Louise said, frowning, "I'm not sure the daughter's system is any better than the father's."

"Neither one of them is very romantic," said Ethel. "Shouldn't a princess story have some romance, Florence?"

But Florence uncharacteristically ignored the criticisms and continued.

"And so the great prince consort hunt began. Promising young men from all over the kingdom—not just knights—came to the palace to test their mettle via a battery of tests. They were asked what a given shape would look like unfolded, and what the relationship of black was to white; they were asked to analyze a business problem related to foreign trade; they were asked about a horse leaving point A at five miles per hour and another horse leaving point B at ten miles per hour and where they would meet.

"They were asked questions about history, literature, mathematics, practical governance and diplomacy. They were asked to demonstrate both the breadth of their interests and the depths of their knowledge in some favorite field of inquiry. They were asked to analyze poetry, to calculate the food needs of a province and to plan the seating for a diplomatic dinner. They were asked about their families, their hobbies and their secret desires.

"All their answers, and all the evaluations on their performances in practical examinations, were calculated and graded; and when that was done, Princess Faith had a thick dossier on most of the talented men in the country, and a short list of those whose talents and abilities were in some way extraordinary.

"Her father came to her as she and Sir David were reviewing this list. 'So,' the king asked, rubbing his hands together, 'who's the winner?'

"In response, Princess Faith handed him the list of outstanding individuals and began a recitation of the particular strengths and qualities of each.

"When she was less than halfway through, her father dropped the list on the table impatiently. 'Yes, yes, that's all well and good, but you haven't told me which of these outstanding young men you are going to marry.'

"'Oh,' said the princess, caught up short. 'Well, I'm going to marry Sir David, of course.' She grabbed the young man's hand in hers.

"Her father's mouth dropped open. 'Sir David,' he repeated incredulously.

"'Yes, well, I figure the question of my marriage constitutes a kind of test for me, as a princess and a future queen. It's a test of my ability to determine the appropriate standards to apply in making a particular decision. In this case, the appropriate standards are those of the heart. I've loved Sir David ever since I knocked him off his horse.'

"Her father, for a moment, was speechless. Then he finally said, 'Well, since I wanted you to marry him all along, I guess I'm delighted. But, but what about all this?' He waved his hand at the stacks of reports that resulted from the tests the princess had given. 'Was this all for nothing?'

"'Father, do you jest?' asked his daughter. She picked up the list of highly qualified individuals and shook it at him. 'Look at this. Don't you see? This information will be the basis for one of the best, most effective civil-service systems in history.'"

The men on the bus laughed heartily. "You're right, Florence," said Cyril, "that is certainly a very different kind of fairy-tale princess, and a most admirable one."

Florence beamed.

Louise had to admit that she found Princess Faith to be quite appealing as well, an opinion that Ethel shared.

"That is a young woman who is going places," remarked Lloyd.

"And speaking of going places," said Harry, "we are just arriving on the outskirts of Portland."

Chapter Seventeen

*J*ohn Gaunt pulled out a cell phone and punched some buttons to call his nephew. He informed Jeremy of their imminent arrival and then called to the front of the bus, "Harry, do you need directions to the seminary?"

"No, thank you, sir. We're all set. Unless," he added, "we need directions within the grounds themselves."

John checked with Jeremy and then reported, "No, the layout is pretty obvious, he says." Harry nodded and John returned to his conversation with his nephew.

The Maine Theological Seminary was located on the outskirts of Portland in an upscale area. It had once been the home of a rich industrialist, and the main building sat on extensive grounds with scattered outbuildings. A stone arch marked the main entrance, and a long, smooth, tree-lined drive led to the front of the seminary and a small parking lot set off to one side.

Jeremy Gaunt stood on the steps of the seminary, waiting to greet them, wearing a broad smile. Tall and straight like his uncle, he was a handsome young man whose wavy brown hair and gray eyes were particularly appealing features.

Jeremy helped each of the pilgrims to climb out of the bus. His uncle came first, and the two embraced warmly. Then John turned and named his fellow travelers. Jeremy had met most of them before, but only on a few occasions. Each offered him congratulations.

After the greetings, the visitors stretched their legs—all feeling a little creaky after such a long ride—and soon found themselves enthralled by the intense wash of gold and red and yellow autumn leaves. The stately maples and fiery sumacs seemed to be holding their hands up in the air in an arboreal prayer. Jeremy laughed in delight at the collective oohs and ahhs.

"It's so nice of you all to come all this way for the ceremony," said Jeremy. "I really appreciate it. Uncle John is lucky to have such caring friends and neighbors."

"We all think pretty highly of your uncle," said Lloyd.

Jeremy grinned. "Yes, so do I." He turned and indicated the buildings and grounds with a sweep of his arm. "I'd like to you show around, but I imagine that first you'd like to settle in and freshen up. We have a couple of guesthouses where you'll be staying, one for the men and one for the women. It'll be close quarters for the men, I'm afraid, but I think you'll manage.

"Mr. Bailey, if you'd like, you can drive the bus down the drive and take that right-hand turn through the trees down there. You can just make out the guesthouses, do you see?"

Harry nodded. "Sounds good to me."

"The rest of us can walk along this path, if you like. It's more direct, and you all might enjoy walking for a change."

Set in a copse of evergreen trees, the guesthouses were two wooden cottages with green shutters and trim. They were dark but not dreary. If anything, they seemed quiet and inviting. Still,

Louise wondered if they might prove rather chilly, especially at night, but the seminary had installed furnaces in both buildings, and they turned out to be warm and snug.

"I'm glad they have indoor plumbing," joked Ethel as she, Louise and Florence settled into rooms in the women's cottage. In fact, each room had its own bathroom, and the fixtures, while not new, were in good shape. Florence took the only single room, while Louise and Ethel shared one of the two doubles.

Superficially, thought Louise, it didn't look all that different from the hotel room that they'd shared: a couple of beds, a lamp on the bedside table, a desk. But the feel of the room was different. The hotel room had been clean but generic. Here, the bedspreads were mismatched—one was blue and one was cream colored—and underneath were mismatched plaid wool blankets. A small bookcase held an assortment of paperbacks and a Bible that had been underlined and annotated by previous guests. This room had more character than the hotel room, and everything in it felt homey.

"Reminds me of the camp I went to as a little girl," Ethel said with obvious approval. "I was in the Hemlock Cottage. Now if you want material for stories . . ." She winked at Louise.

"The room does have a reassuring feel," Louise replied. It was the same feeling that Louise hoped their own guests experienced at Grace Chapel Inn.

That night, John Gaunt took them all out for a celebratory dinner at a local restaurant.

Louise, who hadn't seen Jeremy for some time, marveled at the way the young man had matured. He was not talkative or showy, and he seemed genuinely modest when his uncle made mention of his accomplishments. He possessed a quiet dignity and gravity that drew the eye and made him the center around which the talk and activity at the table swirled. Louise felt this would have been the case even if he weren't the person being celebrated, and she thought that this power of presence would prove useful to him as a minister.

That wasn't to say he was overly solemn. He was clearly enjoying the company and the occasion. From time to time, he would sweep the table with his glance, and Louise would detect the light of good humor deep in his eyes. And as much as possible, he kept the conversation directed away from himself. He peppered the travelers with questions about Acorn Hill and about their trip.

He was particularly delighted with the notion of the storytelling activity, and he smiled as he expressed the opinion that the trip north must have been enriched by his visitors' tales.

Chapter Eighteen

Wednesday, Alice and Jane were enjoying some tea, having cleaned all the rooms and completed their other chores for the day.

"So you're going back to your mysterious project this afternoon?" Alice asked.

"Yes," said Jane, "if that's still convenient for you?"

"Oh yes," said Alice. She desperately tried to think of a way to prolong the conversation. Jane had already made it clear that she wouldn't answer a direct question, but Alice was hoping that if she could draw out Jane somehow, she might be able to guess what the activity was. Or maybe Jane would even slip and tell her outright.

Jane, who knew perfectly well what her sister was up to, sat and watched her with amusement.

Alice pursed her lips and stared down into her teacup. Finally, she said, "I noticed you took your car the other day when you went on your secret mission." Then, struck by her own transparency, she laughed out loud.

"Yes," said Jane, laughing also. "Yes, I did. Did you check the odometer? With a little effort you could figure out how far I traveled."

"Oh no," Alice demurred. "You're much too clever for that. I'm sure you drove far out of your way, just to rack up extra miles and throw me off the scent."

Jane lowered her voice to a confidential whisper. "You could always have me tailed."

"But who could I get to do it? I'd ask Lloyd, but he's gone off to Maine." They laughed at the notion, because Lloyd drove a large and distinctive SUV, unsuitable for tailing anyone.

"I'll tell you what," said Jane after a moment. "If you can guess what my project is, I'll tell you if you're right." Almost immediately, she regretted the offer. What if Alice did guess it?

Alice raised her eyebrows. "Well now, that does make things interesting. How many guesses can I make?"

Since she'd made the offer, Jane had to go along. Nevertheless, she was eager to limit her risk. "Three?"

Alice made a face. "Just three? When it could be anything? That's not very sporting."

Jane shrugged. "You're going to find out soon anyway."

"That's right, you said that, didn't you? Friday morning? Is that what you said?" Jane nodded. "Still, I think a few more than three guesses between now and then would only be fair. How about three this morning and, if I don't get it, three more tomorrow morning? And then, as you say, on Friday I'll know regardless."

Jane smiled. "Okay. Are you going to make your first three right now?"

Alice hesitated, torn between her eagerness to know and her desire not to waste half her guesses. Finally, she nodded. "Yes. Let's see. Are you shopping for something?"

"That's awfully open-ended," protested Jane. "I think you should have to make your questions specific."

Alice frowned but acquiesced. "Are you shopping for new things for the kitchen? New pots and pans and such?"

Jane smiled. "You don't think Louise approves of pots and pans?"

Alice had forgotten that the mystery project somehow required Louise's absence so that Jane would not face her disapproval. "Well, something expensive then. A new dishwasher? But no, it can't be something for the inn. We would discuss it together. So it would have to be something personal, but sufficiently expensive that Louise would disapprove." She shook her head in bewilderment. "Jewelry? A fur coat? I can't imagine you wanting things like that."

Jane was shaking her head and laughing. "You're going down the wrong track altogether, dear sister. But I think all of that speculation should count as at least one of your guesses."

Alice fell silent and stared at her sister, trying to think more logically. More to herself than to Jane, she muttered, "Some dangerous new hobby, perhaps?" and in a louder voice, she asked, "Have you taken up rock climbing or something?"

"I have not taken up rock climbing."

If Alice had been paying more attention, she might have noted the careful specificity of that answer, but she was distracted by a long-simmering fear that had bubbled to the surface. Indeed, it was one of the first ideas to occur to her about Jane's mystery project, and she had been struggling mightily to suppress it. She found she could no longer avoid it, however.

"Jane," she said with some hesitation, "are you looking for a job outside the inn?"

Alice frequently worried that Jane would someday regret having given up her cooking career in California to return to Acorn Hill and help her sisters run Grace Chapel Inn. Perhaps Jane no longer felt sufficiently challenged by the demands of a bed-and-breakfast and its limited menu.

If Jane did find an outside job, certainly both Alice and Louise would be affected, but Alice thought that Louise would indeed be the one to feel such a change more deeply. Therefore, if Jane was going out for job interviews, Alice could see why she might want to do so while Louise was away.

Jane shook her head. "No," she said, "I'm not looking for a second job. I've got plenty to do here." She paused and smiled. "That's three," she pointed out.

Alice, feeling more relieved than she might have expected, gave a long sigh. "I'll have to give more thought to this," she said. Then she stood and began clearing away the tea things. "If you're going to go gallivanting this afternoon, I'm going to take the opportunity now to run down and see how Vera and Fred are doing. I'll be back before you have to go."

"Are they still at odds over the doohickey?" Jane asked with concern.

"They both can be stubborn when they want to be," said Alice, "and, of course, they're both miserable over the tension between them. But I'm afraid that won't be resolved until Fred's contest runs its course. Another reason to look forward to Friday," she added grimly.

○

Down at the hardware store, Alice found Fred frowning at a large cardboard box he had set on the counter. "Look at this," he said as she approached. Alice thought she detected a note of frustration in his voice.

Peering into the box, Alice saw that it was three-quarters filled with folded slips of paper. Immediately, she recalled Vera's plan to stuff Fred's contest box with outrageous guesses. She wondered if Vera had put her idea into action. Rather than voice that suspicion, she merely asked, "More than you expected?"

"This is just from two days," Fred complained. "I didn't count on anything like this."

"Surely that's a good thing," Alice said hopefully. "It's drawing a lot of interest."

Fred sighed. "I suppose." After brooding a minute longer, he said, "The thing is, I told myself that I wasn't going to look at any of the guesses until the end of the contest. I didn't want to give even the appearance of manipulating the process in any way.

"But when I started to get so many, well, I scanned them, wondering how many people really know what the doohickey is. I mean, I expected that one or two people might know, but since the response was this heavy, I figured maybe more people know than I thought."

Alice realized with a start that Fred's claim to know the identity of the doohickey was a point of pride for him. He regarded the object's purpose to be a matter of esoteric knowledge. Now he worried that the knowledge might not be as rare and interesting as he thought.

Alice considered Vera's theory that the contest was just a ruse for Fred to learn what the thing was, without admitting his ignorance of it. But this new realization of the pleasure that the knowledge could give him put the final nail in that theory's coffin, at least as far as Alice was concerned.

She gestured at the box. "So you looked after all, and all these people know what the doohickey is?" she asked sympathetically.

"I looked, yes. But no, that's just it, it's clear that they don't know. There are some of the most bizarre, unlikely guesses you can imagine here."

Vera! thought Alice.

As if he had read her mind, Fred said, "And no, it's not Vera. I heard about her plan, and she swears that she didn't do this. Obviously, something's up. This doesn't just happen on its own." He cast a suspicious glance at Alice. "Vera didn't put you up to implementing her plan, did she?"

Alice laughed. "Fred, I love Vera dearly, but I'm staying out of this. Do you really think I have the time, or the desire, to produce all these?"

"No," Fred admitted, frowning. "But some folks do. I wish I knew who."

"Does it really matter? It's a tribute to you that so many people are interested in your contest. It's all the town talks about. If you've got some crazy guesses in there, even a lot of crazy guesses, what difference does it make? It's all part of the fun. And as long as you know what it is... You do know, Fred, right?"

Fred gave a sly smile. "Have a nice day, Alice."

Just to be sure about the box stuffing, Alice sought out Vera. "Not me," said Vera, shaking her head and spreading her hands.

"But it's just what you talked about doing."

"I know," said Vera, "but really, do I have that kind of time? You made it clear that you weren't going to help me with it. I gave up on the idea and confessed to Fred. You were the only other person I mentioned it to. Whatever's going on, I had nothing to do with it."

Alice was silent for a moment. "So you told Fred?"

"Yes, I thought my candor would inspire him to tell me what the doohickey is—or admit that he doesn't know himself."

"Did it work?"

Vera scowled. "No!"

Jane walked into the same building at the little airfield and was surprised to find *something* hanging from the ceiling. It was a tangle of straps, ropes and buckles, and it looked rather like a large spider suspended in the middle of the room. After a moment, Jane realized it must be the harness of a parachute.

They had it rigged up with a pulley, so that it could be lowered to the floor and raised again. Miranda had warned them at the last class that they would be practicing with a harness today, but the thought of actually strapping herself in to that rig made Jane's heart beat a little faster.

"Okay," Miranda said when she had gathered everyone together. "Monday, we talked about all aspects of the jumps you'll be doing: how to use the equipment, exiting the aircraft, proper body position during free fall, hand signals from the instructors, steering the parachute and landing. We also reviewed what to do in the unlikely event of an unexpected situation. But that was all talk.

"Today, as far as it's possible to do on the ground, we're going to practice these techniques. We're going to take you out to a parked plane and have you practice stepping out in the proper manner. We're going to rig you up in this harness here so you can feel what it's like to have it on and to hold the proper body position in midair.

"Also, if you have any problems with the actual jump schedules we worked out on Monday, or if you haven't been assigned a day yet, please speak to us and get it worked out before you leave. We want to do it while your training here is still fresh in your mind."

Jane looked around with growing excitement. The sight of the harness had made the whole idea of skydiving more concrete for her. The startling thought occurred to her, as it had periodically over the past few days: *I'm going to jump out of an airplane.*

When Jane returned home that night, Alice met her with a worried expression. "Jane," she said, "I'd like to take my other three guesses now."

Surprised, Jane said, "Are you sure? You don't want to wait for tomorrow? You might think of better ones this evening." Alice shook her head and sat down at the kitchen table, gesturing for Jane to do the same. Seeing how solemn her sister looked, Jane said in a subdued tone, "All right then, go ahead."

Alice took a deep breath and waited a few moments, as if gathering her nerve. Finally, she said, "Jane, are you . . . are you seeing someone Louise might not approve of?"

This was so unexpected that it took Jane a moment to realize what Alice was asking. But her blank stare seemed to make Alice think she had guessed the secret.

"Because you know," Alice said, "there's no need to keep something like that secret. You know that Louise and I would support—"

Jane's hoots of laughter cut her off. For a minute, Jane couldn't even control her hilarity long enough to answer.

Alice sat back, her expression a mixture of relief and chagrin. "I'll take that as a no," she said.

When Jane finally regained her self-control, she looked at her sister and said in as serious a tone as she could muster, "Alice, you've got two guesses left." But this only sent her off into gales of laughter again.

Finally, Alice snapped, "It's not out of the realm of possibility, you know."

"Oh, I hope not," Jane said, eyes still tearing, "but it's just so far from my secret objective. I'm sorry, Alice." She paused before adding, "Why would I want to keep that from Louise?"

"Well, if you had some reason to think that she might disapprove of . . . the gentleman in question."

"I see. You think I'm likely to take up with a member of some motorcycle gang or something?" Jane teased. "You've still only got two guesses left."

While Jane subdued the last of her chuckles, Alice sat frowning in concentration. "Okay," she said finally, "how about this. Are you doing some sort of dangerous volunteer work? Teaching cooking classes in a prison or something? Putting yourself at risk?"

"I'm not sure I agree that that would be particularly dangerous," said Jane, "but still, it's very kind of you to think of that as a possibility. As a matter of fact, the thing I'm doing is just for me and my own satisfaction. No prisons are involved."

Alice frowned. Her next guess was to be her last, and she had only a long shot to try. "Have you started painting again?" Painting, she reasoned, had once meant so much to Jane, and it had been so long since she'd done it on a formal basis that she might be intimidated about taking it up again. Louise often expressed concern that Jane tended to over-extend herself.

At that, Jane's features softened. She was recalling how she had originally left Acorn Hill to attend art school. "No," she said softly. "But it's an idea worth thinking about."

Chapter Nineteen

*J*eremy's ordination was to be held at a Portland church, where he had been assisting during his course of studies and which he was now to join as associate pastor. It would be followed by a reception in the church hall.

When the visitors from Pennsylvania arrived, they found a large sanctuary with little adornment, though with lots of warm woodwork, smoothed and polished by years of faithful congregants. The most decorative elements were the tall, narrow stained-glass windows, though even they featured subtle, cooler colors rather than anything deep or striking in hue. The walls were painted in a warm off-white, and the overall effect was understated but not chilly or uninviting.

For this occasion the sanctuary was awash in flowers. As was the case for the decor overall, they had been chosen with an eye for warm but subdued tones. Louise felt they added a restrained festiveness to the church.

There was a low buzz of happy conversation among the attendees already gathered, and for a moment, the group was self-conscious about being strangers in this place. But Jeremy soon spotted the guests. He excused himself from a conversation with an older couple and walked toward the rear of the church to welcome them. He had reserved a pew near the front for the group, as it turned out, and he escorted the party there personally. Once there, he introduced his guests to some of his friends and teachers who were seated nearby.

Louise found herself sitting next to a Rev. Dunwoody, who had been Jeremy's mentor in a program that the seminary ran. "A remarkable young man," Dunwoody said. "I can't think of anyone I'd rather see take this position."

Louise gave him a questioning glance.

"I'm retiring as associate pastor here," he explained. "That's why the position is open. For a number of years I have held both that post and my teaching job at the seminary, but I just can't do both any longer.

"Jeremy's work here began as part of our regular mentoring program, which is designed to familiarize the students with the practical aspects of pastoral work. Like anything else in teaching, the classroom work is essential, but you also have to learn to integrate theory with the day-to-day realities of actual ministry. Through the mentoring program, the students get to observe and participate in the practical side, under the guidance of someone with experience."

Louise smiled at her companion's dedication and enthusiasm.

"When Jeremy hit it off so well with the congregation here, I realized he was an answer to my own prayers as well. The dual responsibilities of the church and the seminary have been weighing on me." He lowered his voice to a confidential tone. "I had a small heart attack last year, you know, and the doctor said I absolutely had to cut back on some of my activities." He sighed.

"But there is always so much to be done. So, when I saw just how well Jeremy was fitting in, I realized I had the opportunity to put my doctor's advice into practice, leave the church in good hands, and do something helpful for a promising young man, all at once.

"As you can see," he concluded with a chuckle, "today is a great culmination for me."

"God's will," said Louise simply.

"Indeed." The aging minister nodded.

The rich, sonorous notes of the organ filled the church, and everyone settled down for the ceremony.

Louise felt that the ordination was conducted with just the right balance of gravity and joy. At one point, members of the congregation were invited to rise and speak, and several stood to describe admirable works that Jeremy had already done in his association with the church. In addition, several of his teachers and fellow students rose to describe the contributions he had made to the life of the seminary. Glancing down the pew, she saw tears of joy in the eyes of her friend John, but he seemed unaware of them as he lost himself in the beauty of the occasion.

After the laying on of hands by the church's pastor, Jeremy delivered his first sermon as an ordained minister. Louise was amused when he began to speak about storytelling and the use of parables as teaching tools, which enabled him to mention his uncle's trip to Maine to attend this ceremony. He paid a gracious and loving tribute to his uncle, who then looked, if possible, even happier.

At the conclusion of the ceremony, the church's magnificent bells pealed in one of the most joyful sounds that Louise had ever heard. Deeply affected, she was moved to say a prayer of thanks that she'd had the opportunity to attend this ordination.

The reception was held in the church's basement. A steady stream of parishioners, teachers and colleagues offered Jeremy their congratulations and best wishes. John Gaunt knew some of these people from previous visits to his nephew, but the rest of the Pennsylvanians gathered in a knot because they knew no one else there.

After a while, Louise decided that she ought to try to mingle a bit more, and she had hardly turned away from Ethel and Florence when she once again encountered Rev. Dunwoody.

"It's funny that Jeremy should choose to preach on stories and storytelling," he said with a smile. "There are a few stories that might be told about *him*, most of them, I'm pleased to say, of a very positive nature. Let me provide an example." With that he guided Louise to a relatively quiet corner.

"Last Christmas there was a family from this church whose daughter Cindy had to have an operation, and she was a very scared little girl. I think she absorbed the nervousness of her parents, but how could they help being nervous? It was some sort of hereditary condition that made the operation necessary, and their niece, who had the same condition, had died on the operating table during the same procedure two years before.

"Now, the doctors assured the parents that there had been unusual complications in that case, but the parents, of course, were still worried sick. And their daughter continued to be afraid, though I don't think she'd been told the details about her cousin.

"In any event, she was distressed, and every time the parents tried to comfort her, they were unsuccessful. Jeremy and I went by to see if there was anything we could do. This was the evening of the day after Christmas—Boxing Day, as they call it in England—and Cindy was scheduled for surgery the next morning.

"Do you remember how those Twisty Bears were a hot gift for Christmas? Looked like regular teddy bears, but you could bend them around in odd ways? Well, the little girl had gotten one as a present. I think her father had to drive to New Hampshire to find it, but she wanted one badly, and, of course, her parents wanted to do whatever they could to take her mind off the surgery.

"Cindy was clutching her Twisty Bear when Jeremy and I arrived. When you're trying to comfort children, asking them about their toys is always a good icebreaker, and Jeremy is a natural at that sort of thing, so he asked her about the bear. It was clear that she was quite taken with it.

"So Jeremy said, 'I know a story about a Twisty Bear. Only this Twisty Bear couldn't twist right.' And he told her a story about how the Twisty Bear went to the doctor to get his twist fixed, and the doctor said the Twisty Bear was going to need an operation. Twisty Bear was frightened, but he went into the hospital as the doctor told him to, and he had the operation. After it, he could twist perfectly again. Jeremy's story idea was ingenious and the little girl was delighted.

"But it's what happened next that I really treasure: Cindy begged him for another story about Twisty Bear. Jeremy looked up at me, and he had this happy little gleam in his eye. He pulled up a stool that was nearby, then said, 'Oh well, I know lots of stories about Twisty Bear, because after his operation, he went on to have many adventures. How many would you like to hear?'

"'All of them!' cried the little girl.

"'In that case,' said Jeremy, 'we'd better get started.'

"And he went on to tell her a whole series of stories about Twisty Bear.

"Twisty Bear went to school and helped the children with their math problems, because he could twist himself into the shapes of numbers. Twisty Bear went to the zoo, where the keepers made a mistake and tried to put him into a cage. He amazed them by twisting his way out, and then they realized who he was. Twisty Bear went to the park and had a twisty picnic, where all the food—except for the pretzels—was twisted into strange shapes.

"After a while, I couldn't stay awake any longer. I went to a room they keep at the hospital where old fellows like me can rest and have a nap. When I woke up later and returned to the room, he was still telling her stories.

"Cindy stayed awake so long listening to those stories that she no longer dwelled on her fear, and when she finally drifted off, she slept peacefully until the hour of her operation.

"Jeremy returned to the hospital after catching a few winks, and he was there when she woke up after the surgery. He had one last story to tell her, about how Twisty Bear had finally returned from all his adventures and was so happy to be reunited with the little girl who loved him that he just wanted to rest by her on her pillow.

"That is the sort of kindness that I think we can look forward to from Jeremy throughout his ministry."

Chapter Twenty

Thursday morning, the friends gathered for breakfast with Jeremy before starting the return trip. They all had been deeply impressed with the ordination ceremony and with the standing that Jeremy had already earned in his community.

During a quiet moment when Louise happened to be standing next to Jeremy, she asked him if he knew any good Twisty Bear stories. The surprise on his face quickly changed to a grin. "That bear sure gets around," he said, giving her a wink. Louise thought that, some time after they returned to Acorn Hill, she'd have to make a point of telling Jeremy's uncle about Twisty Bear.

As Harry loaded their bags into the bus, the visitors said their good-byes to Jeremy, with many promises of future visits on both sides. Finally, bags and people were all on board, and Harry maneuvered the bus down the seminary's long drive and out beneath the stone arch.

The passengers were quiet awhile as they reflected on their experiences of the day before, but soon they began to share their thoughts on the ordination and to congratulate John Gaunt once again on his nephew's achievements. Though the conversation ebbed and flowed, the silences contained none of the awkwardness that the travelers had experienced at the trip's beginning. All were happy to relax and enjoy one another's company.

But after a while time began to hang a bit heavy for them, and at that point, it seemed the most natural thing in the world when John said, "Well, when are we going to resume our storytelling? I, for one, would love to hear a new tale."

Florence, who had been thoroughly enjoying the colorful scenery, said, "Yes. I'd like to hear a story about Maine. Especially since we just had such a wonderful time there." Several others spoke up in favor of a story about Maine.

Finally, Harry said, "If you don't think I'm interfering by telling a second tale, I have a story about Maine. In fact, it's about the famous Maine coast, and it's one of the most popular kinds of stories." He paused for dramatic effect. "It's a ghost story, and though we are driving down the highway on a sunny day rather than sitting around a campfire in the dark of night, well, I think I'll tell it anyway. It takes place during Prohibition.

"Nell Cahill had been neglectful of her husband's wishes only once, and that was when she was packing her trunk in preparation for a trip to an island off the Maine coast. Before James left for work that morning, he asked her to go to the post office and mail a packet of letters. He said they were just some notes to distant relatives, but he wanted them to go out that day.

"The letters were going to Canada, and in order to get the international postage, Nell would have had to stand in a long line, and she didn't understand why she couldn't wait until she got to

Maine to mail them. Therefore, she packed the letters in her trunk, tucking them underneath her personal items.

"James was a true and good husband, and Nell loved him dearly, even if his whims—like insisting the silly old letters had to be mailed at once or like insisting that she go ahead of him to their summer cottage—didn't always make sense to her.

"Oh, she looked forward to the little cottage that James had rented for just the two of them, and to the rocky coast and the fresh salt air. She looked forward to arranging the cottage and decorating it with the little trinkets she was sure to find in town. But she was only twenty-three and recently married, and she did not relish the prospect of a month alone while James wrapped up his affairs at the office.

"Nell and James made an unlikely pair. They were both Boston-bred, but whereas Nell was a solid almost-Brahmin, James came from rougher stock. But he'd made good. His dapper clothing alone would indicate as much. Nell would tell you that he worked 'just below the president' of a small bank, because those were the words James used to describe his job to Nell, and later to her parents, who approved of James's good manners and his prospects.

"Nell arrived in Stonyport, Maine, on a sunny June day. The Boston air had been muggy and stifling, but fresh ocean breezes cooled the coastal town almost to the point of its being chilly. From Stonyport, Nell took the Granite Island ferry, an old steamboat that had seen better days, out to the island. Despite the clear sky, cool breeze, and generally smooth sailing, the moderate pitching and rolling of the ship caused Nell to spend that hour suffering from a queasy stomach, unable to enjoy the beautiful coastal vista.

"Upon reaching the island, she practically stumbled down the gangway, grasping the rope rails, until the captain, with an avuncular chuckle, offered her his arm and guided her to a bench on the path that led to the grand hotel. He offered to have her trunk sent on there, but she managed to choke out that she was staying in a cottage, so he had it placed at her side. As she sat, head down and miserable, trying to steel herself to move along, she heard a woman's voice say, 'Don't tell me the island has disappointed you.'

"Nell looked up and squinted into the sun. All she could see was a dark, narrow shape bearing down on her. 'Oh dear,' said the wraithlike woman. 'I guess that's not it. Here, here.' She sat down next to Nell and draped an arm around her shoulders. 'My boy Wallace is ready with a pony and cart. We'll get you home in no time.'

"'Wh—who . . .' Nell stammered.

"'I'm Enid, of course. Enid Skillings. Why, child, I'm your landlady—unless perchance you aren't Jimmy Cahill's bride. But if you ain't, then I'm teched.'

"A young boy about ten or twelve appeared, leading a weathered old pony that pulled a small cart. Enid introduced Nell, then stuck her fingers in her mouth and produced a long, shrill whistle. Before Nell could cringe in embarrassment, a sunburned sailor biting on an unlit pipe sauntered over. With a flick of her eyes, Enid ordered him to heft the trunk onto the cart.

"'Thar you go, ma'am,' he said with a nod toward Nell, who could barely express her thanks. The sailor sauntered off to join his friends at the pier.

"Enid pulled a handkerchief out of her sleeve and dabbed Nell's forehead with it. 'There, child, you'll be feeling better in no time, now that you're on land.'

"Mercifully, it was a short ride to the cottage.

"Indeed, the cottage was so close to the village that Nell would be able to walk to the general store or pharmacy for whatever she might need, or to the Hotel Pimm to sit in the pleasant drawing room and have a cup of tea.

"The cottage was set back from the road on a lot crowded with pines and woolly hemlocks, and it was situated at the top of a rocky cliff not visible from the village despite its proximity. It offered solitude, but with easy access to civilized comforts.

"On the ride up, Enid explained that she was the owner of this cottage and a few others on the outskirts of the village. Her own was practically within shouting distance.

"When Nell wondered out loud how James had ever come across a place like this, Enid explained that she and 'little Jimmy' went way back. Perhaps Enid knew Jimmy's parents, Nell thought. She'd never met them herself.

"Clad in weathered brown and gray shingles, the cottage was a narrow, two-story building with a turretlike structure in a rear corner. The house was a patchwork of odd rooms at odd angles, as if it had been built one room at a time, as extra space was needed.

"'This is the house the crazy old captain built,' Enid said. 'And over there, you see'—she pointed to the turret—'is his observatory. The captain had a telescope in there, and at times he used to watch the sea for the arrival of his lost love.'

"'The old captain,' Nell echoed. 'Did you know him?'

"The boy giggled.

"'Naw,' Enid said. 'He was dead by the time my ma was born. But everybody round here knows of him. He's a part of the island, as much as Killick Hill, over yonder.'

"'What was he to the island, a local hero?'

"Wallace, the boy, *pshawed* and smiled in the way of a child who is surprised to find he knows something an adult doesn't.

"'No, dear,' Enid answered. 'His map of the harbor is the best one made to this day, but people was here when he got here. He was from far away.'

"Wallace added, 'He didn't come here until he retired. Then it's said he never left because his heart was broke, and he haunts the place still.' When Nell raised her eyebrows, Wallace told her the whole story, and Enid nodded as he went along.

"'The old captain, Hiram Sutton, sailed whaling ships around the world, so he'd been up in these parts and all along the Atlantic coast, but he liked it here the best. He built a little house and wrote to a woman in Baltimore that he wanted to marry to invite her to come up here and be his wife. She said yes and set sail for Granite Island in the spring. Every afternoon the captain would go down to the docks and watch for her boat. It never arrived, and no word was ever heard of it. It was presumed lost, with all aboard.

"'After that, the captain never left the island. He spent his time in the turret, watching the horizon. He died of a broken heart, in this very house, and his ghost now keeps watch on the sea.'

"Nell's small hand flew to her heart. 'My word, that is a sad story.'

"'Well,' Wallace said slyly. 'It's kind of a folktale now, something the summer people like to hear.'

"When she entered the cottage, Nell looked around at the shadowy interior with its spider webs clinging to the corners, while Enid set about opening the curtains, revealing the most marvelous view of the harbor. Though she'd been feeling uncertain up to that point, then and there Nell was quite sure she would enjoy her stay. The coast was wild and impressive, and it appealed to her young heart.

"Enid showed Nell how to light the little potbellied stove in the kitchen, and she set a kettle of water on for tea. As she did so, she explained that the ferries came in the morning and evening, and told Nell that if she needed anything from the mainland, she could tell Sarah at the general store in the morning, and she would have it by the time the evening ferry arrived. 'Though you might be surprised,' she added, 'at all the things she keeps in stock, regular.' She gave a wink whose significance Nell was unable to fathom.

"'Sarah,' Enid continued, 'was young Wallace's aunt, his father's sister.' Nell looked down at the freckle-faced youngster, so young but already possessed of a quiet intensity. She tipped him a dime and a piece of striped candy she'd brought up from Boston. His eyes lit up when he saw the candy, suggesting a boyish spirit, after all.

"Tired after her long trip, Nell slept soundly that first night.

"At dawn she arose hungry and thought she would get a little breakfast at the hotel in town. Then she would see about picking up some groceries. She dressed quickly and made her way down while the sun was barely above the horizon. At the Hotel Pimm, she chose a seat that gave her a view of the harbor, where she could see the bustle of passengers lining up to travel to the mainland on the first ferry of the day. The boat had already arrived, and the visitors to the island were disembarking.

"If she was feeling at all lonesome, seeing the happy faces, eager to greet returning family members, warmed her heart. One father was met by three children and their mother. The charming part of the tableau for Nell was the obvious joy on the face of the youngest toddler. *One day*, she assured herself, *that will be James and me and our happy brood.* The family soon passed on, to be replaced in Nell's observations by other joyful reunions.

"A rustling of paper at the next table brought another matter to mind. A gentleman had just opened an envelope and was reading the contents, causing her to realize her error. The letters! She had forgotten to bring them with her to post. She felt a flicker of guilt but then realized she would have an excuse to wander back into town in the afternoon.

"As she ambled back toward her own little cottage, she passed the general store that Enid had described, and she realized that she had forgotten another reason for walking into town, to purchase provisions, and perhaps to see about having ice delivered.

"She stepped inside, but after the bright sun, she was momentarily unable to see clearly, and she stood awkwardly holding onto the doorframe. Once she was able to make out a few shapes, she took small, cautious steps into the store. Sullen faces loomed out of the darkness, then bodies to go with them. An old man sat on a stool in the corner. A young woman was shelving dry goods. A hard-looking woman with wiry salt-and-pepper hair rested an elbow on the cash register. She had rough, chalky skin and a walleye. All three stopped what they were doing to stare silently at the newcomer. As Nell moved uneasily around the store, the hard woman followed her with one eye or the other.

"No one spoke. No other tourists or locals came in. Nell roamed the aisles, at times picking up some things, which she cradled in her arms like a baby.

"Finally stepping to the counter, Nell caught sight of a tattered and yellowed poster: Drink—A Great Cause of Immorality, it announced. She certainly agreed with that. She'd seen that poster a hundred times in Boston. And through volunteering at a church soup kitchen, she had seen what the ravages of drink could do. She started to comment on it, just to make small talk, but she couldn't tell whether the woman at the counter was glaring at her, or at some specter in the dark recesses of the old store.

"'And will that be all?' asked the walleyed woman in a voice that seemed heavy with expectation. She started to reach under the counter, but when Nell nodded, she stopped, gave her a strange look, and then shrugged.

"Nell put her money on the counter and waited while the strange woman counted out her change, then wrapped up Nell's purchases in old newspaper. Nell did not linger any longer than necessary.

"Once in the fresh air again, Nell hurried up the sidewalk until she was beyond the corner of the store, then paused to take a deep breath.

"'You've been visiting the chamber of commerce, I see,' a disembodied voice said.

"At first, Nell saw nothing but a few trees that gave shade to the odd little store and the street in front. On second glance, though, she saw a woman who nearly blended into the trees. She was tall and tan and wore a nut-brown sleeveless dress. She was sitting on a stump, leaning on one hand and holding a book of poetry with the other. In contrast to Nell's stylish city bob, this wood nymph's light-brown hair brushed her shoulders and was fine enough to be lifted up by the faint island breeze.

"'I meant that sarcastically, you know. Hah! I suppose I'm a little odd myself, though. Aren't we all?' Her laugh was infectious. 'When did you get off the boat? I'm Imogene, by the way.'

"'How do you do? I'm new . . . Nell, I mean. But I'm also new to the island. I just arrived yesterday. You?'

"'Been here a few weeks. Long enough to get the lay of the land.' She nodded as if indicating the little store, though Nell missed her intended meaning. Then Imogene scooted to the side of the stump and patted her hand for Nell to sit down. 'I saw you sitting alone at the hotel this morning. I'm staying there with my sister and her husband, but newlyweds—what bores!'

"'Oh, ah . . .' Nell stammered a little bit, and reflexively touched her wedding ring.

"'Oh, dear me! I've gone and offended you. This mouth of mine will be the death of me one day. How long you been married?'

"'Please, I wasn't offended. It's funny, and I suppose James and I may be boring as well. We've been married just three months. Well, it's not that we try to be homebodies, but James works so hard, and well, you know.'

"Imogene had a relaxing smile, and as she was just Nell's age, the two talked easily. Imogene was from Hartford, and her father was in finance. Still chatting, they left their seat and walked up the hill to Nell's cottage, where they lunched together, then sat out by the cliff on old blankets and watched the horizon. Eventually Imogene thought it would be prudent to return to the hotel, 'before the dull, married folk start worrying.'

"'Will you be all right walking alone?' Nell asked. Imogene raised an eyebrow.

"'What's to fear? Ghosts? But I tell you what. Tomorrow, I will pick you up in my brother-in-law's touring car and we can go sightseeing. You'll see, this old island does have some special features.'

"Nell spent the rest of the day reading and relaxing. She was snug in bed before she remembered the letters once again. She felt a stab of guilt and her heart pounded. Well, she had tomorrow."

"Our Nell sounds a mite naïve," Cyril observed.

"Every ghost story needs someone naïve," said John. "You know, the person who will go up into the dark and haunted attic, when common sense would tell most people to run away as fast as possible."

Harry smiled and continued the story without responding.

"Nell slept fitfully that night, and as she lay awake some time after midnight, she decided to go down to the kitchen and heat up milk and make cocoa. As she was pulling on her housecoat and slipping on an extra pair of wool socks—the nights held an unseasonable chill—she heard a knocking sound. It was faint and irregular, and she couldn't tell if it came from inside or outside the house. She peered out the window, but that night the moon was obscured by clouds, and she could see nothing.

"Then she heard the knocking again. Louder this time. Perhaps from the basement? Her heart was pounding, and for a long moment she was too frightened to move. She recalled little Wallace's story about the ghost of Captain Sutton. She grabbed a quilt off the foot of the bed and carried it with her into the closet, where she spent the night huddled in a corner. She didn't remember falling asleep, but she certainly remembered waking to a cramp in her leg and a feeling of embarrassed foolishness.

"She'd washed up and picked at some breakfast when she heard a car horn toot. She looked out the window and saw Imogene at the wheel of a roadster, coming up the drive in a cloud of dust. She wore goggles and a green toque dotted with embroidered leaves.

"'Jump in!' she shouted over the roar of the engine. She tossed a pair of goggles into Nell's lap when she climbed into the car.

"Imogene gave her the full tour of the island, showing her caves and granite quarries, deserted sandy beaches and the best farm stands. At one of the beaches they walked barefoot and spotted seals and puffins, and even, Nell thought, an eagle. They settled on a warm rock, watching the waves, each woman eating an apple.

"Out of the blue, Nell said, 'Imogene, do you believe in ghosts?'

"'What? No! Do you?'

"Nell laughed a little. Imogene's down-to-earth reaction was reassuring. 'Well,' she started to explain, 'that boy, Wallace—'

"'Wally with the pony cart, I know him,' Imogene interjected.

"'He told me the story of an old captain, Hiram Sutton, who went mad, apparently, when the love of his life was lost at sea while coming to the island to marry him. He built the cottage James and I are renting this summer.'

"'*Hmm*. I've heard that story. Very tragic. Fit for an opera. Didn't know about the cottage, though. But no, love, I don't believe in what I can't see in front of me. Perhaps you saw a wisp of fog—you know how the weather is here.'

"'I didn't see anything. But . . . I heard noises, a knocking sound.' Nell described spending the night in the closet, much to Imogene's amusement.

"'Let's see. There's thunder, wind, gulls. For Pete's sake, raccoons will come around at night looking for scraps. There's all sorts of things that make noises in the night.' Imogene sat up. 'Which reminds me. There's going to be a clambake at the hotel Thursday evening. My sister and brother-in-law and I would love it if you joined us. Be a dear and say yes.'

"'Yes.' Nell laughed.

"'All right then. I'll pick you up at six. Now back to the road. I have to get this ghastly machine back to Mr. and Mrs. Woodbury before Mr. Woodbury has a fit.'

"Back at home, in the quiet of the afternoon, Nell sat down to write a letter to James. Two days and already she had enough to tell him to fill six pages. When she was done, she stretched her cramped hands and carefully addressed the envelope. Then she collected James's letters for Canada and headed into town.

"Once at the post office, she learned that she had missed that day's outgoing collection, but the postmaster promised that her letters would go out with the first ferry in the morning. With James's letters finally in the mail, Nell felt relieved.

"That night and the next, she again slept fitfully, snapping awake at every creak and groan of the house. The old house creaked and groaned a lot. The slightest wind caused an unnerving sound, and periodically, there would be odd thumpings and bangings that Nell, try as she might, couldn't quite ascribe to old wood and wind. Nevertheless, she forced herself to stay in bed rather than bolt once again for the closet, and each morning would dawn in due course, sunny and safe.

"Thursday evening, the long sloping lawn of the Hotel Pimm was dotted with chattering guests. Dorothea and Teddy Woodbury turned out to be as stuffy as Imogene portrayed them, yet they were gracious to Nell and obviously adoring of Little Sister, as they called Imogene. Wandering among the other guests with Imogene, Nell realized that most of them knew each other from previous summers on the island.

"Nell had felt tired and blue earlier in the day as she walked alone along the shore. But the party buoyed her spirits, and she began to feel more lively. The party itself was certainly animated, festive even, in no small part thanks to good music and congenial company . . . and probably to the consumption by some of an amber refreshment referred to as 'seawater.'

"Nell knew that the Prohibition laws were flouted regularly and flagrantly in Boston, but somehow she had assumed that things would be different in rural Maine.

"Despite her opposition to the 'seawater,' Nell was enjoying the sensation of officially becoming one of the summer people. She couldn't wait for James to join her and meet everyone. Oh, he might feel a little uneasy at first, mixing with these people, but Nell was convinced that city prejudices dropped away on the island, and so everyone would see James as she did—as a smart, hardworking young fellow, every bit as fit to be a financier as any man born in Newport.

"'What's this I hear about ghosts?' Teddy Woodbury appeared at her side.

"'Oh, that,' Nell murmured, turning toward Imogene's brother-in-law. 'Well, it's just that I've heard some strange sounds in the night, and I'm in the house where an old captain went mad, or so they tell me.' She gave a hollow laugh. 'It's a place that leads to morbid thoughts.'

"'I say, I'm quite envious. I've heard about that captain. Never seen a ghost myself. Perhaps the captain thinks you're his lady love, finally come in from the sea.'

"'I'm sure there's a good explanation for the noises,' Nell said, trying to sound brisk and commonsensical. 'Imogene thinks it might be a raccoon in the basement.'

"'*Pshaw!*' Mr. Woodbury flapped his hand in Imogene's direction. 'My wife's sister has no sense of the romantic. She's a born headmistress, that one, ruler in one hand, book in the other.' And with that pronouncement, Teddy Woodbury walked away.

"Nell reflected that she saw none of that in the fun-loving Imogene she knew, but then, unlike Teddy, she wasn't drinking 'seawater.'

"As the evening wore on, the fog rolled in so suddenly that some of the guests actually bumped into each other. Imogene offered to drive Nell home, and she gratefully accepted. The fog was so thick Imogene drove at a snail's pace. Nell could have walked home quicker than the auto took them, but she felt safer with Imogene.

"Imogene drove all the way up into the yard and up to the doorstep. Then she followed Nell inside and helped her light the stove and a few candles. 'I hope Teddy didn't pester you. He is fond of the sound of his own voice, I'm afraid, but he's not a bad sort.'

"'He didn't bother me at all,' Nell reassured her. 'Where does the "seawater" come from, I wonder. I hardly expected to see people drinking it so openly.'

"'The local folks supply it to the island's visitors. I hear it comes down from Canada. It's stored on Granite Island, hidden in one of the caves, I believe, and from here it's distributed throughout northern New England and all the way down to Boston.'

"'My goodness!' Nell was taken aback by Imogene's revelations. What she had just heard certainly colored her impressions of the island.

"'Well, I better be off. You will come hiking with us tomorrow, won't you?' Imogene tooted the horn once, then drove carefully back down the drive, disappearing quickly in the foul weather.

"The fog thickened around the house, and Nell now felt somewhat apprehensive about going to bed, even though she was exhausted. She set the latch and slowly made her way upstairs. From the captain's observation window, Nell could barely see beyond the windowpane. Too tired even to undress, Nell slipped off her shoes and curled up on the bed, asleep before she pulled the quilt over her legs.

"An hour later she awoke with a start. Her eyes wide and her heart pounding, she wasn't even sure if she'd actually heard noises in the house. Perhaps she only dreamed that she had. Nell clutched at the bedcovers. Then she heard what sounded like muffled thumps and scrapings, like something moving about in the basement.

"She listened intently. There was wind in the trees. That was one sound. There was a branch scraping the siding of the house, making a whistling sound. That was another sound. Then all was dead silence . . . until the footsteps started.

"Yes! She was sure now that was what they were—slow footsteps, soft at first but growing louder, climbing the cellar stairs, then sounding in the downstairs hall. Nell grabbed the quilt and hurried once more into the closet.

"'Oh, James,' she said silently. 'Come to me now. I've never needed you more.' The footsteps stopped. Nell thought she heard a rustle of papers, but then all was silent and that was the last thing she heard that night."

"She should get out of that house," Florence said with a worried tone.

"Where's she going to go?" asked Cyril. "She's on an island." He chuckled.

Florence, flushed, turned around to respond to Cyril, but Harry continued with his tale before there might be a heated exchange.

"Nell awoke the next morning to a knock on the cottage door. She bolted upright in the dark closet, then quickly went downstairs. When she saw Imogene at the door, she burst into tears.

"'Nell, whatever is the matter?' Imogene asked, entering the house. 'Has your ghost been back? You're a fright to look at.'

"Nell nodded, unable to summon words.

"'Well then, let me help you get dressed for a hike. I think it will do you good to get out of the house. And when we come back,' she added thoughtfully, 'we'll all go from room to room to find that old raccoon—or whatever it is—and roust it out.'

"The hike did much to lift Nell's spirits and to mute her fearful imaginings. Even better, Imogene and Teddy conducted a thorough examination of the house while Dorothea sat with her in the kitchen. When they were done, they informed Nell that they had found no evidence of anything strange in the house.

"'There's some junk in the basement that previous tenants seem to have left,' Teddy reported. 'You might want to speak to your landlady about that, lest you end up being held responsible for it. But we found no evidence that any animals have gotten in to upset things.'

"That night all was quiet, but on Saturday the noises returned, and though she kept to her bed, Nell did not sleep well at all.

"On Sunday, suffering a splitting headache, Nell did not seek out the local church. Instead she rested in a chair outside and read from her Bible. In the afternoon, she made her way over to Enid Skillings' to complain to her landlady about the noises. She didn't dare call it a ghost, but Mrs. Skillings took a look at her haggard condition and asked if the old captain had been visiting again.

"'No!' Nell almost shouted, then apologized for her outburst. 'I'm sure there is an explanation. I'm sure a good carpenter can do something to eliminate the noise. But if it's not fixed, I will have to give up the house, ask for our rental funds back and move into the Hotel Pimm. It is driving me to distraction.'

"'Hah!' Enid laughed. 'Jimmy didn't put any money down, so I can't help you there. And handymen are hard to come by in the high season. All booked up, and three times the off-season rate when you can get one.' She shrugged unsympathetically. 'It's a bit of noise. You must have noise in the city.' Enid gave her a look full of mysterious meaning. 'Jimmy wanted that cottage in particular,' she said, 'and he had his reasons. I don't think he'd take to the idea of you moving out.'

"'My husband would support my decision,' Nell said. 'I don't know why you think you know so much about it.'

"Enid looked steadily at Nell and said, 'Go ahead and let on that you've heard a ghost. You'll be the talk of the town; everyone wants that place to be haunted anyway. And I'll get another five dollars a week more for that cottage next season.'

"Enid Skillings laughed harder this time and snapped her fingers for Wallace to bring around the pony and cart. He had the good manners to pretend he hadn't heard a thing.

"'I'll give you a lift down the hill,' she said, 'but I can't help you about the house. You'll just have to wait for Jimmy to show up.' She gave an odd laugh. 'After this, I wouldn't be surprised if it clears up by itself. But if you do think you hear the captain moving about again, well, he won't hurt you, you can take my word for that.'

"Her head pounding, Nell was unable to argue her point any further. Maybe she *should* just wait for Jimmy—James!—to arrive. He'd take care of everything. She took a shaky breath and pressed her hand to her forehead. *At least*, she thought, *with the way I feel, if there's any noise tonight, I probably won't be able to hear it.*

"As a matter of fact, there were no noises that night, but Nell's nerves were so frayed that she was able to sleep, though fitfully, and she awoke no better rested than she had for several days. Later in the morning, she wrote a letter to James, begging him to hurry to Maine.

"After she posted the letter, Nell visited the island's small library, looking up accounts of the tormented old captain. The librarian even guided her to one of the library's prized possessions, an oil painting of Captain Hiram Sutton.

"He looked to be about sixty in the painting, with white hair and a white beard, and a piercing, intent stare. Nell studied it a long time and began to imagine that the man in the painting was talking to her, but his lips were moving so slowly, and the sound was so faint, she couldn't discern any words.

"'Ma'am, are you okay? Ma'am?'

"Nell realized the librarian was speaking to her. 'Yes,' she said tentatively, then repeated more forcefully, 'Yes. I only have a headache. It's distracting me a little.'

"'I see,' the bespectacled man said. He leaned in a little closer and dropped his voice. 'If you are having trouble . . . ahem . . . you know Sarah at the general store at the edge of town? She can help you, ah, obtain a little "seawater" for what ails you. Mother swears by it.' He grinned a little.

"Nell was a little slow to catch on to what he was saying. 'Sarah? Wallace's aunt?'

"He nodded.

"'But she has a poster behind the counter that says—'

"'I know. But believe me when I say she can help you.' Then he guided Nell back toward the library entrance, where she thanked him and left the building.

"The sky had darkened, and a storm seemed to be brewing. Though she wanted to return to the cottage before the rain started, Nell wondered if she should try to send a telegram to James or even to her father asking that money be sent so she could move to the hotel. Could she even send a telegram from the island? She had written James a letter, she thought confusedly, why hadn't he responded? Of course, she realized, she had sent the letter earlier that morning. Hadn't she?

"Her thoughts growing ever more confused, Nell trudged up the hill and reached the cottage just as a crack of lightning split the sky.

"The rain battered the windows and the house creaked, but Nell ignored the sounds as she sat at the kitchen table and rested her head on her arms. She dozed that way for an hour or so, and when she awoke, her head was sufficiently clear that she was able to get a fire going in the stove. She brewed herself some tea and sat listening to the sounds of the rain on the house. The initial fury of the thunderstorm had passed, but it was followed by a hard, steady rain.

"Her thoughts raced through her head, sometimes more coherent, sometimes less. Whenever she found them turning to Captain Sutton, however, she tried to push them away.

"In the brief time she had been marooned, so to speak, on the island, she had learned to both love it and fear it. She was awed by the beauty and power of the ocean, the variety of birds and trees, the intricate veins in the rocks that spoke of centuries of pressure and erosion. And yet there was also the indulgence that led some to become tipsy with 'seawater,' the disdain with which the year-rounders often viewed the tourists, and the irritating way in which Enid Skillings called her husband 'Jimmy,' when it just didn't seem possible, as Enid claimed, for her to have known James before he contacted her to rent the cottage.

"Her thoughts racing, Nell continued to sip her tea long after it had gone cold, and she never even realized that she had had nothing solid to eat since toast at breakfast. When night fell, she found she was too upset to go upstairs, so she sat in the hard spindle-backed chair and sought rest there.

"When Imogene came calling the next morning, she found Nell still sitting in her chair, staring straight ahead. She was a fright to look at. Her uncombed hair stuck out at odd angles, her dress was all wrinkled and tea-stained, and there were dark rings under her eyes.

"'Oh, my dear.' Imogene hugged her friend. 'Did that old ghost come back again?'

"'Came back,' Nell said in a faraway voice. 'He came back.'

"'Captain Hiram Sutton,' Imogene said sternly and loudly to the walls and ceiling, shaking her fists, 'I command you to leave this poor girl alone. She is not the cause of your loneliness.' Then Imogene, in an attempt to get Nell to smile, stamped up and down on the floor. 'Go away, go away, go away, ghost!'

"But Nell just looked past her with a vacant stare. Imogene was now truly concerned. She took Nell by the hand and led her upstairs, where she helped her change into fresh clothes. Then she led Nell away from the cottage and walked her to the Hotel

Pimm, where she intended for Nell to sleep in her room for the day and perhaps for the night too—for as long as it was necessary.

"They were nearing the hotel's entrance, when Nell looked out over the dock and called out, 'Where is he? Where is my husband? Oh, James!' She began to sob.

"Imogene hurried the incoherent and weeping Nell into the hotel and asked that a doctor be sent to her room. Then she hustled Nell up the stairs and got her tucked into bed. Nell fell into a light, restless sleep, one that seemed to be punctuated by nightmares. She murmured off and on as she tossed, and Imogene sat anxiously by her side.

"'She's been calling for her husband James,' Imogene explained in whispered tones to the doctor. 'But her husband's in Boston, and not due to arrive until the week after next.'

"The doctor nodded and pronounced, 'Exhaustion.'

"'Give her a little "seawater" to help her sleep,' he suggested. 'She needs sleep more than anything right now.' But when Imogene tried to pour a bit into Nell's mouth, she refused it and turned her head away.

"Day passed into evening, and in the middle of the night, Nell woke Imogene with a cry. Imogene had been sleeping in a chair beside the bed. She awoke to find Nell out of bed and standing by a window, looking down at the docks in the moonlight.

"'James!' Nell screamed, then fainted dead away.

"Grimly, Imogene managed to lift her back into bed and hoped that Nell might finally have a peaceful, uninterrupted sleep.

"The rest of the night passed without incident, and early the next morning, Imogene sat reading by her bedside while Nell continued to sleep. Suddenly, an urgent knocking came at the door.

"Imogene tried to turn the visitor away, but Enid Skillings forced her way into the room. 'She's got to hear this,' said Enid, 'it's about her husband.'

"Nell sat up in bed. 'What about James?'

"Imogene looked concerned, but clearly she couldn't send Enid away now.

"Enid looked suspiciously at Imogene and then turned to Nell. 'It's about Jimmy's . . . business,' she said. 'Maybe we should speak in private.'

"Imogene folded her arms and said, 'I'm not going anywhere.'

"Nell seemed oblivious to this exchange. Instead, she cried again, 'What about James?'

"Enid cast one last look at Imogene and shrugged. Then her face softened. 'I'm sorry child. He . . . asked for you at the end.'

"Imogene's eyes began to show alarm, but Nell only seemed confused. 'Have you seen him?'

"'He's been here right along, child. He didn't want you to worry, but off and on he's been staying in the basement of your own cottage.'

"'What's going on?' demanded Imogene. 'Why on earth wouldn't Nell's husband tell her if he was here?'

"Enid looked at Imogene. 'Jimmy, he worked for gangsters,' she said. 'The bosses in Boston were sending him here to take charge of the bootlegging from Canada down through New England. They'd been using some Canadian fellas, but they found out that those guys were thieves, so they wanted Jimmy to come up and take over.

"'Of course, that wasn't going to make the Canadians too happy. Jimmy sent word of his plans to Canada, and the gang's people there were supposed to square it so that no one would come after him, but Jimmy knew he'd have to lay low for a few weeks while that got . . . settled.

"'But he still had to come up here to get the lay of the land and be on the scene when the change came. He had to be sure there wouldn't be any interruption in supply. Jimmy decided to hide out for a few weeks while everything got squared away. Said he was already paying for that cottage, he might as well live there. He thought he could do it with nobody being the wiser, though that didn't work out so well.

"'For some reason, word didn't get through to the right people in Canada, and the bad guys didn't get taken care of. And meanwhile, Jimmy had to start making himself known to the local dealers and haulers so he could learn how the setup worked. Well, the Canadians figured he was looking to muscle in on his own, and so they did . . . they did what people do in that situation.

"'I found him . . . I found him shot and dying, at the cottage. He said something about some letters, and then he asked about Nell. I'm sorry, child,' Enid said, turning back to Nell, 'I didn't know where you was. Jimmy's dead.'

"This didn't seem to register. Instead, Nell said faintly, 'James is here? Then I did see him! I saw him just last night! Down by the dock. Oh, James.' She broke down sobbing.

"But Enid grimly shook her head, 'Not last night, child. I found him dying about dinner time, and though he struggled to hang on, he gave up the ghost just after sundown.'"

Some of Harry's passengers felt shivers at the conclusion of Harry's ghost story, and for a while there was silence.

"I love a story with reversals like that," said John finally. "You spend most of the story wondering if there's really a ghost or if there's some natural explanation, and just as it appears that there's nothing supernatural going on, you get that twist at the end that makes it mysterious again."

"I don't care for ghost stories," murmured Florence. "I never did." Louise had noticed, however, that Florence sat enthralled the entire time Harry was telling the story.

"I thought it was interesting that the criminals turned out to be their own worst enemies," Lloyd said. "Jimmy was killed by the criminals he was sent to replace, but you can bet that Jimmy's bosses in Boston won't let that mistake go unpunished. 'The weed of crime bears bitter fruit.' I guess you have to assume that they would have killed Nell, too, if they'd found her at the house."

"So in a sense, its being 'haunted' saved her life," said Cyril.

"I'm glad you liked the ghost story," said Harry, "but it does seem a shame to be discussing such dismal subjects in the midst of such glorious scenery."

Rather than take the interstate, Harry had chosen to drive down a road that followed the Maine coast. The famous rocky shoreline was frequently just yards away on their left, and periodically they passed through small vacation resorts with long, sandy beaches.

Once again, they stopped at the seafood restaurant near Portsmouth for lunch. Louise found herself as taken with the herb-cheese muffins as she had been the first time, and even though she worried that it might go stale, she brought away a sample in a Styrofoam container to give to Jane. She was confident that her sister could re-create the savory treat for their own menus.

On the road again, they passed over the tall bridge from Kittery, Maine, to Portsmouth, New Hampshire. Harry pointed out the Portsmouth Naval Shipyard on Seavey Island. "That's the US Navy's oldest functioning shipyard," he reported. "It was established in 1800. Guess what they work on these days?" When none of them could, he told them. "Nuclear submarines. There's always room for the new along with the old."

The new and the old were also on Alice's mind that day when she made another trip to Fred's store to see how his contest was progressing. She was surprised to see that the old box for entries was now gone and had been replaced with two new boxes.

"Still getting a large volume of guesses, Fred?" Alice asked, smiling.

"I've expanded my contest, Alice," said Fred happily. "Guesses now come in two flavors."

"What do you mean?"

"Do you remember how I was getting all those far-out suggestions?" Alice nodded. "Well, apparently my contest was an opportunity for a little game with some of the local kids. They began by challenging each other to come up with the craziest possible guesses that would still be just this side of plausible. Then they had so much fun doing that among themselves that they started writing them down and stuffing them into the box. They were hoping I'd open them for the first time in front of everyone on Friday.

"But now I'm making it an official part of the contest. In addition to a prize for the correct answer, I'm also going to offer a prize for the most creative guess, and I've encouraged the kids to come up with their wildest ideas. I think it'll be fun."

"Maybe," said Vera, coming forward from the back of the store, "except *he's* going to be the one to judge how creative they are, and he without a creative bone in his body."

Fred, however, refused to take the bait and contented himself with rubbing his hands together in anticipation of the outlandish guesses that would be submitted. "This is going to be great."

Chapter Twenty-One

"I was wondering...," began Louise tentatively.

"Yes, Mrs. Smith?" Harry encouraged.

"I was wondering what it would be like if we all tried to work together on a story. A mystery story, say, that we could each contribute to as it went along. Do you think that would work?"

"I think it could be interesting to try," Harry replied, "so long as everyone's willing." But in the rearview mirror, Louise saw a smile on his face that belied his cautious response.

The others, Louise was pleased to find, eagerly agreed to the plan.

"You set things up, Louise," said John. "It was your idea."

Louise thought for a while. "Well, Alice is really the mystery reader in the family, but I know that one thing that's always important to her in a mystery is the setting. So perhaps we should start with that. How about if our mystery is set . . . at a country inn?"

Everyone laughed. "Whatever made you think of that, Louise?" asked Lloyd in a teasing manner.

"But it's classic, though, isn't it," said John enthusiastically. "An inn gives you a chance to mix characters who are local to an area with people from outside. You can see why a writer would like that sort of setup."

"Well then, what is the area?" asked Ethel.

"New England, of course," said Florence.

"Vermont?" suggested Cyril. "During foliage season."

"Okay, so what about people?" said John. "Who are our characters? Louise? Any thoughts on the owners? Three sisters, perhaps?"

"Certainly not," said Louise. "No, I think the owners are a middle-aged couple who have left the city in order to escape the rat race and pursue their dream of becoming innkeepers. The . . . Pattersons. Bill and Sherri. They used to have high-stress jobs in advertising, but they've left all that behind. And they love being innkeepers, even when it's so busy they are run off their feet, such as during foliage season."

"So the inn is full of leaf-peepers," said John. "Who are they?"

"I think there's a young couple on their honeymoon," said Florence. "Trish and Felix." She nodded with satisfaction at her newly created man and wife.

"And another couple, middle-aged," said Cyril. "Up from the city. The McAvoys?"

"What about a victim?" asked Louise. "I assume this is going to be a murder mystery? If we're going to create a mystery, we might as well go all the way."

"I think the victim should be a very rich, very unpleasant old woman named Hortense," said Florence. "Mrs. Hortense Gunther, but of course she will insist that everyone call her Mrs. Gunther. And she should have a young woman companion with her, Muriel, whom she will treat like a servant—but then, she treats everyone like a servant. Besides rich, she should be miserly." Florence spoke in such deliberate tones that Louise wondered if she had someone in mind.

"Wealth is always a good motive for doing someone in," said John. "And what about a detective? Shall it just happen that the world-famous private detective, Henry Porot, is also staying at the inn?"

Louise smiled. "That would seem to be in the best tradition of the genre. But there must also be a local police officer who will be baffled by the crime."

"Poor Chief Dudley," said Lloyd. "Rufus Dudley, that is. Never was necessarily the brightest bulb in the box, but a good steady policeman, like his father before him, for a small Vermont town. Who would ever have dreamed that he'd be faced with investigating a murder?"

"I think there ought to be at least one more local," said Ethel. "How about a handyman named Bert? He's not regularly employed by the inn, but he's often to be found here."

After a moment's silence, Louise asked, "Any more? Well, I guess that'll do to start with. If we need more characters, we can add them as we go along. Now then, where do we start? With the murder itself?"

"Oh no," said Florence. "You have to introduce the characters, especially the victim. Oh, I'll take care of that part."

To Louise's surprise, Florence plunged in to begin the story.

"Bill and Sherri Patterson were standing outside their inn in rural Vermont on a sunny autumn day, inspecting the facade with

Bert Vallier, who was going to be doing some work on the clapboards for them. The resplendent red and gold of the fall foliage shone brightly about them in the warm sunshine.

"'You think they'll last till spring, Bert?' asked Bill.

"Bert, his nose almost as red as some of the leaves, nodded. 'Oh, sure, they'll be fine. No point doin' most of this work now, anyway. It'll just get all banged up in the winter. Wait till spring. Then it'll be all nice lookin' for the new season.'

"Bill and Sherri were nodding their heads in agreement when they heard the sound of a car entering the driveway. They turned to see a large, black SUV pulling in. At first glance, it appeared that the SUV was driving itself, but as they looked more closely, they could see a diminutive, white-haired figure behind the wheel. In the passenger seat, a younger woman clung grimly to her shoulder harness.

"The Pattersons cast apprehensive glances at each other. 'Mrs. Gunther,' said Sherri in a resigned tone.

"'Didn't know you was expecting her today,' muttered Bert.

"'She's been up every year for the foliage,' Bill reminded him, 'ever since we bought the place.'

"'I remember,' Bert replied grimly. He took a step back.

"The SUV inched its way up the inclined driveway and finally stopped by the front entrance. Once the engine was turned off, everything was silent for a few moments, and then Bill gave Sherri a resigned look, cleared his throat, stepped up to the vehicle and opened the driver's door. 'Welcome back, Mrs. Gunther. What happened to the Lincoln?'

"Hortense Gunther glared at him as she clambered down from the throne of the SUV. 'I like the height it gives me,' she snapped. 'These are much safer too.'

"'Safer for you, anyway,' said her passenger, coming around the front of the vehicle. 'Not necessarily for the other drivers on the road. Hello, Bill, Sherri. Bert.'

"'Of course safer for me,' muttered Mrs. Gunther, who had heard only the first part of her passenger's comment, 'Who else am I buying the thing for?'

"'Hello, Muriel,' said Bill to the old woman's companion. She was already preparing to climb up into the driver's seat herself, but Bill stopped her. 'I'll park it,' he said, 'you go on in. I'll bring the bags in a minute. You're both in your usual rooms.'

"Muriel looked at him gratefully. 'Thank you, Bill. It's been a long ride.' She paused and shook her head. 'And I thought she was a terror driving her Lincoln.' She handed him the keys and turned to walk with Sherri into the house.

"Bert said his good-byes and headed toward his pickup truck, while Bill prepared to move the SUV into the inn's parking lot."

"That's good," exclaimed John. "I like that idea of making her a regular guest. She's not a local, but she's not a complete stranger, either." Florence smiled almost shyly at the praise. "Now, how will we bring the rest of our players on stage?"

"Well," said Louise, "there's every chance that they would meet each other at breakfast the next morning." She thought for a moment before taking her turn.

"Bill liked cooking eggs, and he was good at it. One of the distinctions of their inn was the quality of the breakfasts, especially Bill's wide variety of omelets. He was in a good mood because the young couple on their honeymoon, Trish and Felix, had been there almost a week, and they had already tried several different omelets. Bill had been pushing himself to come up with creative celebratory offerings for them.

"And this fellow Porot, their celebrity guest, was also a man who liked his food. He'd been effusive with his compliments about the breakfasts.

"Trish and Felix, with the enthusiasm of the young, were the first ones in the breakfast room, soon followed by Porot. Mrs. Gunther, he knew, would be down at 7:35 on the dot, Muriel trailing, and they would each have a soft-boiled egg. But the other couple, who had arrived late the day before, Ross and Norma McAvoy, were still a question mark. He was interested to see what they might order.

"The McAvoys were the next to arrive. He ordered two eggs over easy, and she wanted hers scrambled. Because it was their first morning, Sherri was making a point of chatting with them, trying to determine if they would want suggestions about places to go or things to do.

"Bill was always amazed at the number of people who were grateful for such advice but would not ask for it on their own account. It became a bit of a guessing game. You didn't want to give the impression you were prying, but if they did want suggestions, and you were able to determine that and supply helpful hints, they would always comment later on the wonderful service. It never failed.

"Sherri must have decided these folks were pretty sociable, Bill thought, because he could hear her introducing them to the newlyweds. That was another minor matter that required a degree of sensitivity and tact. Some people loved meeting their fellow lodgers and were delighted to be introduced. Some just wanted to keep to themselves. Hosts didn't really want to initiate any introductions unless they felt they'd be welcome by all parties.

"Sherri wouldn't try introducing any of them to Mrs. Gunther and Muriel, Bill knew.

"At 7:35 precisely, Mrs. Gunther swept into the breakfast room. Sherri had unobtrusively steered the other guests away from her favorite table, and the old woman descended on it with a proprietary air. Not until she was seated did she even glance at the other people in the room, though when she did so, Bill thought he saw her give a little start and then knit her brows. He glanced around at the others, wondering who had provoked this reaction. Perhaps she had recognized Porot, the famous detective.

"But Sherri was already collecting their soft-boiled eggs, and both Mrs. Gunther and Muriel seemed to focus on preparing their tea. The room was quite a bit quieter after their arrival."

"This is very mysterious already," exclaimed Lloyd. "Are you suggesting that one of the other guests already knows our victim, Mrs. Gunther?"

"I think Louise is doing a wonderful job of setting up some possibilities," said John. "But with your permission, I'll move to the event that will put the investigation in motion."

"The inn's guests were blessed with another day of bright sunshine and warm weather in which to enjoy the spectacular foliage. The McAvoys and the newlyweds both asked about places where they could do some hiking, and Bill had provided recommendations, tactfully suggesting an easier trail for the McAvoys. The other guests were content to enjoy the show from a car.

"The inn was blissfully quiet for much of the day, but in the midafternoon, all began to return, most of the guests eager for a chance to rest and freshen up before going out to dinner. Breakfast was the only meal regularly provided by the inn. For those who wanted a recommendation, Bill usually suggested a nearby restaurant, the Fatted Goose. It was within walking distance, it commanded a lovely view of the village green, and it was a picture-perfect example of what a quaint Vermont restaurant ought to be.

"As he'd been working in his office at the back of the house during the afternoon, Bill heard the sounds of the various guests returning. He did not consciously keep tabs on their comings and goings, but his sense was that if they were not all back, more had returned than not. He'd spent about an hour going over the bills and accounts, and as he sat tapping a pencil on the cover of the ledger book, a frown creased his face.

"It was five o'clock, and he needed to make himself accessible to his guests in case they wanted restaurant suggestions or the like. He picked up his newspaper and moved out to the front of the house. This way, he would be available to answer questions without appearing to hover.

"Just as he sat down with the paper in the front parlor, however, the quiet afternoon was pierced by a shrill scream.

"Instantly, Bill bolted up the stairs. His sense was that the scream had come from the third floor, but he paused on the second to take stock. The guests on that floor had all rushed out into the corridor and were staring at him in confusion. Next, he heard loud sobbing coming from the floor above.

"At the top of the stairs, he found Muriel standing outside Mrs. Gunther's room, just this side of hysterical. Mr. Porot, whose room was also on that floor, was doing his best to comfort her. As Bill moved toward the door of the room, Porot put out a restraining arm. 'Don't go in,' he said. 'We mustn't disturb the crime scene.' When Bill turned an uncomprehending look at him, he explained, 'She's dead.'"

"How did she die?" asked Cyril eagerly.

But John gave him a broad smile. "I don't know, Cyril. How *did* she die? I think you might be able to enlighten us."

Cyril took his cue.

"Two hours later, Bill returned to the third floor and peered into Mrs. Gunther's room. Yellow crime-scene tape had been stretched across the doorway, just like on TV, but the body had not yet been removed. Mrs. Gunther still lay curled around a pool of blood from the knife wound in her abdomen."

Louise gave a small shudder, and Florence asked querulously, "Does it have to be so disgusting?"

"What would you prefer?" asked Cyril.

"How about poison?" suggested Ethel.

"If it's poison, they might not realize right away that she's been murdered. They might assume that she's had a heart attack or stroke."

"And what's the matter with that?" demanded Florence.

Cyril shrugged. "Nothing, I suppose. Just seems like it drags out the story, though. We don't want Porot going home from his vacation before he has a chance to get involved. Besides, a knife just seems to suggest a crime of opportunity and passion. Gives us a broader field to work in."

The debate over the appropriate method of death continued for a bit, with the women arguing for poison and the men rather more strongly preferring a knife. Ethel was the first to tire of the discussion. "Oh, let's let it be a knife and get on with it."

"Gladly," said Cyril.

"What surprised Bill was the amount of time everything took. The local police had to be called, and they had to look over the crime scene, and then they determined that the state police had to be called, and the state police had to look it over as well, and then they required that their forensics lab had to be called. It was endless.

"Fortunately, Bill succeeded in keeping the second-floor guests from coming up the stairs, so he at least kept them from the grotesque sight. He had tried to spare Sherri as well, but she insisted on looking. Poor Muriel had been given a sedative, and Porot, well, Bill supposed Porot must be accustomed to that sort of thing.

"Indeed, more accustomed than their local chief of police. Poor Rufus Dudley had gone striding right into the room, and even though Bill had warned him what to expect, he stumbled when he saw the body and had to catch himself by reaching out and grabbing what he could find. 'Careful,' Porot nearly shouted from the doorway. 'Fingerprints.' But Chief Dudley had been so upset that Bill didn't think he'd heard Porot.

"That was the beginning of the parade. Now the forensics people were waiting for the state medical examiner to remove the body so that they could continue their examination of the room. Through it all, Porot stood quietly by, watching every move. The one piece of information that Bill was able to pick up was the estimate that Mrs. Gunther had been dead for about an hour at the time she'd been found.

"The state police were able to supply the technical assistance, but the troopers told Chief Dudley that he would be in charge of the investigation. 'Your patch, your problem,' one of the troopers said tersely. 'There's a list of specific criteria the crime has to meet before we can come in, and so far, this one hasn't met them.' Chief Dudley looked resigned to his fate.

"Without thinking, Bill spoke up. 'Perhaps Mr. Porot here can help.'

"'Porot?' said the trooper. 'Henry Porot?'

"Porot graciously acknowledged the man's recognition and enthusiasm and then said, 'Of course, since I am right here, I'd be willing to help.'

"Chief Dudley looked blankly for a moment between Bill and Porot, but then a light seemed to go off for him, and he gave a grateful smile. 'That'd be great. Thanks, Mr. Porot.'

"Well, Bill hadn't intended to offend Chief Dudley's sensibilities, but he was sure the chief would appreciate the assistance before it was all over."

"Now what?" asked Ethel.

"This is the best part," said Lloyd. "Now the investigation begins."

Chapter Twenty-Two

*L*loyd picked up the story.

"At Porot's suggestion, Chief Dudley asked Bill to have the guests assemble downstairs in the front parlor. While they were gathering, Porot took Bill aside. 'Did these people eat dinner?' he asked.

"Bill was somewhat startled to be reminded that life went on. 'No, I don't think so,' he said. 'I know I never did. I think most of them went back to their rooms after . . .'

"'Well, is there a pizza delivery place or the like around here? I don't think it will help our investigation if the witnesses are distracted by hunger. Don't bother trying to take orders or anything, just go ahead and get something brought in. Take my word for it: They will appreciate it.'

"Once everyone had assembled, Chief Dudley stood up before the group. But as the officer struggled for words, Bill thought he looked even worse than when he'd first seen the body. Finally, the chief looked in Porot's direction and said, 'Mr. Porot, would you . . . ?'

"Porot addressed them with an air of quiet authority. 'Ladies and gentlemen, as you know, a tragedy has occurred. Mrs. Gunther, one of your fellow guests, was murdered this afternoon in her room on the third floor.

"'Chief Dudley here will be conducting a thorough investigation. One of the first and most important steps in such an investigation is constructing a timeline of all the events that occurred in the vicinity of the crime during the day. To that end, we will be interviewing each of you as to your own actions and whereabouts today, and most importantly, what you may have seen or heard here at the inn, especially in the afternoon.

"'We will appreciate your cooperation. But first, as none of you has eaten dinner, our host Mr. Patterson has made some arrangements.'"

"What's all the fuss about the pizza?" asked Cyril. "Is that a clue? Did the delivery man do it?"

"It's character development," said Lloyd in affronted tones. "I wanted to show that our hero, the detective, is a considerate person. Also, it demonstrates his greater familiarity with crime and tragedy. While everyone else is still shocked by the crime, he knows from experience that, eventually, people are going to remember they've missed their dinners."

"I think it's a smart idea," said Ethel.

"Every story goes better with pizza," said John, "but allow me to take you back to the investigation.

"Bill and Sherri set up Mr. Porot and Chief Dudley in their office so that they would have a place to conduct their interviews. A state trooper agreed to stay with the other guests in the parlor while they waited their turns, ostensibly to provide information and comfort but also to overhear any incriminating remarks that might be made.

"In the office, Bill, Sherri and Porot finished their pizza before getting on with the business at hand. Chief Dudley refused any food. Porot said casually, 'We might as well start with the two of you, since you're here.' Bill and Sherri sat up a bit straighter in their chairs. With a sidelong look, Porot asked them, 'How well did you know Mrs. Gunther?'

"Bill and Sherri exchanged nervous glances. Then Bill said, 'She was a regular guest. Came up every year for a week during foliage season. She was nice enough.'

"Porot arched an eyebrow, and Sherri said, 'Bill,' in a warning tone.

"Bill sighed and his shoulders drooped slightly. 'Okay, she was a mean old bat. We've known her for years, since we lived in the city. She knew Sherri's mother, and she knew . . . a secret about her, one that—'

"'My mother had an affair,' said Sherri. 'Unfortunately, I am not my father's child.' Bill reached over and clutched her hand.

"'Her mother was always so ashamed,' said Bill. 'She would have been mortified if the truth had gotten out. And even though she's dead now, Sherri's dad is still alive and, well, we don't know if he suspects—he's never said anything—but we don't see any reason to upset him by bringing it up at this late date.'

"'And you're certain Mrs. Gunther knew?' asked Porot. Bill nodded. 'And are you saying she made use of this knowledge? Did she blackmail you?'

"'Well, I don't know if you could call it that,' Bill replied. 'She never asked for money or anything. But for years, she has made demands for little favors and services, gifts. One of the reasons we wanted to leave the city was to put some distance between us and her, though that didn't work out as planned either.'

"'What do you mean?'

"'As soon she learned about our plan to open an inn someplace, she started putting tremendous pressure on us to buy this place. She owned it, you see, but hardly ever used it. She wanted the convenience of being able to come here without the expense and bother of being responsible for the house.

"'I don't know what would have happened if push had ever come to shove,' Bill said thoughtfully. 'The power of a shameful secret only goes so far. But the fact is, this house, this town was exactly the kind of thing we were looking for anyway, and even though she asked top dollar, we managed to bring her down a little bit. In the end, it didn't work out so badly.

"'Of course, she didn't tell us until after the deal was done that she expected to stay for free whenever she came, and that she'd be here at our busiest, most profitable season. But even at that, we'd had much less contact with her here than we did in the city.' He shrugged. 'It may not be the ideal arrangement, but it was an improvement.'

"'Which is why,' said Sherri, 'we didn't have any motive to want her dead. A few years ago, before we moved here, we would have been much better suspects.' Porot smiled at that, but Bill blanched: He'd forgotten for a moment the reason they were having this conversation.

"Porot questioned them closely about their own movements that day. Both had been busy around the house: It was Sherri's washing day, and Bill had done a lot of maintenance work with Bert's help. Later in the afternoon, Bill focused on paperwork in his office, and Sherri went to her small studio to do some painting. Neither made a special effort to keep track of the comings and goings of the guests. It was their policy to allow them as much privacy as possible.

"Finally, Porot said, 'Tell me about Muriel.'

"Both Bill and Sherri shook their heads. 'She came on the scene just as we were leaving the city,' said Bill. 'We don't know her that well. We've always assumed that she was some sort of paid companion. Hortense wasn't getting any younger after all. We figured she hired Muriel to do all the things that we used to do for her.'

"'So she was an employee?' asked Porot.

"Bill shrugged. 'That's always been our assumption, but we don't know for sure. When they came up here, Hortense expected us to give Muriel a free room, same as her, and on the third floor so there would be less traffic outside their rooms.'"

"I think one of the Pattersons did it," said Florence. "The way she treated them all those years? You can build up a lot of resentment in that time. The wife's comment that they would have been better suspects a few years ago is just a clever ruse. By admitting that they *look* guilty, she's trying to make the detectives think that they *aren't* guilty."

"Okay," said Cyril, "but what about her point? If they wanted to kill her, why didn't they do it years before?"

"Maybe," Florence's voice rose with the excitement of a new idea, "maybe they aren't so happy as innkeepers as they let on.

Maybe they're having a bad year, and having to give up two rooms in their busy season is going to put them into a hole they can't climb out of. Maybe Hortense finally made one demand too many."

"Sounds like a plausible theory," said John, "but we may find that they're not the only suspects. What do you think, Louise?"

Louise smiled and said, "Well, you know, I've been wondering about the newlyweds. Allow me to give you a look at them.

"Trish and Felix sat close together, holding hands and nervously glancing back and forth between Mr. Porot and Chief Dudley. Porot was watching them intently without speaking. Dudley paced restlessly back and forth behind him.

"'Chief,' said Porot finally, 'are you sure you wouldn't like a little something to eat?' He kept his eyes fixed on the couple.

"'I'm fine,' said the chief.

"'Trish, Felix,' said Porot in an avuncular tone, 'this is a terrible way for you to be spending your honeymoon. Congratulations, by the way.' They murmured their thanks. 'So tell me about your day.'

"'We went hiking,' said Felix.

"'To see the foliage,' added Trish.

"There was a pause, which Porot allowed to stretch out to an uncomfortable length. When the young people were all but squirming in their seats, Porot said quietly, 'You went hiking to see the foliage.'

"'We didn't kill her!' Trish exclaimed.

"Porot calmly arched one eyebrow. 'I didn't suggest that you did. I merely asked you to tell me about your day.' He paused slightly. 'Is there some reason I might think of you as suspects? Did you have any interaction with Mrs. Gunther during the day?'

"Trish sagged in her chair, and Felix put his arm around her. 'She was a hateful old woman,' said Trish bitterly.

"This time, Porot allowed both eyebrows to rise. 'You knew her?'

"'Yes. Well, no. Sort of. She was my grandmother Eunice's sister, my mother's aunt. But Hortense and Eunice never got along, and when my grandmother died, Hortense directed her hatred toward my mother. My grandmother died when my mother was still a teenager, but even though Hortense had married a rich man and Eunice had left my mother with nothing, the old bat would only offer my mother scraps.

"'She wouldn't brush off my mother altogether. Oh no, there was no sport in that. Instead, she gave her a miserly allowance until she was twenty-one, and she felt this gave her the right to treat my mother like a servant. Even after Mother turned twenty-one, Hortense would make all sorts of demands on her, saying my mother owed her for her support in her time of need. Finally, my mother just cut off all contact with her.'

"'What about your mother's father, your grandfather?' asked Porot. 'Where was he when your grandmother died?'

"Trish hesitated. 'He was long out of the picture. I don't know the details, but I gather he was the cause of the breach between Eunice and Hortense.'

"Porot nodded thoughtfully. 'You'll forgive me, Trish, but it seems to strain the limits of credibility to think that you just happened to be visiting this particular country inn at the same time as your estranged grandaunt.'

"Trish sighed. 'Well, of course, Hortense and Eunice had family connections to this area, though my mother stopped coming here long ago. But did you know that this house used to belong to Hortense? It should have been half ours, but Hortense had better lawyers.' Porot stared at her with a mild expression. 'Oh, okay, Mr. Porot, we knew she would be here. My mother maintains a little contact with her. We planned it so that we would be here when she was.'

"'To what end?'

"Trish sighed deeply. 'We wanted to ask for a loan. We want to run our own business. There's a video-rental shop for sale in the town where we live, and we'd like to buy it. But we can't get a bank loan. We thought, hey, we just got married, it's the time for family members to pitch in and show a little support, right? We wanted a loan, not a gift.'

"'And did you ask her?'

"Trish nodded. 'When we first saw her at breakfast, she pretended she didn't recognize me. But even though the family's not close, she ought to know me by sight. One thing my mother *has* done is keep Hortense supplied with pictures. I even invited her to the wedding, not that she came.

"'Anyway, after breakfast, we caught up with her out in the parking lot. She and that other woman were getting ready to go for a drive. I must say, she was hustling right along for an old woman. When we walked up, I thought at first she was going to keep pretending she didn't know me, but when I said, "Aunt Hortense," she turned to the other woman and said, "Muriel, wait in the car."

"'When she turned back, I introduced Felix, but she just frowned and wouldn't even shake his hand. Finally, she asked, "Well, what do you want?" I was very nervous by this time, and I tried to explain about the video-store opportunity, but I got all messed up, and Felix had to finish for me.' She smiled at her husband.

"'When we finished, she didn't say anything for a while. Then she said, "It's remarkable the degree to which you resemble your grandmother." I was trying to figure out whether that was good or bad when she said, "I will certainly not give you a loan. I wouldn't even if I thought you had some chance of repaying it, which I do not. I'm surprised you have the gall to ask me. I suppose your mother put you up to it. She always had her share of nerve. Well, let her give you the loan. I don't wish to be bothered again." And with that, she turned her back on us, climbed into her SUV and drove off without another glance.'

"'And how did you feel about that?'

"'We were pretty angry, of course.'

"'Not so much that she turned us down,' Felix finally spoke up. 'I never thought there was much chance she'd agree. But she was so rude about it.'

"'And what did you do?'

"Trish shrugged. 'We went on the hike that we'd been planning to take. It was just beautiful, and the exercise was a good way to wash the anger out of our systems. By the time we had returned to the inn, we were back to normal.'

"'And what were you doing when the body was discovered?'

"'We were packing. We had decided to leave the inn early and go somewhere else. It clearly wasn't going to be very pleasant hanging around near Hortense, and we are still on our honeymoon, after all.'

"'Of course,' said Porot. 'Tell me, Trish, have you informed your mother of her aunt's death?'

"'No,' said Trish with dismay. 'I suppose I'd better.'

"'And what about other family? Did Mrs. Gunther have children of her own who should be notified?'

"'Oh no. Since her husband died, she's had no real family except my mother. Which made their estrangement all the sadder.'

"'I see,' said Porot thoughtfully. 'And so your mother now probably stands to inherit Mrs. Gunther's estate?'

"Trish's face blanched, but she did not have an answer."

"There you go," said Ethel with conviction. "Old festering resentments, *and* money. That sounds like a recipe for a motive to me."

"They did go to some trouble to arrange that 'chance' meeting with their aunt," said Lloyd thoughtfully. "Perhaps they were counting on that loan more than they let on. Why didn't they just call her on the phone to ask? Perhaps they weren't willing to take no for an answer."

"Maybe they just thought a personal appeal would be more effective," said John. "And people are more relaxed and receptive when they're on vacation. Are you suggesting that they planned to kill her if she turned them down?"

Lloyd shrugged. "It sounds a little cold-blooded, I know. But . . ."

"Well," said Ethel, "it's always been my understanding that the first place you look for a suspect is close to home, as I'll make clear.

"They deliberately delayed questioning Muriel in order to give her more time to recover from the shock. She was no longer weeping, but she sat with a glazed look in her eyes, while her tremulous lips suggested that the tears could return at any second. They provided her with food, and though she ate mechanically, it seemed to do her some good.

"'We're very sorry for your loss,' began Porot quietly, and Muriel nodded. For a moment, Porot said nothing more. Then he said, 'How long had you worked for Mrs. Gunther?'

"Drawing a shuddering breath, Muriel replied, 'Five years.'

"'So you were her employee?'

"'Technically, yes, though I like to think that I was also her friend.'

"'And what exactly were the terms of your employment? What were your day-to-day duties?'

"Muriel shrugged. 'Companionship. Assistance. Mrs. Gunther was getting old, and she had no family who could be relied on. She was independent, but she realized that she had her limits. She used to ask what would happen if she ever fell and broke her hip. Without someone like me around, she might not be found until it was . . . too late.'

"'How had she been lately? Did you notice any change in her behavior? Did she say anything about being concerned for her safety?'

"'No, nothing like that. I don't think I ever heard her express concerns like that. She worried about accidents or her health, but not other people.'

"'Can you think of anyone who would want to kill her?'

"Muriel hesitated, apparently probing the gap between candor and loyalty. 'She wasn't necessarily an easy person to get along with. She could certainly . . . rub people the wrong way. But no, I can't think of anyone who would want to kill her.'

"'Any new people or new developments in her life?'

"'No, she led a very quiet life. Unless,' Muriel added with dawning awareness, 'you mean that young woman who is staying here. She approached Mrs. Gunther in the parking lot this morning and called her "Aunt Hortense." Mrs. Gunther sent me away, and they talked for a little while.'

"'About what?'

"'Mrs. Gunther later said the young woman wanted her to give her money so that she and her husband could open a business, I believe.'

"'And you hadn't seen this young woman before?'

"Muriel shook her head. 'Not before this trip. I was aware that Mrs. Gunther had a niece, but I'd been under the impression that she was older than this woman.'

"'And how did Mrs. Gunther explain that?'

"'Apparently, this young woman is the daughter of that niece.'

"'Did she say anything else about the encounter? Or her family?'

"'She just seemed rather disgusted that they would ask her for money.'

"'Has anything else out of the ordinary happened on this trip? You come up every year, yes? Anything else different this year?'

"Muriel shook her head. 'You know that Mrs. Gunther used to own this house, don't you? She felt that the Pattersons rather took advantage of her when they bought it, but she just couldn't do the work of keeping it up any longer. And she's been forgiving enough to keep coming up every year for a visit. Of course, her mother's family had come from this area, so she has roots here, though I think that after she married Mr. Gunther, she stopped spending much time here.

"'But we returned yesterday, and it all seemed usual. Bill and Sherri were here, and Bert of course, though he left just after we arrived. He usually does, though I saw him again today working with Bill out back.'

"'Bert?'

"Muriel shrugged. 'Local handyman, a jack-of-all-trades type.' Porot recalled Bill's mentioning this Bert as well. 'Of course,' continued Muriel, 'we don't usually get pulled over by the police when we come up.' Her eyes traveled up to Chief Dudley, standing behind Porot.

"Porot craned his neck around to look at the chief. 'You pulled over the victim?'

"Chief Dudley shrugged. 'She was driving so slowly out on 12A that she constituted a hazard. Mostly I pulled her over just to let the traffic by. In that new SUV, I didn't realize it was her. I didn't even give her a ticket, though that didn't stop her from reading me the riot act.'

"'Yes, she was certainly upset,' Muriel said. She paused before asking, 'What did she mean about you being just like your father?'

"Dudley glanced off to one side. 'My father was also the chief of police in this town, in his day. So, Muriel,' he continued, 'that was about three thirty that I pulled you over, and you were headed back in this direction. Did you return to the inn at that point?'

"'Yes, we came straight back here, and we each went to our rooms to rest. I was to wake her at five so she could get ready for dinner, but when I went to her room . . .' She came close to breaking down again but controlled herself.

"'Tell me, Muriel,' said Porot, 'when you got to the room, was the door open or closed?'

"'It was closed. I knocked a couple of times and called for her, but I didn't hear any answer. So I tried the knob and the door was unlocked. As soon as I opened it, I saw . . . I saw her lying there, and I guess I screamed. And then you were there, Mr. Porot, and then the others. It's all something of a blur.'

"'But did you enter the room?'

"'I don't think so, no.'

"'I don't think so, either,' said Porot. 'I found you standing on the threshold, but I wanted to make sure.' He glanced down at the pad on which he'd been taking notes. 'One last thing, Muriel. Do you know who will inherit Mrs. Gunther's estate?'

"'I believe she had set up some sort of foundation, and that most of her money will go to that. In fact, I think she already turned over much of what she had to it, for tax reasons.'

"'And were there no other beneficiaries?'

"Muriel looked somewhat flustered. 'Well, she always told me that she had made some provisions for me in her will, but she didn't tell me the details. She just said I'd be "taken care of." It seemed crass to pry.'

"'And what about her family? Will the niece that you mentioned receive anything?'

"'I had the impression that her niece would get little or nothing, but I don't really know.'

"'And do you know if the niece herself was privy to her aunt's plans?'

"'I'm afraid I don't know.'"

Chapter Twenty-Three

"Well, that confuses the issue of a motive for Trish," said Cyril.

"I suspect she knew," said Lloyd.

"And what about Muriel herself?" said Louise. "She admits that she stands to benefit from the will. Perhaps her settlement is more generous than she's letting on."

"Okay, but Muriel had plenty of opportunity," said John. "If she wanted to kill Hortense, she could have done it any time. Why now?"

"Because this is the only time when she would not be the most obvious suspect," said Louise. "At any other time, she would be about the only person with opportunity, but here, the victim is in a house full of other people who might also be suspects. And maybe there's also an opportunistic element here. Perhaps when she realized that Trish was there and would make an obvious suspect, she decided to seize her chance to do something that she had wanted to do for a long time."

"We have several strong theories already," noted John, "and we've not even made it through our cast of characters yet."

"Who else have we got?" asked Cyril. "The McAvoys? They couldn't have any motive to kill Hortense, could they?"

"Well," Lloyd said with a smile, "I'm not so sure of that. When Ross and Norma McAvoy were ushered into the office, they found Chief Dudley talking on the phone while Porot looked on. 'Well, pick him up and bring him down to the inn, will you?' the chief said, and after listening a moment, he hung up the phone.

"'Thank you, Chief,' said Porot. Then he turned in his chair to greet the newcomers. 'Mr. and Mrs. McAvoy, please sit down. I'm sorry for the inconvenience this is causing. I hope you had something to eat?'

"The couple sat down, and Ross McAvoy shuffled his feet nervously for a few moments. Then he abruptly spoke up. 'Look, I don't know what you know already, but I want to make a clean breast of it.'

"Porot sat back in his chair and looked up at Chief Dudley, who was staring intently at McAvoy. 'All right, Mr. McAvoy, go ahead. Make a clean breast of it.'

"McAvoy nodded. 'Right. Well then, it's true: We knew Hortense Gunther and her thieving husband, and we had no cause to be fond of either of them. Some might even say we had cause to hate them. And if you've had a chance to do any sort of background check on me, you'll know that I . . . I have a criminal record.' Porot glanced again at Dudley. They'd done no record checks on anyone, at least not yet. 'I want you to know I didn't do that crime,' continued McAvoy, 'even though I spent six years in jail for it. And I want you to know too that I didn't kill that wicked old woman.' He sat back and heaved a deep sigh. His wife grabbed his hand and patted it, and he gave her a grateful smile.

"'I see,' Porot said slowly. 'All right then, why might some people feel you have cause to hate Mr. and Mrs. Gunther?'

"McAvoy leaned forward again, his beefy face flushed. 'Because Giles Gunther was the reason I ended up going to jail for a crime I didn't commit.' After a pause, he said, 'Will you hear my side of it?'

"'Of course.'

"McAvoy nodded with satisfaction. 'Well then. Giles Gunther and I were partners in a small brokerage house. Even though Giles was a lot older, we made a good team. I knew the market and Giles was a born salesman. Together we made our clients, and ourselves, some decent money.' He smiled proudly at the memory of their success.

"Norma McAvoy spoke up for the first time. 'But then Giles got cocky. And greedy. He started taking on clients of his own, ones that Ross didn't know about, and handling their trades himself.'

"'They were on the books as clients of the company,' Ross clarified, 'but I'd always let Giles handle that stuff anyway. I just knew the markets.

"'But Giles thought that he knew the markets too, and he started making trades on behalf of these private clients of his that were not any trades I'd recommended. He was off on his own, flying solo. And he crashed.'

"'He started stealing from their other clients because he didn't want to admit that he had lost his private group's money,' Norma said.

"'For one thing, he would have had to admit that he *had* the private group,' continued Ross. 'And of course, he thought he could dig his way out. Unbeknownst to me, he was doing all of this in my name, since I was the trader.

"'Well, as you can imagine, it all collapsed. And my friend and trusted partner set it up to make it look like my doing. As I say, I went to jail for six years. Giles, as it happened, died of a heart attack before my trial ever started. I still wonder if he would have lied on the stand in order to save his own skin. He never had to.'

"'Okay,' said Porot, 'let's say we believe you. Why are you here? To take revenge on the widow of the man who sent you to jail?'

"'No,' said Ross quickly. 'No. I just . . . wanted to see her. Giles had been my partner. We'd all been friends. I didn't understand how he could have done that to me.'

"'Giles died and Hortense never came to the trial,' said Norma. 'She never said a word about what happened, never even spoke to us again.'

"'I just wanted to make her face it,' Ross concluded with a helpless tone in his voice.

"'How did you know she would be here?'

"Ross laughed. 'When I got out of jail a couple months ago, I tried to call her, but that Muriel woman answered. She didn't know who I was—I guess Hortense never told her that story. But it was easy enough to convince her that I'd known Giles, and she was happy to tell me all about Hortense's schedule. It was easy for her to avoid us in the city, but we thought up here she'd be unable to.'

"'And did you confront her?'

"Ross shrugged. 'Didn't have the chance. I could see it gave her a start to find us having breakfast when she came in, but then she just pretended not to recognize us. But she did, because I tried to go see her after breakfast, and she and that Muriel had already scooted out of the house to avoid us. I figured I'd try again tomorrow, assuming she didn't leave.'

"Chief Dudley spoke up impatiently. 'I still don't see what you expected to accomplish by confronting her. You sure came a long way for what sounds like a pretty vague plan.'

"Ross shrugged again. 'I know, but that's just what I did. I don't know what I wanted her to say. I just wanted some acknowledgment from her of what her husband did. What else have I got to do with my time?' he added bitterly."

"I'm with Chief Dudley," said Ethel. "I think this McAvoy fellow had a more definite plan in mind. Maybe he thought he could force Hortense to give up some evidence that would exonerate him."

"But why now?" asked John. "He's already served his time."

"Because it would clear his name," Lloyd said. "Also, if he's been convicted of a crime, he's probably no longer allowed to be a broker. So if he could challenge the conviction and get it overturned, he might be able to get his livelihood back."

"So you think he confronted Hortense, failed to get what he wanted, then killed her out of anger and frustration," Cyril said. "I suppose it's plausible."

"Or maybe it turned out that the evidence never existed," said Louise, "and he had nurtured a false hope. Or even worse, that

Giles, or even Hortense, had deliberately destroyed the evidence. That might send him into a murderous rage."

"Does that exhaust our suspects?" Ethel asked.

"I don't think so," said John, and the others looked at him in surprise. "You're forgetting a very important principle of the mystery novel," he said. "The notion of the least obvious suspect. And in this case, that would be someone we met back at the beginning of the story. I'll refresh your memory.

"As Porot and Dudley were showing the McAvoys out of the office, Bill Patterson approached. 'Oliver's here,' he said, meaning Oliver Thompson, Dudley's deputy. With a note of confusion in his voice, he added, 'He's got Bert Vallier with him.'

"Oliver Thompson escorted Bert into the office, then left to cover the station in the chief's absence.

"'Have you heard what happened?' Dudley asked Bert.

"Bert nodded. 'Hortense Gunther was killed. Stabbed to death, I hear.'

"Porot looked at him sharply. 'How do you know that?' he demanded.

"Bert shrugged. 'It's a small town. Everyone knows.'

"Porot grimaced and flung an angry look at Dudley, but the chief merely spread his hands. As Bert had said, it was a small town.

"'We're trying to trace the movements of everyone who was in the vicinity of the inn this afternoon,' Porot said. 'I understand you were here today?'

"'That's right. I was helpin' Bill get the place tightened up for winter. Sherri gave us lunch, and then I worked till about four or so.'

"'The body was discovered at five, and we believe the murder occurred about an hour earlier. So we are particularly interested in what was happening about four or so.'

"Bert thought. 'Well, the last thing I was doin' was puttin' away all the window screens in the big storage shed out back. There's a lot of windows on this house, as you can see. I was out there about half an hour or so, gettin' those put away and straightening up generally, so I don't know what was going on up at the house.

"'I'd already told Bill I'd be clearing off, so when I was done, I didn't bother to go back inside. I came around the house and down to the parking lot and got in my truck.' He paused to recall the scene. 'I didn't see anyone coming or going at the house. Mrs. Gunther's big SUV was in the parking lot, and I'm pretty sure there were two other cars as well.' He closed his eyes. 'One was blue or black, and I think the other was green. As I pulled out, I saw the chief's squad car parked down the street in front of the donut shop.' He grinned at Dudley. 'But I don't recall seeing any people out and about at the time I left.'

"Porot nodded absently. 'How well did you know Mrs. Gunther?' he asked.

"Bert looked back and forth between the two of them. 'I knew her.'

"'Come on, Bert,' exclaimed Chief Dudley, causing Porot to look at him in surprise. 'You're going to have to tell him.' Porot looked at Bert with renewed interest.

"Bert looked down at his lap and shuffled his feet before saying, 'I used to work for her.'

"When Bert seemed disinclined to continue, Chief Dudley said, 'You used to live in this house, didn't you, Bert? You used to be the official caretaker. And since your father was caretaker before you, you pretty much grew up in this house, didn't you? This house was in Mrs. Gunther's family for many years, up until she sold it five years ago, fired you and kicked you out. Kinda left you high and dry, didn't she?' Then, with real curiosity in his voice, he softened and asked, 'Do Bill and Sherri know?'

"'No,' mumbled Bert. 'They know I've done a lot of work on the house over the years, but that's it.'

"'Where do you live now?' asked Porot.

"'Trailer park,' mumbled Bert.

"'The less desirable one of the two in the area,' added Dudley.

"'And what do you do now?'

"'Handyman.'

"'He drinks, is what he does,' said Dudley. 'I've had you drying out in my cell more and more frequently over the past year, Bert.' Bert glared at him but said nothing.

"'There's no love lost between you two, I gather?' Porot asked.

"Dudley deflated a little. 'We've always been oil and water, Bert and I. But,' he looked at Bert, 'he didn't do this.'

"Bert stared at him in astonishment."

"Just because he's a local, he can't be a suspect?" asked Cyril. "Just because the police chief has known him all his life? I'm not sure we can trust Chief Dudley's opinion on this one."

"Does the chief really believe that anyway?" asked Florence. "He's the one who brought out all the incriminating information in the first place. Maybe he's trying to be subtle in setting Bert up."

"How are we going to wrap this up?" asked John. "I like Bert for the murder. Hortense completely upended his life, apparently without a second thought. He's been on a decline ever since she did, as shown by the increase in his drinking. And he's the most likely person to kill her, because he has the opportunity when she's in town. And as I said before, he's the least obvious suspect."

"Well, I think it was McAvoy," declared Cyril. "A betrayal of trust, a prison term . . . that's a lot of motive. Since he couldn't get at Giles, Hortense was the next best thing."

"I'm picking Muriel," said Louise. "Not only did she have to endure Hortense Gunther on a daily basis—and who knows everything that she had to put up with?—she admits that she stands to gain financially from her death."

"Ah, but Trish and Felix stand to gain as well," said Ethel, "or at least they have every reason to think that they would. And they admit that they need the money. I think this murder is a family affair."

"I agree," said Lloyd.

"I'm sticking with the Pattersons," said Florence. "Since they owned the place, they had the best access and opportunity. And they had the most immediate problem"—Florence kept a straight face—"she was taking up two rooms that they needed."

"Good one, Florence!" said Lloyd, slapping his knee.

"Well," said John, smiling. "I see that every suspect has his or her backer. How shall we resolve this? Which one will be the true murderer?"

The argument went round and round for some minutes, but each passenger clung doggedly to his or her preferred solution. Finally, John said, "Let's have Harry settle it." Everyone else quickly agreed with that suggestion. "Well, how about it, Harry?" John called. "Which of our solutions is correct?"

Harry waited just a moment before replying, and then in a mournful tone said, "I'm very sorry, Mr. Gaunt, but I'm afraid none of them is."

Surprised smiles broke out on all the faces in the bus. "Well, go on, Harry," said John. "Don't leave us hanging."

"Certainly," said Harry.

"Mr. Porot and Chief Dudley were alone in the inn's office, reviewing all the evidence that they had heard. Porot sat behind the desk and leaned back slightly in the chair. Chief Dudley paced, but he was now in front of the desk rather than behind Porot.

"'Well, Chief,' Porot said, 'what do you think?'

"Dudley's agitated pace quickened. 'I don't know, I don't know. They all seem to have reason to want the old woman dead. But nobody seems to have been out and about at the right time to see anything. Late afternoon, broad daylight, but nobody saw anything.'

"Porot shrugged. 'It's like that more often than you'd think. Even when there are a fair number of people around, you'll have these quiet periods when nobody is in a given area. More to the point, people only take note of the unexpected. If you expect to see lots of people about, then the presence of any given individual is less likely to register.'

"Dudley shot Porot a glance. 'So you think somebody saw something and they didn't realize it?'

"'And probably won't remember it, either. For most of us, it's the unusual that registers with our awareness, not the expected.' Porot watched Dudley through narrowed eyes. 'So tell me, Chief, how well did you know Mrs. Gunther?'

"Dudley abruptly stopped his pacing. 'What makes you think I knew her?' he demanded.

"'You said so yourself. When you described pulling her over, you said you hadn't realized it was she because she was driving an SUV. That implies not only that you knew her, but that you knew her well enough to have an expectation about the kind of car she drives.'

"Dudley looked away and shrugged. 'Well, of course, I knew who she was. She grew up around here and came back every summer. And as police chief, I tend to know what everyone drives. Part of the job.' He now stood rigidly still.

"'It's just that she seems to have behaved in a rather familiar fashion when you pulled her over. Granted, she was under a lot of stress, having encountered both her estranged grandniece and her late husband's ex-partner at breakfast. Still, most people, no matter how unpleasant, would not be quick to give a tongue-lashing to a police officer who has just pulled them over. I thought perhaps that she knew you well enough to feel that she could get away with such behavior.'

"'As a matter of fact, I had as little contact with her as I could. I knew how nasty she could be.'

"Porot nodded thoughtfully. 'And how well did your father know her?'

"Dudley stiffened even further and slowly sat in the chair on the other side of the desk. He kept his eyes averted, but all he said was, 'My father.'

"'According to Muriel, Mrs. Gunther said that you're "as bad as your father." It sounds like she knew him as well. He was chief of police himself, was he not?'

"'My father'—Dudley choked on the words—'my father loved her.'

"As if finally receiving a gift he had long expected, Porot let out a soft 'Ah.' Then he waited.

"'They were sweethearts when they were young,' Dudley said, 'but she threw him over to marry that summer person, Giles Gunther, because he was rich. I'm not sure she ever had any feelings for my dad. I think she just led him on because she knew her sister Eunice was sweet on him. My dad behaved properly toward Eunice, everyone says so, even though he didn't love her as she loved him. Hortense saw an opportunity to break her sister's heart, so she set her sights on my dad, and she succeeded where Eunice had failed in making Dad fall in love.

"'My dad fell hard. Then Eunice left home and moved away, Giles Gunther came along, and there was no more sport for Hortense in leading my dad around.

"'Well, life went on. Dad married my mother, and they had me. But Hortense still kept returning every summer. And after a while, things soured between my parents. It's not unusual. Like most people back then, they stayed together. But he became obsessed with his lost love.

"'He would follow her around, whether on duty or off. He would arrange little "accidental" encounters with her. He sometimes took me along on these spying missions, until I got old enough to refuse to go along. Today we would call it stalking, but he was the chief of police. More than one selectman tried to speak to him about it, but it didn't do any good.

"'He never did anything. Never got violent or anything like that. He just humiliated my mother and me, made us a laughingstock. And then he had a heart attack and died, and it was the best thing for everyone, really. The story still gets told, but it's ancient history now, and as I say, I've avoided Mrs. Gunther completely. When she got old, she didn't come up as often or stay as long. But if I'd known it was her in that SUV, I never would have pulled her over.

"'When she had the nerve to mention my father, I just walked away. But after I drove around and cooled down a bit, I decided I would go set her straight about my father. So I came to the inn, parked down the street and walked right in. Didn't see anyone at first, and I didn't know which room she was in, but then I saw Mrs. Gunther herself going up the stairs.'

"His eyes found Porot's. 'I was calm and quiet as I followed Mrs. Gunther up to her room. I was calm and quiet as I talked to her, and as she said all kinds of vile, hateful things about my father, about both my parents actually. And I was calm and quiet as I took out my knife and stabbed her.' He indicated a knife in a pocket of his uniform.

"'At that point, I thought it was all over. I thought there would be screams and people would come running, but everything was quiet. After a few minutes, I left the room, left the inn and returned to my car. And an hour later, I was called about a dead body that had been found. When I walked in, part of me felt like I was seeing it for the first time.' All at once, his rigidity gave way and he slumped back in the chair. 'How did you know?'

"Porot shook his head. 'I didn't. But you wouldn't have anything to eat, and that just seemed odd. It made me watch you more carefully after that.' Dudley nodded. 'So, may I have that knife?'

"Dudley nodded again, pulled the knife from his pocket and set it on the desk. Porot used a handkerchief to pick it up and set it on a file cabinet behind him. Keeping his voice as even as he could, he added, 'I think you'd better give me your gun as well.'

"Slowly, Dudley unholstered the firearm, but Porot could see the wheels spinning in the man's head. The chief's fingers found their way around the grip of the gun, and he slowly began to lift it in the direction of his temple.

"Porot could not lunge at him: There was a desk between them. Instead, he said, 'Do you have a family of your own, Chief?' The gun stopped and wavered while Dudley gave a small nod. 'Think of them,' urged Porot.

"But after a moment, the gun began to rise again, and Porot saw tears forming in Dudley's eyes. 'Chief,' he said in a low, urgent tone. 'Your father gave in to his weakness. He failed to act responsibly. I think you can do better than that.'

"Once again, the gun stopped and hovered for a moment. Finally, ever so slowly, Dudley leaned forward and set it on the desk. Smoothly, Porot scooped it up and dropped it in the pocket of his coat. Then he stood and stepped to the door of the office.

"Opening the door, he called, 'Mr. Patterson.' When Bill quickly arrived, he said, 'Please ask the state trooper in the front parlor to step in here. It looks like he will need to make the arrest in this case after all.'

"With a confused look on his face, Bill hurried off to deliver the message."

"Bravo, Harry!" called John. "You wrapped up the case in fine style."

The other storytellers shared John's appraisal. Then all reviewed the tale to reexamine clues, to evaluate the suspects' behavior, and to congratulate one another on a job well done.

Finally, Lloyd called out, "I have just one last question: When are we going to eat dinner?"

Chapter Twenty-Four

"You'll be glad to know," Jane said on Friday morning, "that I've arranged for you to have some company." She and Alice were sitting in the kitchen of Grace Chapel Inn. Jane had just finished writing something on a piece of paper, which she folded in half. Now she was rummaging through her purse, checking to see that she had her car keys.

Alice gave her a puzzled look. "What do you mean? Company for what?"

"For finding out what my big secret is," Jane replied as she stood and began shrugging into a light jacket.

"Why do I need company? Aren't you just going to tell me?"

Jane gave her a look of mock horror. "Where's the fun in that?"

"Where's the fun in being kept in the dark?" Alice muttered in frustration.

"That's the nature of surprises, dear sister," Jane said unsympathetically. "Now"—she handed Alice the folded piece of paper—"in one hour, you and Sylvia—"

"Sylvia?"

"Didn't I just say that I'd arranged company for you?" Jane cocked an eyebrow, and then continued. "In one hour you and Sylvia will drive to a certain spot, following these directions. It should take you about thirty minutes. Don't get lost! The timing is important."

Alice glanced at the directions as Jane spoke. "This is going to put us in the middle of nowhere," she said.

Jane continued as if Alice hadn't spoken. "Sylvia will meet you here some time before you need to leave. Don't worry about the inn. I've arranged for Justine to keep an eye on things while we're both gone."

Alice shook her head in bewilderment.

"Oh, and take these along," said Jane, handing Alice a pair of binoculars. "You might find them useful."

"Useful for what?"

"Bird watching," Jane said with a perfectly straight face.

Alice sighed. Of course Jane wasn't going to give her a genuine answer.

"I'll meet you there," said Jane as she headed out the door.

"You will?" wondered Alice out loud to herself.

About fifteen minutes later, Jane's good friend Sylvia Songer arrived, her strawberry-blonde hair pulled back and held in place by a tortoiseshell barrette. When Alice greeted her, Sylvia looked about with an expression of confusion. "Did she leave already?"

"Yes," said Alice. "Do you know what this is all about?"

Sylvia shook her head. "I just know that you and I are supposed to drive out and meet her someplace. She said she'd give you the directions." Alice nodded to confirm she had them. "And she said to bring these." Sylvia held up her own pair of binoculars.

Alice shook her head and sighed. "Well, you and I are not to leave for another forty-five minutes. Would you like some tea?"

~

As Alice had predicted, Jane's directions did indeed seem to be taking them to the middle of nowhere. They drove in silence, and Sylvia could sense Alice's mounting tension.

Finally, Alice said, "Are you sure you don't know what's going on, Sylvia?"

"I really don't, Alice. Why, what's wrong?"

"Are you . . . concerned at all about all this?"

"No. Do you think there's reason to be?"

Alice frowned and said, "Jane admitted to me that she's doing this"—she waved a hand vaguely in the air—"*project* now because Louise is away. Apparently, it's something that Louise would object to. And yet I'm not allowed to object to it or even to know what it is. What if I'm making a mistake by allowing her to do this?"

Sylvia considered this for a moment, her dark eyes staring straight ahead. "I don't know that 'allow' is really the operative concept here," she said. "Jane is an adult. She has good judgment. She's responsible for her own actions. Even if Louise were here, and even if she somehow prevented Jane from . . . doing whatever it is she's doing, that still doesn't mean she'd be justified in stopping Jane.

"Look, Alice, don't take offense. I have a lot of respect for Louise. But she can be . . . a bit forceful when it comes to you and Jane. She acts like, well, a big sister."

"But I'm a big sister too," complained Alice.

"Yes, but that's not all you are. I think Jane feels that there are some things about which you're more sympathetic, because you also have been on the receiving end of the big-sisterliness. That isn't to say that she doesn't love and respect Louise. Of course she does. It's just that there are going to be some occasions where she thinks you will be more understanding."

Alice pursed her lips, but she looked somewhat mollified.

"For what it's worth," Sylvia continued, "Jane seems fine to me. She's obviously excited about whatever this project is, but otherwise, I see no cause for alarm in her behavior."

Alice felt reassured. "Thank you, Sylvia."

"Oh," Sylvia suddenly called, "turn here, turn here!"

"Are you sure?" asked Alice, but she obediently turned the wheel.

They found themselves driving along a dirt road that ran along a large, open field. Glancing back down at the directions, Sylvia said, "Yes, a dirt road is what we want. She says it's a quarter of a mile to the 'rendezvous point.'"

A short distance down the road, they could see a pickup truck pulled off to the side, a man leaning against it. When he saw their car coming, he straightened, and as they got close, he gave them a wave of his hand.

"Do you think it's okay?" asked Alice hesitantly.

"Probably," said Sylvia, "just one more part of Jane's puzzle. Still, let's stay in the car until we know more."

As they pulled up behind the pickup, they could see he was an older man, dressed in a flannel shirt and blue jeans. He walked slowly up to the driver's side and leaned down as Alice opened the window.

"You must be Alice and Sylvia," said the man with a bit of a drawl. "My name's Buck Eton. Jane asked me to meet you."

Alice and Sylvia looked at one another, a last trace of apprehension making them hesitate. Buck smiled. "Jane wanted me to ask if you remembered to bring your binoculars."

The two women smiled and relaxed. As they climbed from the car, Alice introduced herself and said, "I'm sorry, we weren't really expecting to see someone else."

"Not a problem. She told me she was planning a surprise for you."

"So do you know what this is all about?" asked Sylvia.

"Now, ma'am," smiled Buck, "that would be tellin'."

"Is Jane on her way then?" asked Alice.

"Yes, ma'am. We're gonna stay right here and wait for her. It may be a few minutes yet, but not too long. Your sister, Miss Howard, has got some spunk to her."

"That she does," said Alice. "Well, if we can't ask about Jane, can we ask about you?"

"Certainly," replied Buck with a smile. "I'm a farmer. In fact, this here field belongs to me. If you look all the way yonder"—he pointed to the far corner of the field—"you can see my barn and silo." They squinted in the direction he indicated. "Maybe you want to try it with your glasses," he suggested.

Alice and Sylvia both raised their binoculars and focused. "Oh yes," said Sylvia, "I see it."

"Do you use this field for pasture, Mr. Eton?" asked Alice. At the edge of her hearing, she became aware of a faint droning sound.

"Not this one, ma'am," Buck replied. "This field now . . . has a special use." Alice wondered what that could be; it looked like an empty field to her.

Sylvia had been looking up and down the road with her binoculars. "Which direction will she be coming from, Mr. Eton?" she asked.

"Well, ma'am," replied Buck slowly, "neither of those."

Sylvia pulled the field glasses away from her eyes and gave Buck a questioning look. Meanwhile, the droning continued to tug at Alice's consciousness; it was getting louder, she realized. Frowning, she scanned the sky.

Smiling, Buck said, "Miss Howard has the right idea," which prompted both women to turn and stare at him. In response, Buck pointed once again to the far corner of the field. High above his barn, a small plane had come into view. "You might want to train your glasses on that plane," he suggested.

Both women quickly did so.

The plane was coming toward them and rapidly grew larger and clearer in the glasses. Despite its considerable altitude, Alice could see the windows, the struts on the wings, and red markings on the fuselage. The propellers were just a blur of motion. She saw something dark on the side of the plane. No, it was an open door. And there was a person standing in it.

Both Alice and Sylvia gasped as three figures dropped together out of the plane and into the open sky. The two figures on either side seemed to be holding the third one between them. "Is that Jane?" gasped Alice.

Unseen by the women, Buck nodded. "She'll be the one in the middle. The two instructors on either side are helping her to maintain the correct body position during free fall."

"Free fall," Alice repeated with a quiet gulp. "There's another one," she said, when a fourth figure followed the other three in their descent.

"That'll be Raffi, the cameraman," said Buck. "He's filming your sister's jump."

Somehow the cameraman moved his body about in midair so that he circled the falling trio and filmed them from different angles. Alice, however, tried to focus on Jane. She was wearing a helmet and a blue jumpsuit, but somehow she still looked like Jane. She was dropping front down—as in a belly flop—with her feet, arms and head arched up above the plane of her body. The two instructors were helping to hold her in that position. Oddly, she looked more like she was floating than falling.

Alice realized that she had been holding her breath since her first sight of her sister in the air.

Suddenly, Jane's parachute blossomed out behind her, and the two instructors immediately dropped away to either side, their own chutes opening a few moments later. Alice almost lost sight of her when the opening chute produced a rapid deceleration. Only then did Alice have a sense of just how fast Jane had been falling.

Nevertheless, as she watched the rainbow-colored, rectangular chute turn in the air, Alice felt a greater sensation of Jane's speed now than she had watching the free fall.

She saw Jane turn and look up at her chute, apparently checking the deployment. It appeared that Jane had quite a bit of control over the parachute's flight because after a few moments, she began to curve across the sky in wide arcs, like a great bird. It seemed to Alice that her speed through the air was alternately increasing and decreasing, but she couldn't be sure.

The instructors and the cameraman were navigating their own chutes in a similar fashion.

"Beautiful," said Buck, looking into the sky. "Just perfect. Your sister is having a great jump. The instructors are talking to her now over radios, helping her to steer the chute. They'll be able to fly around like that some more before they come down."

"And they'll land in the field?" asked Sylvia.

"Yup, that's the drop zone."

Alice tried to imagine what Jane was feeling, looking down on the landscape from that great height. Could she see her sister and her friend looking up at her? Apparently she could: She gave them a wave.

"Here they come," said Buck softly, and with a start, Alice realized that Jane was almost to the ground. She lowered her glasses and stepped forward to start across the field toward her, but Buck held up a warning hand. "Hold on," he said, "don't go rushing out until they're all down. We don't want anyone to land on ya."

Jane, who tumbled forward when she landed, was the first to touch down, but as requested, Alice and Sylvia waited, impatiently, for the others to land before rushing toward Jane. She had stumbled to her knees, and they were eager to make sure she was okay.

By the time they reached her, however, Jane was back on her feet and laughing with the excitement of her experience. She let out a great whoop and pumped her fist into the air when she saw them coming toward her. She turned and made a halfhearted effort to start collecting the fabric of her chute, but she was too excited. When Alice and Sylvia reached them, she hugged each of them.

"That was amazing!" she cried. "I've never felt anything like it. What an experience! I'm so glad I did it."

Buck Eton came striding up behind Alice and Sylvia. He helped Jane unfasten her harness and then began efficiently bundling up the parachute. The other skydivers had quickly rounded up their own gear and were approaching to congratulate Jane.

A small woman with a compact build and dark hair had removed her helmet and goggles, and she was smiling broadly. "Well done, Jane," she said. "Was it everything you hoped for?"

"Oh yes," said Jane. "I can't begin to thank you all enough, especially you, Miranda. You were very patient with me." She turned to Alice. "So, what do you think? Were you surprised?"

Alice put her hand over her heart. "My word, I thought I'd faint," she said. "It's not every day that you see your sister fall out of an airplane."

"I didn't fall," Jane said emphatically. "I *jumped*."

"And therein lies all the difference," added Miranda, laughing.

Chapter Twenty-Five

"I'll tell you what it *didn't* feel like," said Jane as she and Alice finished their lunch in the kitchen of Grace Chapel Inn. "It didn't feel like I was falling."

"Very odd," Alice replied. "I would think that the sensation of falling would be overwhelming."

Jane nodded. "I had the same expectation, but no. Looking back, I think it had something to do with the lack of reference points. The ground is so far away that it doesn't mean much to you, and the plane is away where you can't see it. The only objects that are close by are the instructors, and they're dropping more or less at the same rate you are.

"There was certainly a tremendous sense of movement, of air rushing by, but it didn't register as falling. It truly felt like I was flying. It was an amazing experience.

"It was only after the chute deployed that I began to have a sensation of descending, even though at that point I was falling much more slowly, and I also had greater control over my movement through the air. That was incredible, too, having some control over my flight with the parachute. I could turn it, and speed up and slow down."

"I saw you," said Alice, smiling at her sister's lingering excitement.

"And I have to say that, even though I never felt like I was in danger, it was still a very reassuring moment when the chute opened and I felt that sharp tug." She smiled as she replayed the jump in her mind yet again. "I can't wait to see the film they made."

"When will you have that?"

"They said they'd mail it to me. They used a digital camera, and they have to burn it onto a disk in order to send it. I can't wait to show it to Louise."

"*Hmm,*" said Alice, as she stood and began to clean up the lunch dishes. "I think we'd better be sure to prepare her before we spring the video on her."

"I told you my little project was something best done while she was away," Jane said.

Alice agreed, but given the pleasure that Jane had taken from the experience, she had to conclude it would have been wrong to try to stop her from trying it. Perhaps she didn't give Louise enough credit, Alice thought as she loaded plates into the dishwasher; perhaps Louise would not have caused any trouble if she had known about the plan. Alice winced; she had to admit that was unlikely. *Sometimes it's easier to ask forgiveness than permission,* she thought. *Not that Jane needs either one, but . . .*

"You're not angry, are you?" Jane asked quietly.

Alice straightened and smiled at her sister. "No," she said, "no, of course not. Though if you ever decide to do it again," she joked, "I don't think I want to know."

But Jane responded seriously. "It's possible I'd go again some time, but I doubt it. I think I got that one out of my system."

Alice glanced about the kitchen for any additional cleaning up that needed to be done. After a moment, she said, "Well, I have to go down to Fred's. Today is doohickey day, don't forget. Are you going drop by later to see who won the contest?"

Jane laughed. "No, I'll stay and keep an eye on things here. For me, today is all about my jump." She gave Alice a wink. "Surely that's enough excitement for one day?" Alice smiled and nodded. "But I didn't think the contest announcement was until later this afternoon. Are you just going to check how they're doing?"

"No." Alice gave a sigh. "I've been pressed into service to help judge the creative category. Fred's gotten so many responses that he's going to have to start going through them a couple of hours ahead of time. He already announced that the deadline for submissions would be noon. And now I have to go help him wade through them."

"The kids have really taken to his contest idea," Jane observed.

"I wonder if he rather regrets encouraging them now."

"So . . . is Vera going to help read the entries as well?"

"Yes," Alice said, "that was a condition of my participation—that the two of them work together on it as well."

"I see," said Jane, smiling, "so it's a form of therapy. And you're the counselor."

"I just hope I don't end up being the referee."

When Alice arrived at Fred's hardware store, she found Vera and Fred standing in the back at a table covered with a large collection of small pieces of paper. Vera looked up as Alice approached and said, "This will take hours."

"Shouldn't you have a sign on the front door?" Alice teased. "Closed for Doohickey Contest Business?"

Fred grimaced. "I can do this and still wait on my customers," he announced. "Most of them can wait on themselves, anyway," he added in a mutter.

"You certainly got a lot of entries," said Alice brightly. "And these are just the creative ones?"

"Oh, after I separated the categories, there were only a handful of serious ones." Fred took down a shoebox from a shelf behind him and shook it. The rattle suggested there were only a few slips of paper inside.

"Only Captain Doohickey himself gets to look inside that box," said Vera. "Its contents are not for the eyes of you or me."

"This category," said Fred, holding up the shoebox, "only needs one judge, because there's only one right answer. Any given guess is either correct or incorrect. But this category"—he waved his arm over the pile of slips on the table—"is better served by multiple judges, since the 'most creative' title is necessarily a subjective call."

"That's always assuming," Vera replied, "that the judge for the first category *knows* the one correct answer."

Fred gave a smug smile and returned the shoebox to its shelf.

"How are we going to go about this?" asked Alice, pushing some of the slips around on the table.

"When I went through some the other day," said Fred, "I found that there was a certain amount of repetition, with people making the same or similar guesses. For instance, I bet you'll find a lot of guesses saying it's one of those little frames that you set down into your frying pan in order to contain a fried egg, making it suitable for an egg sandwich.

"Not only is that a common guess, but in my opinion it's not particularly creative. So all the guesses that fall into that category can just be set aside in a pile."

Alice—embarrassed but also amused—came close to admitting that this had been her own thought when she first saw the doohickey, but she decided against it.

"I think we'll find some other themes as well that will allow us to separate a lot of these into some broad categories."

"And those will all automatically be dismissed?" asked Vera.

"Not necessarily. It could be that we end up choosing a particularly good example of a common theme. But I think it's more likely that the winner will be one that is unique.

"So"—he cleared one corner of the table—"let's make a pile of the egg-circle guesses here, and as we go through the rest, we'll see what other common guesses emerge."

"'A pasta measurer for very large groups,'" Alice read from a slip of paper. "Well, it's a little different, but I don't think it quite qualifies for the contenders' pile." She instead added it to the pile they had designated for rejects.

"'A the-dog-ate-my-homework maker,'" Vera read. She peered at the piece of paper. "I guess you would use it to mangle your homework somehow? Sounds useful!" With a laugh, she placed that one on the contenders' pile.

"Another egg circle," said Fred, shaking his head. He added it to the pile in the corner.

"'A tool for scraping out chair seats,'" Vera read, a note of puzzlement in her voice. "I'm not sure I quite know what that means."

"It seems kind of pedestrian for a guess," Fred remarked. "Throw it on the rejects pile." When Vera hesitated, he added, "We can't make every guess a strong contender. The point is to whittle these down." And indeed, the contender pile was growing dauntingly large. Vera nodded and added hers to the rejects.

"It doesn't have a name on it, anyway," she said.

"Can't declare a winner if we don't have a name," Fred reminded them for about the tenth time. "No name, automatic reject."

Alice meanwhile had added another two to the egg circle pile. Now she read, "An earring for a troll."

"I didn't know trolls favored jewelry," Fred remarked.

"I think it's original," said Vera.

Alice winced. "Original perhaps, but I think we've seen better." She laid it on the rejects pile, but Vera reached over and moved it to a pile they had designated for maybes. Since the contenders' pile was so large, there seemed little chance they were ever going to get to these maybes, so Alice just shrugged.

But when she reached for another slip, there were no more to be found. "Hey," she said in surprise, "we're all done."

"No," said Fred grimly, "we've just completed the first pass." He moved aside everything but the contenders' pile, and moved that to the center of the table. "Now comes the hard part," he said.

Chapter Twenty-Six

After another night in the same Spruce Grove hotel where they had stopped on the way north, the group gathered for a convivial breakfast together in the hotel restaurant. Afterward, when they piled into the bus for the final day of travel, they were still in high spirits, and though they'd had every intention of making this a final day of storytelling, the conversation and laughter flowed so easily all day, they never got around to it.

Harry—the chief storyteller, as Louise had come to think of him—didn't seem to mind in the least.

They came rolling into Acorn Hill in the late afternoon. As they approached the town, Cyril called out, "Say, isn't this the day Fred's going to end his contest? What time did he say he'd announce the winner?"

"Four o'clock," said Lloyd. "And it's almost four now."

As they drove west on Hill Street and approached Chapel Road, they could already see that there was a great deal of activity at Fred's Hardware, which sat on the corner. As the bus turned right onto Chapel Road, John asked, "Would anybody mind if we stop here before we go on up to the inn? I'd really like to see how this turns out." The suggestion was received enthusiastically, and Harry pulled the bus over to the side of the road to let out the passengers.

"I'll go on up and park the bus at the inn," said Harry, "rather than leave it here in the street."

The passengers climbed out rather stiffly, and as they stood stretching on the sidewalk, the bus continued on up to Grace Chapel Inn. Then the travelers made their way across the street and entered the store.

Inside, quite a crowd had assembled already, but they were still waiting for Fred's awards ceremony to start. Fred was in a corner, conferring with Carlene Moss, the editor of the *Acorn Nutshell*. An event like this was sure to rate extensive coverage in her weekly newspaper, and she clutched a camera in her hand to record the occasion.

Louise surprised Alice by walking up behind her and tapping her on the shoulder. "You're back!" exclaimed Alice, exchanging a loving hug with her sister. Then she held Louise at arm's length and examined her critically.

"Still in one piece, you'll note," Louise said dryly, "and not too much worse for the wear."

Alice smiled broadly. "How was it?"

"Everything was lovely," Louise said. "I can't wait to tell you all about it. But first"—she nodded in Fred's direction—"we all jumped off the bus before we even made it back to the inn in order to find out who the winner of the doohickey contest is."

Louise looked around, giving a wave to Rev. Thompson, who stood near the counter. He smiled and mouthed the words,

"Welcome back," then turned to greet Lloyd and Ethel, who were bearing down on him.

"It seems to have been a popular contest," continued Louise. "What did we miss?"

"Well for one thing," laughed Alice, "it's technically two contests now." She went on to explain about the addition of the creative category.

"My," said Louise, "and you were one of the judges? Were they good? And more importantly, what is that thing really?"

"I still don't know," Alice whispered, just as Fred climbed up onto his sales counter and asked for quiet.

"First of all," said Fred, "I'd like to thank everyone who participated in the contest. It's been a lot of fun for me. And I'd especially like to thank my wife Vera, without whom . . . well, let's say it wouldn't have happened." This provoked a fair amount of laughter. "I'd also like to thank some others."

As Fred was speaking, he was holding the doohickey in his hand, but it was obscured by some papers and other materials that he was also clutching. As he continued with his opening remarks, Louise heard a soft voice say, "Well, well, what *does* he have there?"

Harry had apparently hurried back after parking the bus, and he stood peering intently toward Fred.

Alice had overheard him as well, and she turned to give him a smile. "Hello, Mr. Bailey. Welcome back," she whispered. "Your question is just what we're here to have answered."

"Hello, Miss Howard," Harry said with a warm smile. "Yes, I heard about the contest. Very intriguing, very intriguing." As his voice trailed off, he continued to stare in Fred's direction, cocking his head to one side as if that would help him see better. Then he said, "If you ladies will excuse me, I think I'm going to try to get a closer look." He began to slip through the crowd.

Fred was explaining how the contest had been enlarged with a second category. He was hamming it up considerably, going on about the "overwhelming response" and the "incredible quality" of the entries. *He's having a ball*, thought Alice. From time to time, she would see Harry Bailey's bald head, bobbing and weaving through the crowd.

Finally, Fred approached the crux of the matter. "While the creative entries came in droves, however, the serious guesses were few." He held up a small sheaf of papers. "And in fact, most of them were wrong. It turns out, my friends, that from among all of you, there is only one other person who knows what *this* is." He raised the doohickey with a flourish and paused dramatically.

"Oh," sighed a soft voice, ripe with satisfaction, "it's a scorp." And then Harry, realizing that he had spoken this thought out loud, clapped his hand over his mouth and looked about in a comical fashion.

Fred froze and stared at Harry for a moment, but Rev. Thompson burst into a great shout of laughter. Fred quickly recovered and said, "Only *two* other people know that this is indeed a scorp." Rev. Thompson's infectious laughter was causing him to chuckle as well. "A closed scorp to be specific. And those two people are both before me here . . . though I only recognize one of them."

Fred knelt on the counter as Rev. Thompson stepped up and introduced him to Harry Bailey. Harry tried to back away, but Fred said, "No, no, Mr. Bailey. Any man who knows his scorps is welcome here."

Straightening, he again addressed the crowd. "I am pleased to announce cowinners of the contest, because the other person to correctly identify the scorp, as you probably have guessed by now, was Rev. Thompson." The crowd cheered and applauded, and Carlene Moss stepped forward to take their picture.

"As a matter of fact, this works out well," continued Fred, "because we ended up with a tie in the creative category as well. So I'd like now to invite our two winners to each read one of the winning entries in the creative category. Are you willing?" He looked down at Harry and Rev. Thompson, who both nodded.

"Okay then," said Fred. "The first cowinner in the creative category."

He handed a slip of paper to Rev. Thompson, who looked down at it and said, "This one comes from Bobby Dawson—whom I think I saw standing right over there. He suggests, 'A monocle for a giant, missing its lens.'" Everyone cheered and applauded.

"And our second cowinner . . ." Fred handed a piece of paper to Harry.

"This is from Danny Bodillo." He looked around briefly, but everyone else knew that Danny was standing right next to his friend Bobby, "and he suggests that the doohickey is 'An ice-cream scoop for dieters.'" There was even more laughter for this one, abetted by Harry's miming of the frustration of trying to scoop ice cream with the scorp.

Fred brought both boys forward so that Carlene Moss could take their picture as well.

Fred seemed about ready to wrap up the ceremonies, when Cyril Overstreet called out, "And what about you, Fred? Do you still maintain that you knew what the scorp was all along? I understand there have been some doubts expressed on that point."

Fred struck his forehead with the heel of his hand, as if he'd been on the verge of forgetting something important. "Carlene," he called out. "Carlene, I need your assistance please." Carlene stepped to the front with the air of someone who knew what was about to happen.

"Carlene," said Fred in a mock conversational tone. "Do you happen to have with you an envelope that I gave you recently?"

"Why, yes I do, Fred," she replied, holding it in the air.

"And would you be so good as to explain to our friends and neighbors the circumstances under which I gave you this envelope?"

"It was first thing Monday morning," she said, "shortly after you decided on the doohickey contest."

"And what is the condition of the envelope, Carlene?"

"It is sealed."

"And it's been in your possession, sealed, ever since I gave it to you?"

"Yes."

"Well, then," said Fred, "I think it's time we opened it. But wait! We need a suitable volunteer." He made a show of scanning the room and then exclaimed, "Vera! My darling wife, perhaps you would do the honors?"

Before her husband could drag out the performance any longer, Vera marched up to the counter, took the envelope from Carlene and ripped it open. She glanced quickly at the piece of paper inside and then held it up so everyone could see that it had a single word on it. "Scorp," she said, her voice heavy with mock disgust.

Many in the crowd lingered in the store after the ceremony was over. Alice, Louise and Rev. Thompson were congratulating Fred and Vera on a successful event. Vera remarked jokingly that she might have enjoyed it more if it had been a little less successful.

"But what is a scorp, anyway?" asked Alice. "What is it used for?"

"You're not the first person who's asked me that. It's a woodworking tool, a kind of drawknife," said Rev. Thompson. "You use it to scoop out the seat of a chair, particularly a Windsor chair. It shapes those indentations that accommodate . . . that allow a person to sit more comfortably."

Vera turned in astonishment to her husband. "So there was *another* correct answer! Don't you remember? Someone put that very answer into the creative response box."

"Who submitted it?" Fred asked mildly.

Vera frowned. "It didn't have a name on it. But still, you were wrong when you said that you three were the only ones who knew what it was. *Somebody* else knew."

"No, I don't think I was wrong." Fred smiled. "I just think that I know enough to disguise my handwriting when my wife will be one of the people reading the entries."

Chapter Twenty-Seven

After the conclusion of activities at Fred's store, Harry hurried back to Grace Chapel Inn so that he could unload the bags for his passengers and be part of the round of good-byes and good wishes that were in order after a successful tour. Ethel, Lloyd and Florence soon followed, with John and Cyril arriving a little while later. When Louise did not return immediately, he hefted her bag from the bus and carried it into the inn.

Setting the suitcase by the front desk, he made his way back to the kitchen. "Ms. Howard?" he said to Jane as he stuck his head through the door. "I just wanted to let you know that I've put your sister's bag out by the front desk." He gave her a wink. "I didn't want you to think I'd driven off with it."

Jane, who had already welcomed him back, was busily preparing dinner, but she was still able to stop and offer him a smile. "Why thank you, Mr. Bailey. Can I offer you something before you go? A cup of tea? Or some apple cider?"

Harry hesitated a moment, then came into the room. "Thank you, Ms. Howard. A glass of cider would be very nice."

Even as Jane was pouring the cider, they could hear the voices of Louise and Alice as they returned to the inn. "Thank you,

Mr. Bailey," said Louise when she entered the kitchen, "for bringing in my bag."

"My pleasure, Mrs. Smith," Harry said graciously.

"You know, Jane, you're in the presence of the cowinner of Fred's doohickey contest," Alice said with a smile.

Jane looked at her with a puzzled expression. "You, Louise? Oh, you meant Mr. Bailey. I'm sorry. I didn't even realize you had entered. In fact, how did . . . ?"

Harry grinned. "It was a spur-of-the-moment thing." He drained his glass and then saluted them with it before setting it in the sink. "Mrs. Smith, I thoroughly enjoyed your group. Fine people. If you ever need an excursion bus again, just call Tabard Tours and ask for Harry. And thank you, ladies, for the hospitality. A blessing on your inn!"

And with that he bounded out of the room with the same energy that Louise had noticed the first time she saw him.

That evening, Ethel joined the sisters for dinner, and they sat at the table for a long time afterward while Louise and Ethel described the trip.

They spoke glowingly of Jeremy and the ordination ceremony, of his friends and teachers up in Maine and of John Gaunt's obvious love for his nephew. Louise recounted the story that Rev. Dunwoody had told her about the Twisty Bear, and this prompted Ethel to describe how the idea of storytelling had first come up on the trip.

Alice and Jane were fascinated with the idea of the storytelling game, and they demanded that each tale be described. Louise noticed that Ethel "summarized" John's shaggy-dog story at almost the same length at which he had told it, yet it produced the desired groans from Alice and Jane.

But Louise had to prompt Ethel to describe her own story about gossiping, and even then, Ethel gave only a very condensed version of it. Nevertheless, Louise thought she saw the same light of recognition in her sisters' eyes that she herself had felt when Ethel first told the story. In a rush of affection for her aunt, she proceeded to recount the story Lloyd had told in defense of gossip.

Both sisters thoroughly enjoyed learning about Florence's princess fairy tale, and they thought she had offered a fine rebuke to the adventure tales of the men. Privately, though, Louise thought that in recounting the tales, neither she nor Ethel did justice to the stories the men had told.

Ethel praised Louise's Roman story to great effect, and Louise described how the whole group had contributed to creating the "Mystery at the Vermont Inn." Jane and Alice were thoroughly impressed with Harry Bailey's unexpected solution to the mystery.

"Mr. Bailey seems like quite a character," Alice remarked. "I'm sorry now that I didn't get to know him better."

"You heard him, Alice," Jane said. "All you have to do is book a bus with Tabard Tours, and you can go on a storytelling adventure of your own."

"It might be worth it." Alice laughed.

"But that's enough about us," said Ethel. "We want to hear all about you girls. What have you been up to while we were away? Getting into any trouble?"

"I'm sure they've had a very quiet time of it, Aunt Ethel," Louise said with confidence.

Alice and Jane looked at each other and smiled. After a moment, Jane inclined her head, inviting Alice to take up the tale.

"Well," said Alice emphatically. "Have *we* got a story for *you*."

About the Authors

Jolyn and William Sharp work as editors in magazine and book publishing, respectively. After a number of years in New York City, they now live in New Hampshire with an energetic dog and a senior cat. Jolyn enjoys knitting, weaving and gardening; William is constantly awed by her energy. They are active in the Women's National Book Association and the New Hampshire Writers' Project, as well as a local book-discussion group. They read more detective novels than is good for them.

A Note from the Editors

We hope you enjoy Tales from Grace Chapel Inn, created by the Books and Inspirational Media Division of Guideposts. In all of our books, magazines and outreach efforts, we aim to deliver inspiration and encouragement, help you grow in your faith, and celebrate God's love in every aspect of your daily life.

Thank you for making a difference with your purchase of this book, which helps fund our many outreach programs to the military, prisons, hospitals, nursing homes and schools. To learn more, visit GuidepostsFoundation.org.

We also maintain many useful and uplifting online resources. Visit Guideposts.org to read true stories of hope and inspiration, access OurPrayer network, sign up for free newsletters, join our Facebook community, and follow our stimulating blogs.

To order your favorite Guideposts publications, go to ShopGuideposts.org, call (800) 932-2145 or write to Guideposts, PO Box 5815, Harlan, Iowa 51593.

Tales from Grace Chapel Inn

Recipes & Wooden Spoons
by Judy Baer

Hidden History
by Melody Carlson

Ready to Wed
by Melody Carlson

The Price of Fame
by Carolyne Aarsen

We Have This Moment
by Diann Hunt

The Way We Were
by Judy Baer

The Spirit of the Season
by Dana Corbit

The Start of Something Big
by Sunni Jeffers

Spring Is in the Air
by Jane Orcutt

Home for the Holidays
by Rebecca Kelly

Eyes on the Prize
by Sunni Jeffers

Summer Breezes
by Jane Orcutt

Tempest in a Teapot
by Judy Baer

Mystery at the Inn
by Carolyne Aarsen

Saints Among Us
by Anne Marie Rodgers

Never Give Up
by Pam Hanson
& Barbara Andrews

Keeping the Faith
by Pam Hanson
& Barbara Andrews

Rally Round the Flag
by Jane Orcutt

Sing a New Song
by Sunni Jeffers

Prayers and Pawprints
by Diann Hunt

Empty Nest
by Pam Hanson
& Barbara Andrews

Once you visit the charming village of Acorn Hill, you'll never want to leave. Here, the three Howard sisters reunite after their father's death and turn the family home into a bed-and-breakfast. They rekindle old memories, rediscover the bonds of sisterhood, revel in the blessings of friendship and meet many fascinating guests along the way.